"Don't make a stupid mistake."

Lily's voice was hard. "I don't measure my worth in terms of how I disappoint or satisfy your expectations, Sam. I don't do that for any man." She pivoted and headed into the darkness.

He followed. "I'm not asking you to do that. All I want to know is why you're willing to give up." He grabbed her by the shoulder and forced her to turn around. "Lily, look at me."

"Yes," she agreed. "Look at you." The cool mask of anger dropped away. One trembling hand touched his face. "You've been bludgeoned, kicked, poisoned.... How much more of this can you take?"

Sam closed his eyes. Here she was, worried about his safety at the hands of an unknown enemy— oblivious to the damage she was inflicting on him all by herself.

Dear Reader,

Be prepared to meet another "Woman of Mystery"!

This month we're proud to bring you another book in our ongoing WOMAN OF MYSTERY program, designed to bring you the debut books of writers new to Harlequin Intrigue.

Meet Laura Kenner, author of *Someone To Watch Over Me*.

Born and raised in Birmingham, Laura is a military wife and mother of two. She's lived in Alabama, Texas, Virginia, Colorado and now Kansas. Laura used to think living north of the Mason-Dixon line should be considered an overseas tour of duty, however the air force has never agreed with her. Now she looks forward to assignments in far-flung places, seeing each new location as a possible setting for another book. Laura is a Golden Heart Winner.

We're dedicated to bringing you the best new authors, the freshest new voices. Be on the lookout for more "women of mystery!"

Sincerely,

Debra Matteucci
Senior Editor & Editorial Coordinator
Harlequin
300 E. 42nd St., Sixth Floor,
New York, NY 10017

Someone To Watch Over Me
Laura Kenner

Harlequin Books

TORONTO • NEW YORK • LONDON
AMSTERDAM • PARIS • SYDNEY • HAMBURG
STOCKHOLM • ATHENS • TOKYO • MILAN
MADRID • WARSAW • BUDAPEST • AUCKLAND

To Colorado Romance Writers Chris Pacheco and the C/Kathys, with love, gratitude and admiration; to Pike's Peak RW for giving me a second home; and finally to Cindy Nicholls and Dawn Malcolm, with special thanks. Set the phasers on stun!

ISBN 0-373-22263-7

SOMEONE TO WATCH OVER ME

Copyright © 1994 by Laura Hayden

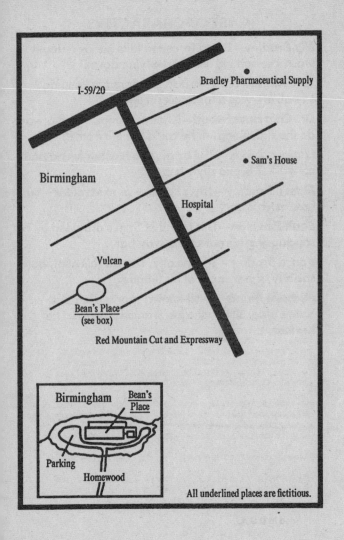

I-59/20

Bradley Pharmaceutical Supply

Birmingham

• Sam's House

Hospital

Vulcan •

Bean's Place
(see box)

Red Mountain Cut and Expressway

Birmingham   Bean's
Place

Parking

Homewood

All underlined places are fictitious.

CAST OF CHARACTERS

Lily Bradley—Being forced to fake her own death wasn't something she'd take lying down.

Sam Markstrom—He had an interest in keeping Lily alive—was it for love or money?

Dr. Chip Hazelwood—Lily's ex-fiancé would always do the right thing—if he could benefit from it.

Lamarr Moody—The tragic death of her friend and co-worker broke Lily's heart.

Mason Bradley—Lily's cousin was much older—but how much wiser?

Bean Emerson—This friend of Sam's provided a sanctuary in his out-of-the-way bar.

Vance Bradley—Technically, Lily was his aunt, but socially, she was out of his league.

Michelle Marks—Well-known sportscaster and Sam's older sister, she just wanted to protect her brother.

Chapter One

Growing shadows overtook the valley, moving across the landscape with the speed of kudzu on a hot summer's day. Sam Markstrom glanced out the side window of his car at the tangled bank of brown withered leaves. Winter had forced the legendary vine to temporarily release its choke hold on the South, but Sam knew the plant would resurrect itself at the first hint of spring.

If spring ever gets here. He fought a shiver by turning up the heater and switching on the car's heated seats.

I hate winter.

Scanning the horizon, he spotted the familiar silhouette of Vulcan, serenely watching over the city of Birmingham from a perch on Red Mountain. The torch in the statue's cast-iron fist burned red, meaning someone had died in an automobile wreck during the day. Sam shook his head. With Mardi Gras coming up, the torch would probably stay red all weekend long.

Seeking distraction, he switched on the radio. A blast of Beach Boys music filled the car, and the thought of summer at the beach made him curse the cold once more.

He pulled from the deserted side street onto the main road where a lone vehicle traveled ahead of him. As the gap between them narrowed, he admired the smooth lines of the white Jaguar, highlighted by the faint glow from an approaching vehicle.

Now that's the type of car I wish I could— A sudden flare of light blinded him. Sam raised his arm, shielding his eyes from the headlights of a vehicle that crested a rise in the road. Ahead, the Jag reacted to the imminent threat of the oncoming truck by swerving to the right where it hit the shoulder, rose in the air and tumbled down a small embankment. When the truck veered into his lane, Sam punched his horn, then gripped the steering wheel, struggling to keep his car on the narrow safety of the sloping shoulder.

The truck swerved back into its proper lane and stopped only after traveling another hundred feet or so.

Sam skidded to a stop and turned around in his seat, expecting to see the driver jump out of the cab and respond to the accident. The incandescent flame from a cigarette lighter briefly highlighted a figure in the driver's window. Sam could see three metallic letters shining in the faint glow from the vehicle's rear running lights: RBS. The truck revved its engine and disappeared into the darkness.

Sam turned back to face the wreck. The Beach Boys continued to blare their praises of surf and sand until he switched off the radio. The sound reverberated in his ears. At the last echo, Sam's consciousness jolted to life.

He snatched the cellular phone from its cradle and efficiently reported the sketchy details of the accident to the calm voice on the other end of the line. After the call, he stumbled down the graveled bank, praying he would find survivors, not bodies. He mentally calculated the driver's chances. Over a ton and a half of metal, going forty-five, maybe fifty miles an hour when it left the road...

It looked as if the Jaguar had been purposely centered on the thickest pine tree in the stand. An angry cloud of steam rose from the car's pleated hood. Sam sniffed at the air, relieved he couldn't detect the telltale and dangerous odor of gasoline. At first the only sound he could hear was the hissing radiator. Then he became aware of vague noises from the driver's side.

Someone's alive in there.

Unable to see through the shattered glass, Sam tried to pull open the warped door. When that failed, he wrapped his wool scarf around his hand and punched a hole through the cracked window. Pebbles of glass covered his shoes as he cleared the frame. The driver groaned, and the sound shot through his self-control.

A woman?

Sam strained to see in the dark, wondering how much blood was concealed in the camouflage of the shadows. He fought against the surge of panic that threatened his self-control. "Don't try...don't try to move, ma'am. I can't get the door open, but help's coming." *Real help,* he added to himself.

The clouds broke apart and moonlight filtered through the shattered windshield. The woman turned her head toward Sam and slowly opened her eyes. "Don't... leave...me."

For a moment, he stood still, mesmerized by her pale gray eyes, the color reminding him of the stormy halo of clouds ringing the moon. A lone drop trickled down her cheek, not a tear but blood, leaving a vivid crimson trail against her pallid skin. His fingers tightened around the edge of the doorframe. He'd seen blood before, more blood than this.

And where there was blood, there was pain. And death.

Sam fought to reclaim his initial detachment, but her silvery gaze demanded his attention, his sympathy and something else from deep within him. Sam's objectivity returned only after she closed her eyes. Old instincts forced their way through his protective shell, and he began to assess the situation. In the emergency room, they called it triage; in the field, they called it survival.

He sniffed the air again. If the gas tank had breached, his first priority was to move her to safety. The only odors he noticed were the cloying scent of pine tar from the splintered tree and the metallic tang of blood.

When he pulled at the door again, the woman groaned at the movement of the car. Sam searched her ashen features for signs of comprehension. "Don't worry. I have a phone in my car, and I've called for the paramedics." He waited for some sort of response, anticipating incoherence or even hysteria.

A trickle of blood trailed slowly down her forehead and her cheek, then dropped and stained her white blouse a rusty red. "Thank God for..." She shifted, then grimaced. "F-for cellular technology." When she looked up at him, he saw the beginnings of a strained smile.

Surprised by her shaky but relatively calm voice, Sam nodded. "The wonders of a modern society," he agreed. He'd expected her initial shock to disintegrate into delirium, certainly not whimsy.

"Tell me..." She paused, her voice low and raspy. "Tell me you're not the idiot who ran me off the road."

"I'm not the idiot who ran you off the road," he repeated. "Just an innocent witness."

Her pinched features relaxed. "Good."

He didn't have to look hard to see the elegance beneath the pain and fear. "Do you think you could handle being by yourself for just a minute?"

A look of panic flashed across her face, knocking away what little composure she'd recovered. "Don't leave me here by myself."

Sam tried to give her a reassuring smile. "Only long enough for me to get the first-aid kit out of my car. Okay?"

She swallowed hard. "Just as l-long as I know you're coming back."

"Promise." He solemnly drew a cross over his jacket pocket with his forefinger. "Be right back." Sam scrambled up the embankment, painfully aware of the frosty clouds formed by his breath. He appreciated the lingering warmth of his car as he dialed 911 and gave the operator an update on the situation.

"Sir, you have to keep the victim calm and make sure she can breathe all right. You're not equipped to deal with the internal bleeding which may start if you try to get her out of the car. Just wait for the paramedics."

Yeah... wait for the professionals.

Sam fished his first-aid kit out of the trunk and returned to the wrecked car and its captive victim. He balanced his flashlight on the corrugated hood, shining the light through the shattered windshield. "The paramedics will be here in just a few minutes."

"I'm not going anywhere." She offered him a small smile, then shivered. "I'm stuck. That is...unless..." She tried to shift in her seat. The flashlight illuminated her blood-streaked hand as she stretched her fingers toward a series of buttons along the car's center console.

"What are you trying to do?"

"If I can reach the controls—that is, if they work—I can move my seat back."

"No!" The word echoed through the silent night like a gunshot. Sam lowered his voice, hoping he could defuse the tension in that word with a watered-down explanation. "That's not a good idea. I know you're not comfortable, but we need to let the paramedics handle this. Okay?"

"Okay," she echoed. "So...let's talk. What brings you out here, on this godforsaken road?" Lit by the flashlight, her drawn face reflected a determination to survive.

He pried open the blue metal box and tried to concentrate on its contents, instead of her pale features. "I was headed to the Civic Center."

"To a concert?"

"No, state basketball championship."

"I'm sorry you're m-missing the game."

"No problem." He gently pressed a piece of cotton gauze against her head to stem the flow of blood. His heart contracted when she grimaced at his touch. For a fleeting moment, he felt her pain as clearly as if it were his own. The sense of empathy cut another deep furrow through his control. Sam pushed away the invading emotion and tried to present an unruffled facade.

"Anyway," he tried to say in a matter-of-fact voice, "I'm not into basketball. One of the coaches, a friend of mine, wanted me to meet his girlfriend's sister. I was supposed to accidentally bump into them at the game." He paused for a moment, watching the woman's eyes flutter, then start to close.

She needed to stay awake.

And he needed to know more about her.

He spoke louder. "It wasn't an official blind date, you understand, but it was too close for my liking. So how about you? Where were you headed?"

"What?" She seemed to wake up a little. "Oh, goin' to meet some friends at the Press Box Club. We...we..." Her head began to sag forward against the wheel.

"C'mon...wake up." He brushed her hair out of her face, alarmed as his fingertips skimmed chilled flesh. He had to keep her talking. "The Press Box Club? The place beside the Convention Center? Don't tell me you were supposed to meet your sister there. I'd hate to think I was standing *you* up."

She managed to give him a tight-lipped smile. "D-don't have any sisters. Only child. Just goin' to meet...friends."

"Tell me what you and your friends were going to do." Even in the dark, Sam could see the strength draining from her eyes.

She sighed, coughed and spoke slowly, deliberating on each word. "We meet every...every Friday. Just to unwind and to..." She seemed to lose her concentration, then regain it. "We talk. About work. About family. About relationsh—"

The sound of cracking wood filled the air. A large tree branch struck the front of the car. Sam ducked, protecting himself from the shower of sticks and dead leaves that bounced off the hood and knocked the flashlight to the ground. A loud clang echoed through the darkness, followed by the slow whine of fatigued metal under pressure. The car shifted, and Sam watched the steering column push forward, pinning the woman more tightly to the seat.

Alarmed by the terror on her face, he reached into the car with both hands and tried to force the steering wheel back. He could hear nothing but her uneven gasps for breath and the pounding of his own heart. Bracing his feet, he called on a forgotten reserve of physical strength and reached out with fervent prayers to whoever would listen. *Don't let her die... please. Not another death.*

The wheel didn't move. Sam felt her hand flutter against his. At first he thought she was reacting with sheer panic, but then he realized she was fumbling with a collar located on the underside of the steering column. Sam cursed his unfamiliarity with the expensive car. He reached between the bloody folds of her skirt, imitating her gesture and pushing at the metal collar.

Nothing happened.

Sam repositioned himself against the window frame and, once braced, tried again. After a tense moment, he felt a slight movement. The steering wheel began to retract into the dash, allowing her to breathe more easily.

A hand touched his shoulder, and he became aware of the dying echo of a siren. During their crisis, he'd noticed nothing other than the all-too-important task at hand. No sounds. No flashing lights from the ambulance, the police or the three fire vehicles parked on the roadside above him. He glanced up into the calm face of the uniformed man.

"Sir, if you'll move, we'll handle it from here."

Stepping back, Sam let the professionals direct the rescue. In moments, the paramedics freed the woman from the wreckage, strapped her to a stretcher, then packed her into the ambulance. The howl of the siren faded into the distance, and a harried young patrolman approached Sam. "We need to get a statement from you, sir."

The adrenaline, which had surged through Sam, began to fade away, leaving him feeling drained. His description of the accident was precise and factual. He left out the details that wouldn't fit in the blanks on an accident report. The police didn't care about the way she faced her pain or how she managed to stay relatively calm despite the fact she couldn't draw a full breath. He knew from the past that official reports never mentioned the sound of shattering glass or the smell of blood.

A horn blared in the distance, playing the opening notes to "Dixie." The patrolman scratched his head and stretched to see over the rise of the road. "What the hell?" They both watched as a line of cars appeared on the dark horizon and crawled toward them.

Sam recognized the school colors and the rhythmic chants of high-pitched voices. "It's the pep-rally caravan from one of the high schools. They usually use a back road to get to the Civic Center."

The young man straightened his tie and positioned himself in the road to direct the column of honking, crepe-papered cars and buses. Students dangled out every window, screaming school cheers and craning for a better view of the possible carnage.

With the officer sufficiently distracted, Sam felt free to make his own inspection of the accident site. The patrolman had brushed off a paramedic's earlier request for the woman's identification by saying he hadn't found her purse yet. Sam recognized inexperience when he saw it, and he decided his own examination might reveal much that the rookie had missed.

After sliding down the embankment, Sam winced as he viewed the Jaguar. The car door hung drunkenly on its hinges, and the severed steering wheel lay on the ground next to the front tire. The firemen had tossed it there after their powerful saw had sliced through the column, releasing the woman. Inside the car, Sam examined the metal stump of the steering column and shook his head. He had thought of a Jaguar as merely an expensive car, but the luxury of a retractable steering wheel had probably saved the woman's life.

Sam used his flashlight to shine around in the dark recesses of the front seat, but the splintered wooden dash dug into the leather upholstery of the passenger seat, making any retrieval impossible. He tugged at the rear door, and it opened with a noisy, metallic groan. Something shiny reflected the flashlight's beam: a brass tag in the shape of a dog bone attached to a leather briefcase. Grasping the case's handle, he discovered the case was trapped between the front and back seats on the carpeted floorboards. Bracing a hand against the driver's headrest, he tugged the briefcase loose.

When the brass locks sprang open unexpectedly, Sam juggled the case, trying not to spill its contents. Several manila folders stuffed with computer printouts plopped onto the ground. After he replaced them, he crawled back into the cramped rear seat, discovering the missing purse had been hidden beneath the briefcase. As he pushed himself back out of the car, the ragged edges of a small hole in the headrest scraped across his skin. He ran his forefinger over the symmetrical perforation in the upholstery and fought the feeling of recognition.

Sam glanced back to street level where a carload of admiring cheerleaders had captivated the young patrolman's attention. "Damn rookies," Sam muttered. Using the thinnest blade of his utility knife, he probed the small hole. A lump of cold metal rolled into the palm of his hand. He examined the back windshield and found a neat corresponding hole in the cracked glass. Line-of-sight triangulation placed the weapon at street level.

"I'll be damned! Not only did the driver run her off the road, he took a shot at—"

A clap of thunder ricocheted painfully through Sam's skull. As he fell to the ground, his last thoughts were of Vulcan, God of the Forge, wielding his cast-iron hammer like a baseball bat.

Chapter Two

Lily Bradley flexed her fingers, feeling the cool, rough material beneath her palms. *This isn't my bed.* A friend had given her blue satin sheets for Christmas, and Lily had quickly fallen in love with the sensation of the slick fabric on her skin. Before she opened her eyes, she knew the coarse sheet tucked beneath her chin was white. She squinted at the blurry hospital name stenciled on the hem. *Hospital?*

"You're awake." The voice came from across the room.

Lily drew a deep breath and winced as it caused a stab of pain to divert her attention for a moment. "Uh...evidently," she managed to say when the discomfort faded. Conversation had never been her strong suit first thing in the morning. When she tried to shake away the cobwebs that blocked her thoughts, the room spun. Once equilibrium had returned, she realized the light from the window held a distinctly silver gleam. Still night.

"Do you know where you are?" The speaker's dark face folded into a gentle smile, revealing a row of white teeth which matched the uniform.

Lily drew in another painful breath and released it in a sigh. "I don't think we're in Kansas anymore."

The woman grew solemn, her words dripping with solace. "Elizabeth, you're in a hospital. In Birmingham. You were in a car accident."

Lily nodded, then instantly regretted the gesture. When the room righted itself, she stretched her fingers again, testing the muscles in her forearms. "No one calls me Elizabeth." *And gets away with it.* "It's Lily." Her vision sharpened and she read the faded initials on the sheet. "And I know exactly where I am. Is Dr. Hazelwood on duty?"

The nurse smiled. "No, but he did want to be called as soon as you woke up." The woman started for the door.

Lily raised a hand to stop her and realized she was connected to an IV drip. "Would you do me a favor? Don't call him. He'll insist on holding my hand and make a big nuisance out of himself. He's a great doctor but his bedside manner is a bit...overwhelming."

What a lie! Lily knew Chip Hazelwood had earned his medical license without ever developing a suitable bedside manner. She also realized he'd love a chance to tower over her and remind her of all the things that had gone wrong in her life, in their life together.

The nurse looked doubtful.

"Please. Just tell him I woke up for a moment, said a few incoherent things and fell back to sleep. See? I'll make it even easier." Lily closed her eyes. "All I want to do is get some rest."

"Well...okay." The nurse made a few adjustments to the sheet and draped the call button within easy reach. "But you have to promise to ring the nurses' station if you start feeling worse."

"Deal." Lily opened her eyes for a moment and smiled. "And thanks."

The last thing Lily needed was Chip Hazelwood hovering over her. His authoritarian needs had overwhelmed their once-upon-a-time relationship. She often wondered how their lackluster romance had proceeded to the engagement level. But, five years after they had broken up, Chip had found a wife to dominate, a formidable father-in-law to return the favor, and three stepchildren, along with a hefty mortgage for good measure.

And Lily had found consolation in her work.

Of course, the rumors suggested that marriage had changed him, not necessarily for the good. But in her case, the family business always provided twice the distractions she actually required. After all, who needed an outside life when family and work were all rolled up in one?

Work, she thought. *I have to get back to work. What time is it?* Lily glanced at her bare arm, where her watch should have been. *Better yet, what* day *is it? Friday? Or maybe it's Saturday by now.* When she sighed, a band of pain wrapped around her.

Morbid curiosity dared her to take a glimpse at the explosion of bruises that mottled her chest and stomach. After a wary examination, she decided that despite the discomfort none of her ribs were broken. She'd hung around too many stables as a kid not to remember with uncanny accuracy the feeling of a broken rib.

If bad things always happen in threes... She blinked away the wet, prickly sensation in her eyes and begged for sleep to relieve the ache in her body as well as her heart. *First Lamarr, now this. What else is going to happen?*

Memories of her late assistant freed the tears she tried to restrain. Lamarr Moody was the one person who had brought variety into her otherwise routine work life. An insatiable collector of the unusual, he had always had a new gimmick or gadget to entertain her. Just that summer he'd become engaged to Barbara Jean, Lily's second cousin twice removed. Now, B.J. avoided the computer room as if the sight of the equipment or even the lone occupant served only to remind her of her lost love.

Last week Lily had finally found the strength to pack up his eclectic belongings. Without Lamarr's junk strewn around, the computer room seemed cold and impersonal. Sterile. Only that morning she had found the coffee cup that she'd overlooked when she'd boxed up his things. She tried to recall the amusement in his face when he first showed the mug to her. *Beware of Computer Programmers—They Byte.*

Lily remembered how they'd argued about the cup hook he'd wanted to install near the coffee machine—a purple ceramic hand making a rude gesture. It was so . . . so typical of Lamarr.

She hadn't laughed since his death, three short weeks ago, and she desperately wanted to do so now. But the laughter eluded her. Instead, a hot tear trickled into her ear. *Don't think about him. Think about anything else but Lamarr. Think about . . .*

A vision of a dark-haired man stepped silently into her thoughts. Lily remembered his calm command, his quiet expression and the way he helped her deal with an otherwise impossible situation. He'd radiated an unruffled strength which reassured her without being overpowering. She closed her eyes, willing herself to create a mental image of her dark knight. *Did he tell me his name? I don't remember. I wish I could see him again and thank him. . . .*

There was no telltale sign of a presence entering her room—no sounds from the hallway, no scrape of the door, no muffled cough to announce his entrance. Yet Lily knew he was there. Opening her eyes merely confirmed it.

He sat on the edge of the empty bed next to hers. He wore a set of faded scrubs with a stethoscope carefully tucked in the shirt pocket. His dark hair was slightly tousled, as if he had pulled a long duty night. Although he looked comfortably rumpled in his utilitarian uniform, he lacked the slick professionalism which usually went with a medical degree.

His quiet expression turned into one of compassion when their gazes locked. "Hi. Remember me? The wizard of cellular technology?"

Lily's voice deserted her, but he seemed to take her silence in stride. He stood up and stepped closer to her bed. "You don't have to talk. All I wanted to do was make sure you were all right."

"I'm fine. I appreciate . . ." She hesitated, trying to find the right words of thanks, something that didn't sound hackneyed or overly simplified. He deserved better. After all, he'd probably saved her life.

"You're very welcome." His intense gaze captured hers until he seemed to become almost uncomfortably aware of the unwavering attention he gave her. Then he turned suddenly, ducked his head and searched for pockets to hide his hands in. "Uh, my name's Sam. Sam Markstrom."

She tried to smile. "Pleased to meet you. I'm Lily Bradley." She glanced at his uniform. "Are you a doctor here?"

"Me?" He looked surprised at her observation. "Sorry, no." He tugged at a faded sleeve. "I...'liberated' these from the maternity ward. It was the only way I could get in here to check on you since it's after visiting hours."

His brazen ingenuity intrigued her. "Let me get this straight. You posed as an expectant father?"

He shrugged. "Sure. It was the easiest way to walk the corridors unchallenged. I borrowed a little window dressing." He pulled out the stethoscope. "And presto chango, instant medical degree."

Lily laughed in spite of the fiery pain in her chest, but her laughter died away when his face suddenly grew pained. He gripped the railing of her bed, bracing himself. When he turned away from her for a brief moment, she saw the tape and gauze which made a stark contrast against his dark hair. Lily felt a flush of guilt redden her face. "What's wrong? Were you hurt in the wreck, too?"

"No." He ran a hand through his dark hair, wincing as he sat down in the chair next to the bed. He drew a deep breath. "I was involved in a little problem that occurred after you and the ambulance left. I stayed around to make a statement, and I guess curiosity made me go back to your car." He hesitated for another moment, then took a deep breath and continued. "I want you to know I told the cops exactly what I saw—that truck ran you off the road. Deliberately."

"That's what I told them, too." Lily recalled the young patrolman who took her statement while she was still in the emergency room. Between his look of boredom and his tired questions, she knew he considered her version of the accident to be more hysterical fiction than fact. She knew the smile she gave Sam Markstrom was strained. "But I'm sure the police didn't believe me."

"But there's more." He rubbed at a small cut on his chin and sighed. "The patrolman hadn't found your purse so I dug around for it. I found it in the back seat under your briefcase. Then I found . . . well . . ."

"What?" Lily stared at him, growing uneasy with his hesitancy. "There was nothing else back there. I just had the car detailed yesterday—er, Thursday."

"I . . ." He stopped again.

Lily grew impatient. "If there's more bad news, just tell it to me straight, Mr. Markstrom."

His forehead furrowed, bringing his dark brows together as he caught her in his disquieting gaze. "I found a bullet hole in the back glass and a matching hole in your headrest."

Shock extinguished her brief flare of indignation. She repeated the words to herself until the significance hit her. The realization siphoned away her remaining strength. "A b-bullet? Someone tried to k—" She couldn't bring herself to say the word.

He gave her a solemn nod. "It looks that way."

Lily watched the walls begin to shift and inch closer to her. Instead of protecting her, the rails of the bed began to resemble the iron bars of a trap. With the world spinning off on an intolerable tangent, Lily grabbed the only weapon she could to defend herself: disbelief. She looked into her rescuer's face, praying he'd provide the only acceptable answer. "Mr. Markstrom, this is a joke, right?"

His sympathetic silence was almost more than she could bear.

Lily gripped the cold rail, her knuckles whitening. "Please tell me this is nothing more than a stupid prank. I mean, things like that don't happen to someone like—" His grim expression made her stop.

"It's no joke, Miss Bradley." He rubbed his hand across the back of his neck. "There was so much going on—the police, the fire fighters, the paramedics. People everywhere." He leaned back in the chair, his gaze growing unfocused. "I wasn't looking for anything sinister. All I expected to find was your purse. But when I saw the hole, I knew exactly what it was." He held out an open palm. "I even had the bullet in my hand when someone slugged me. I woke up downstairs in the emergency room with one hell of a headache. The officer who found me swore I was only caught in the blast of the explosion."

Her heart contracted at the word. "Ex-explosion?"

He nodded, then winced. "Your Jag. It's gone."

She stared at him. "You don't remember my car blowing up?"

"No. And I don't think it's because I got the memory knocked out of me." He gestured to the back of his head. "I promise you the gas tank didn't rupture of its own accord. I am very sure about that. Whoever he was, he hit me and stole the briefcase first, then the car exploded."

Lily looked down, surprised to see the thin blanket pleated between her white knuckles. She tried to think back to that afternoon. Exactly what had she stuffed into her briefcase during those hurried moments before she left work? A sense of denial still colored her thoughts. A combination of fatigue and fear allowed her to entertain visions of spies and secret formulas.

"Uh..." She hesitated, then couched her wild theories in more acceptable terms. "What exactly did the briefcase look like?"

Sam closed his eyes for a moment, evidently conjuring up a mental picture to describe. "Dark brown leather, brass combination locks on each side, neither one locked. All I saw inside was a bunch of manila folders with papers. No one else saw it and because of this—" he gestured to his wound "—they all but said it was merely my imagination."

Lily gave in to the whisper of doubt, telling herself it was a general description, one which could match virtually any executive's briefcase. And if the police didn't put stock in his explanation—

"Oh, yeah," he added. "It had a brass tag on the outside." He cocked his head in thought. "It . . . it was in the shape of a dog's bone."

Lily closed her eyes. It was hers. Lamarr had had the brass tag engraved for her as a gag gift to accompany the real present, the new briefcase. She had surprised everyone—except Lamarr—by attaching it to the handle immediately.

Sam shifted in his seat, evidently uncomfortable. "If you don't mind me asking—what was in there?" He ran a hand along the back of his neck, finishing his question with a silent *to justify getting slugged in the head*.

Lily's mind threatened to shut down, but she pushed on, struggling to remember. Right before she'd left work that afternoon, Mason had stormed into the computer room, railing about the most recent disaster caused by her nephew. She'd grabbed an indiscriminate handful of files from her desk and shoved them into her briefcase, planning a quick getaway.

She drew in the deepest breath she could manage around the bruises. "I don't remember, exactly. I recall putting files in there, but not which ones." The blood pounded through her body, making her ears buzz. "They were just files from the Pharm," she whispered, her strength fading.

To her relief, Sam didn't press her for more details. In fact, he said nothing, demanded no explanations, offered no trite words of sympathy.

Fatigue washed over her, draining the last of her energy without deadening her fear. "Th-thank you, Mr. Markstrom. I appreciate everything you've done for me." She had a hard time making eye contact with him. "And I'm sorry about your head," she added, her voice cracking.

He seemed to understand the dismissal in her words. "Sure." He stood, letting a concerned gaze linger on her face. "If there's anything I can do, call me...please. My office is at my home." He pulled out a business card from his wallet and placed it on the stand beside the bed. He started toward the door, then paused and turned around. She wondered if he could see her shake. "Miss Bradley, I'd like to come back tomorrow, if I may. I think we should talk some more."

"Sure." Her trembling voice betrayed her fear, sounding small and uncertain. "Sure," she repeated with more control. "I think you're right. Thank you."

Lily watched the heavy door close in a slow, sweeping arc. When it finally shut, she bit her lip, trying to think past the overwhelming sense of panic. According to the only witness of her accident, she'd been deliberately run off the road and shot at. Either Sam Markstrom had a vivid imagination—or someone was trying to kill her. But according to her rescuer, even the police put no credence in his story.

But she did.

She stretched with a grimace and picked up his business card.

Sam Markstrom
Computer System Investigations
Data Protection—System Design
555-1204
Licensed and Confidential Investigator

Lily tucked the card under her pillow and stared at the clear bag of IV fluid that hung next to her bed. Weariness flooded her mind and body, overcoming her attempts to think through the sequence of events. How could she rest at a time like this?

I don't want to sleep. Lily closed her eyes. *I don't want to die....*

SAM DISCARDED his disguise as quickly as he could, abandoning the evidence of his impersonation in a nearby supply closet. He rode down in the elevator, mulling over her words: "Just files from the farm."

He'd never met a farmer's daughter who drove a Jag or dressed in linen and silk. It gave new meaning to the words "cash crop." He tried to concentrate despite the annoying buzz in his head and keep his mind and his car on the road. His head ached, his stomach churned and his body screamed for sleep. Once home, he downed a couple of aspirin and a handful of antacids, showered off the outer layer of grime, and then stretched out on his bed, shifting restlessly to find a comfortable spot. He tried to forget Lily Bradley, but her quiet beauty persisted in haunting him, even invading his sleep.

In his dream, he rushed to her car, finding her wedged between the seat and wheel like before. But this time, her gray eyes were glazed, and her jaw hung slack. The bullet hole wasn't in the back of the headrest. It was in her head.

Sam rolled off the bed, threw himself into a low crouch, and tried to thumb open the snap on his holster. Perspiration trickled down his bare chest, but the remnants of his dream proclaimed it blood. He was covered in blood. Someone else's blood.

Walter's.

When the first shot rocked the car, it rattled him so much that he dropped the mike he had in his hand. He lunged for it on the floorboard, found it, then tried to sit up. Walt's dead weight pinned him down.

Glass and blood were everywhere.

Sam ducked behind the protection of an imaginary squad-car door. He rose cautiously to site his attacker. A blood-stained face loomed in the side mirror, and he dropped down before the next barrage of shots perforated the squad car. Unscathed, he tried to return fire, but when he looked at his hand, he held no revolver. Sam stared at his reflection in the dresser mirror. There was no blood. He carried no gun. No badge. He didn't *have* a badge anymore.

Sam perched on the edge of the bed, holding his throbbing head. What had triggered the nightmare, bringing it back from the deep recesses of his memory where it had lain dormant for eighteen months?

Her blood, the shattered windshield or the bullet?

Sam Markstrom closed his eyes and dreaded the next nightmare.

THE MAN IN WHITE SMILED.

It had been deceptively easy to draw the nurse's attention away from her duty station leaving the computer unmanned. With a few keystrokes, he stared at Elizabeth J. Bradley's medical record. With a few more strokes, he erased the entry listing her medicinal allergies and typed in the word, "None."

Glancing up to assure himself the hallways remained empty, he returned his attention to the computer screen where he scrolled to her pharmaceutical record. *Poor Lily. In so much pain.* He typed in a 20 mg dose of morphine sulfate. Low enough not to ring any internal alarms within the system, but high enough to trigger her allergic reaction when combined with the little surprise he intended to give her.

After printing out the altered pages, he inserted them into her file and replaced the metal folder in its slot. He glanced at his watch. Medication rounds started in precisely fifteen minutes. His work was almost done.

He smiled and began to softly whistle a tune as he strolled toward her room.

LILY ROLLED GINGERLY over in her bed, inexplicably awakened by the presence of someone in her room. A large figure loomed in silhouette on the privacy curtain which separated Lily from her roommate.

Another nurse?

The door swung shut, obliterating the shadow on the curtain. But a moment later, a thin flashlight beam danced across the room, eventually highlighting her roommate's IV bag.

Lily breathed a sigh of relief. Her roommate had spent the better part of the night groaning, keeping Lily awake. It was high time someone came in and gave the poor woman something for the pain. Turning to a more comfortable position, Lily closed her eyes, vaguely aware of the scrape of the closing door and the echo of a whistled tune fading away.

WHEN THE EARLY MORNING sun poured through the open curtains and struck Sam in the face, he realized that not only had he slept, but that the nightmare hadn't returned. He squinted at the overly enthusiastic glow from the window, groaned and rolled over, painfully reminding himself of the tender lump on the back of his head. Unable to escape the morning's brilliance, he rose from the bed and stumbled to the kitchen to fix his ritualistic tea.

After he added a second spoonful of sugar to the steaming mug, he came to a sudden conclusion: he hated Lily Bradley for destroying his peace. Yet the moment after the thought crossed his mind, his sense of justice demanded a retraction. How could he blame her, a victim of random violence?

But exactly how random *was* the violence? The only way to end the speculation was to visit her, just as he had promised to do. He finished his tea, dressed and headed to the garage.

Sam took advantage of one of the florist shops placed strategically near the hospital and bought a small bouquet of mixed flowers. Armed with his purchase, he arrived at the hospital and headed straight for Lily Bradley's room. He expected to see a gaggle of relatives flocked around her bedside when he opened the door. Instead he found a stark bed, stripped of sheets and blanket. Backing out the doorway, he stumbled into a young woman, nearly knocking the stack of folded linens from her arms.

Sam grabbed the nurse's elbow to keep her from falling. "I'm sorry. Are you all right?"

She grimaced but nodded. "It's okay."

"I'm looking for Miss Bradley. She was admitted last night."

The woman dropped the sheets onto the empty bed. "I just came on duty this morning. You'll have to ask at the nurses' station." She turned and began to make up the bed.

Sam strode down the hallway toward the desk and found another nurse stacking metal folders on the counter. "Excuse me, I'm looking for Lily Bradley. She was in Room 304 last night. Could you tell me if she's been moved or released?"

The desk nurse turned to the computer and typed. After staring critically at the screen, she pivoted, facing him with a vague look of sympathy flitting across her face. She eyed the bouquet of flowers in his hand. "Are you a member of the family?"

"Uh, no," he admitted. "I was involved, er, witnessed her accident last night."

"Just a minute, please." She turned and picked up a phone. Sam shifted, hoping to get a view of the computer screen, but it was turned away at an angle. He strained to hear her end of the phone conversation, but he heard nothing conclusive. "If you'll wait here for a moment, sir." The nurse turned back to her charts. He leaned against the counter, picking at the green tissue paper wrapped around the yellow and white blossoms.

A man in a white coat moved down the hallway and approached the station. "Are you looking for Miss Bradley?"

Sam glanced at the man's name tag—Richard Hazelwood, M.D. Internal Medicine. The doctor had the golden good looks that belonged on a medical recruitment poster,

f there was such a thing. But it was the glint of hard reality
in the doctor's eyes that worried Sam. "Yes, sir. I hope
nothing's wrong." Sam began to feel a cold tingle crawl up
his spine. Instinct whispered, *Caution: Bad News Ahead.*

The man wore his arrogance as well as he wore his tai-
ored lab coat. "How in the world do you know Lily?"

Ignoring the doctor's air of disdain, Sam adopted a sim-
lar sense of familiarity, seeing it as an irresistible way to bait
the eminent Dr. Hazelwood. "I witnessed *Lily's* accident
yesterday and stayed with her until the police and ambu-
ance came. We talked last night in her room, and she
seemed all right then." Sam suddenly remembered the neat,
symmetrical hole in the Jag's headrest.

Evidence of an attempted murder.

Evidence which no longer existed.

Sam cleared his throat. "Has something happened?"

"Your name is Markstrom?" The doctor raised one blond
eyebrow and pulled a small rectangle of paper from his
pocket. Sam recognized the business card he had left on the
nightstand in her room.

"Yes, Sam Markstrom." *I don't think I want to hear
this....*

Hazelwood's bronzed face remained eerily impassive.
"Miss Bradley died early this morning from complications
of her internal injuries."

Sam ignored his screaming thoughts and kept his voice
calm and level. "That's impossible, Doctor. I talked to her
last night after she was admitted. I know she wasn't hurt
that badly."

"I'm sorry, Mr.—" the doctor glanced at the card again
"—Markstrom. Last night I would have agreed with you but
around three-thirty this morning, she developed some serious internal bleeding and went into shock. Despite our best
efforts, she slipped into a coma around five, then died at
5:42 a.m." The stone-faced medical man offered not one
shred of sympathy in his words or his expression.

Sam stared at the bunch of flowers in his hand, realizing for the first time that the fragile petals were in danger of being crushed in his white-knuckled grip. He placed the bouquet gently on the counter. "Thanks for the information, Doctor. Please convey my condolences to her family." Sam turned stiffly and headed back to the elevators.

It was all too convenient. Too pat. Were her injuries really that serious? *Or did somebody finish a botched hit?*

As soon as the thought skidded across his mind, Sam pushed it away. Ridiculous. Hazelwood probably had a wall full of expensive degrees to substantiate his high-priced talent. It wasn't likely the doctor would mistake unnatural causes for natural ones. Sam moved blindly out the hospital and threaded his way through the patchwork of parking lots dotting the hillside beside the hospital.

He sat in his car for a while, watching people come and go through the main entrance. Their faces reflected a multitude of emotions: concern, elation, grief. Lily Bradley's death was disturbing—not merely because of the questions it left unanswered, but because it reminded him once more about the fragility of life. If for no other reason, he grieved for a young life taken before its time.

With a deep sigh, he started the car and wound his way through the lot to the tollbooth. His fingers curled tightly around the steering wheel as he sat in the line of cars waiting to pay the parking attendant. When the car in front of him failed to move, he hit his horn. Patience was a scarce commodity at this particular moment in his life. A petite blonde stepped out of the stalled car and raised the hood, staring perplexed at the silent engine.

Sam sighed. *Here we go.*

Although he was no automotive expert, he easily spotted the loose distributor cap. When the woman started her car again, she was effervescent with her praise. He accepted the tissue she offered for his grease-streaked hands, but he declined her suggestion of a drink as repayment for his kindness. Sam climbed back into his Saab and waited impatiently for the parking attendant to fumble with the change.

He headed for the highway entrance ramp and merged into the easy flow of Saturday morning traffic. With the windows open and the radio at full volume, Sam let the cold rushing air ease his churning spirits. He glanced up at the terraced ledges of sheer rock lining either side of the freeway. Years ago, when highway engineers cut a wedge from Red Mountain to make room for the expressway, the ledges were bare. In the intervening years, persistent plants had grown in the fissures, clinging to life against all odds. That's what he'd thought Lily Bradley would do. He had pegged her as a survivor.

Another case where his instincts had failed.

Sam tore his thoughts away from the tenuousness of life and concentrated on the freeway as a speedy avenue of escape from the hospital and the memories it evoked. He headed south, traveling deep into the next county where the highway eventually dwindled from four to two lanes. He turned onto a dirt road which quickly deteriorated into a collection of potholes filled with gravel. Sam tried to focus on the challenge of driving, but his mind kept going back to the hospital.

No matter which theory he chose, fatal injuries or the completion of a botched hit, the ultimate responsibility for her death came back to him. He should have called in a few favors and gotten someone to listen to his story. After all, he'd held the evidence in his hand until the explosion. And he still knew guys on the force who might listen to him.

His attention wavered from the road for a moment as he tried to recall the smell of gasoline or the sound and heat of an explosion. Drawing a blank, he remembered only the cool night punctuated by the noise of exuberant basketball fans. And a pair of pale gray eyes filled with pain. *She just didn't seem that sick to—*

Sam jerked the wheel to avoid a large pothole. Something large and solid bumped against the back of his seat.

Slowing the car, he kept his eyes on the road and snaked his hand into the large, flat box he had picked up the day before. Suddenly, yesterday seemed like an eternity ago.

He reached blindly until his fingers curled around the handle of the lightweight revolver. Slipping the weapon out of the box, he braked to a stop in the middle of the road, then turned toward the back seat and called out, "It's got to be uncomfortable under that blanket. Why don't you just come out? Move very slowly and keep your hands up. I'm armed." He nudged the barrel, feeling it recoil from the jab.

Fingers emerged from the blanket, feeling around until they latched onto the front seat. A blanketed figure rose from the floorboard. Another hand clawed at the covering until it finally fell. Lily Bradley stared blankly at the gun barrel, then gave Sam a weak smile. "Remember me?"

Chapter Three

"I could have killed you," Sam Markstrom stated in a flat voice.

Lily watched the gun barrel waver slightly, then disappear. She released a shuddering sigh. "You wouldn't have been the first person who tried." Their gazes locked for a moment until the intensity grew too strong for Lily to maintain. She turned away and wrapped her arms around herself, trying to contain the sudden chill which danced across her shoulders. "I'm sorry if I scared you. But I had to get out of the hospital." She paused, feeling the chill turn into uncontrollable tremors. "I wasn't safe there."

"You were dead. How much safer can you be?" Although his voice betrayed no emotion, Sam turned and placed a white-knuckled grip on the steering wheel.

Lily glanced up, riveted by the sight of the white bandage half-hidden beneath the dark curls on the back of his head. She tried to deal with the momentary flood of guilt. "The story you told me...about the bullet and the briefcase. I didn't know whether to believe you or not."

"Something changed your mind?" He continued to stare straight ahead.

"Yes." Lily couldn't manage anything louder than a whisper. She drew a deep breath. "S-someone tried to k-kill me last night."

"I know. I was there, remember? But you didn't believe me."

"No. I—" Icy fingers of fear threatened to choke off her explanation. Despite her best efforts, her voice broke. "I mean later last night. Maybe it was this morning. I'm not sure exactly when it happened. It was dark." She squeezed her eyes shut for a moment, trying to collect the words and string them in some sort of coherent structure. "After you left, I got an . . . an inadvertent roommate."

"Inadvertent?"

She nodded. "The orderly put her in the wrong room. In my room. I remember hearing her moan and groan during the night, then someone came in and the noise stopped. I just thought they'd given her something for the pain. I didn't realize—" Uncontrollable tears clouded her eyes, and she fought them with no success. At the moment, the pain and the guilt seemed permanently intertwined.

"Realize what?" he prompted.

She breathed deeply and wiped away her tears. "That she'd received an overdose. Mr. Markstrom, I believe someone killed this woman by mistake, thinking she was me." She watched him shrug. "I know," she said with a sigh. "I can barely believe it myself. But from what we can tell, she received the medication that *I* was scheduled to get." Lily paused, feeling a familiar flood of dread wash over her. "And it killed her."

"Maybe she died of something else, and it's nothing more than an unlucky coincidence." His voice revealed no hint of emotion, as if they weren't discussing the death of another human being.

Lily shook her head vehemently. "You don't know how much I wanted to believe that. And I did believe it until the doctor realized someone had tampered with her IV fluid. The preliminary testing showed the drip solution had been laced with a heavy dose of morphine sulfate. And then she received a second dose of the same medication by injection."

"Which you think was meant for you?"

"Yes. Look at the sequence of events." She raised a hand and willed it not to shake while she counted off her points. "First, I'm forced off the road. Second, you discover the bullet hole. Third, someone attacks you and steals my briefcase. Fourth, my car explodes, destroying every shred of evidence to prove your claims. Then finally, this poor woman dies of a drug overdose." She glanced down at her outstretched hand and self-consciously curled her fingers into a fist. When she looked up and read the shreds of doubt on his face, she made herself release her fist.

"I know...it sounds so unbelievable. I hope to hell it turns out I'm just being paranoid. But I wasn't about to take any more chances. I had to get out of there without anyone knowing."

Sam surprised her by taking up her narrative. "Ah, but here's the big problem. You didn't do this by yourself. You brought others into this. You conned the doctor into telling me—and who knows who else—that you died. Then you arranged for the 'helpless' blonde in the parking lot to stall me so you could sneak into my car while I'm playing Mr. Fixit."

She felt his gaze settle on her, trying to read the existence or absence of guilt in her expression.

He continued. "You've taken a big chance, pretending to be dead. It's the type of lie that compromises more than one person's reputation and career."

Lily understood the unasked questions. How long did she have to argue to persuade the doctor to back her deception? How much money had she used to buy his silence? What promises did she make?

If he only knew Chip Hazelwood. It had taken surprisingly little effort to involve Chip in her situation. He owed her one. After all, the night before his wedding, the good Dr. Hazelwood was the one calling her to join him at his bachelor's party for one last night of fun and games. Lily called him a few choice names and threatened to tell his fiancée about his suggestion for a "last fling."

Later, Chip tried to cite nerves and a bottle of bourbon for his fidelity faux pas, but his momentary lapse in judgment had given Lily powerful leverage. And the fulcrum? His father-in-law, a scion of high social standing and even higher moral values, a man who would still be appalled at his son-in-law's attempted escapade three years earlier. So Chip became a willing conspirator, even coming up with the scheme of her untimely demise himself.

Lily decided it wouldn't be prudent to mention to Sam Markstrom the less-than-ethical terms of the agreement with her ex-fiancé. She felt guilty for watering down her explanation to Sam, but she decided to do it nonetheless.

She took a deep breath. "My doctor is... a longtime acquaintance of mine. I told him everything—about the bullet, the missing briefcase, the attack on you. We considered all the ramifications of faking my death, but neither of us could come up with a better way to protect me."

Sam shifted in his seat, evidently uncomfortable either with his position or Lily's revelation. His voice remained flat and emotionless. "The theory being, if you're dead, then you're no longer a threat to whoever wants you out of the picture?"

She nodded. "That's the plan. It'll give me time to try to make some sense out of this situation." Lily watched the man's shoulders rise as he released a sigh.

A hint of reprimand tinged his words. "Maybe you thought you were playing it safe, hiding in my car, but you'd have been smarter if you let me know you were there. I could've kept a watch for someone tailing us."

Her brief flare of smug satisfaction died away. "Oh, my God, I didn't think about that!" She sat up straight and scanned the woods surrounding them.

Sam released the steering wheel. "It's okay. We're safe."

"Are you sure?"

"Yeah." He gestured toward the window. "If anybody had followed us this far into the countryside, he would've been far too easy to spot. Anyway, why'd you take so long to let me know you were hiding in my car?"

Lily flushed, not quite wanting to reveal exactly how her great plan had failed. But he did deserve the truth. "I . . . I fell asleep."

Sam paused, then made eye contact with her for the first time during their conversation. "Do you know why someone might want to kill you, Lily?"

It was an inevitable question, one she'd asked herself a dozen times already. She drew the blanket around her shoulders and shivered. "If I knew the answer to that, I'd be sitting in a warm police station, spilling my story to an officer instead of in the back seat of a cold car, talking to you."

He hesitated for what seemed an eternity to Lily, then nodded toward the passenger seat. "You might as well be comfortable. C'mon, it's warmer up here." She fought to hide the spasm of pain which enveloped her when she tugged at the stubborn rear door handle. "Let me help—"

"No." She raised one hand to stop him. "It's okay. The only way to work through the stiffness is to meet it head-on."

Sam shrugged, doubt reflecting from his face and his words. "Are you sure you're okay? Are you really well enough to be out of the hospital?"

"The hospital is the last place I want to be right now." Lily allowed herself a strained sigh. "Anyway, dead people don't hang around hospitals."

Sam couldn't help giving her a critical look. "Yeah. They hang around morgues," he commented sarcastically as she opened the front door.

She lowered herself gingerly into the passenger seat, responding to his dubious expression. "I know this sounds a little extreme—"

"Extreme?" Sam echoed. "Try dishonest or unethical or just plain illegal. Any of the three would do."

She braced her palm against the dash. "Now wait just a minute! I don't know if you've ever thought your life was in danger, but I can tell you how I felt. I'd be damned if I was going to stay in that hospital bed and wait for someone to kill me. So what if I screw up some bureaucratic paperwork by pretending to be dead? I'm more important than a ledger of figures." Her bravado abandoned her halfway through her tirade. "You're right," she admitted after a moment's hesitation. "It's a little extreme, but what real options do I have?"

"You could go to the police."

Lily didn't have the strength to yell. She didn't raise her voice above a whisper as she enunciated each word carefully. "And show them what? *You* were the one who so very kindly pointed out that all the real evidence was destroyed in the explosion. No bullet, no bullet hole, no mysterious hit-and-run assassin with a rifle." Anger rose again to give her a few last ounces of energy. "I'm not playing sitting duck in the hospital until the woman's autopsy report comes back and proves me right. If it takes money to buy silence, then I'm willing to pay. Without the influence of the almighty buck, I'm not sure who I can trust."

Sam stiffened perceptibly. "Be careful. More times than not, money is the real reason behind murder." He paused, his gaze trailing down to the gun resting on the console between them. "And what about me? Why do you think you can trust me?"

Lily followed his glance to the polished barrel of the revolver. Her anger sputtered and died. A good question indeed. Why him? Why did she feel she could put her trust—her life—in the hands of a stranger?

Instinct? Intuition?

Ignorance?

She couldn't explain her own decision-making process to him, much less to herself. But he did deserve some sort of explanation. "All I know is if you'd wanted to kill me, you could've at any point. In the car, in the hospital..." She lost her train of thought as she reflected on the accident. His strength, his calmness, his concern—those were the things that had saved her. "Instead you called the paramedics and kept me from going insane while I was trapped. If you hadn't—" She stopped, fighting the flicker of pain that threatened to expose her weaknesses. "I could have still been in the car when it exploded. You saved my life—" she paused, then inhaled deeply "—without asking for any payment or reward."

Sam tried to ignore the uncomfortable flush of heat that began at the collar of his shirt and crept its way up.

"I don't know whether I can ever pay you back for that," she continued, her pale gray eyes flickering from beneath thick black lashes. She caught him in her gaze of gratitude. "Thank you...Sam."

Sam sat, mesmerized by her eyes. Usually the "damsel in distress" routine didn't interest him, but this time he sensed it was no act. Her gratitude was as real as her pain...and her fears.

Before he could stop himself, he stretched toward her, consumed by a sudden need to touch her. Covering his unexpected impulse, he reached around her and fastened her seat belt.

He didn't fool anybody. Not Lily, who rewarded him with a tiny quirk of her lips, a brief smile that did terrible things to his equilibrium as he watched her eyelids close. And he certainly didn't fool himself. Without actually touching her, he could feel her long curls wrapped around his finger, the velvet of her cheek pressed against his. He could hear the whisper of enticing words in his ear, the—

"Are you sure you're okay?" he heard himself asking. Evidently his brain had kicked in when his libido seemed destined to run off with his attention.

Lily opened her eyes and gave him a look of renewed determination. "I'll feel a lot better when we figure this thing out."

"We?" The word stopped him cold. A moment later, he realized that her "we" was a proposition to do with matters of the mind, not of the body and soul.

She pulled a card from her pocket and read aloud. "'Sam Markstrom, Computer System Investigations . . . Licensed and Confidential Investigator.'"

He stared at the familiar rectangle. "That card has certainly made the rounds. Last time I saw it, your doctor had it."

"I asked for it back because I'd like to hire you, Mr. Markstrom."

"Hire me?"

She became suddenly aloof. "I assure you I can afford your rates. Whatever they are."

Fragile thoughts of an idyllic romance shattered at his feet. *I guess I should have wondered when money would figure into this.* Sam thought about the Jag and a physician willing to put his career on the line for "a longtime acquaintance." He made a mental note not to let his imagination loose again.

He cleared his throat. "As much as I'd like to help, I can't. The only type of crime I deal with is to discover how hackers get into a computer system. It's my job to trace them, then close up the holes."

"Then here's your first hole to close." She slipped the card back into her pocket. "Someone used the hospital computer to change my records and remove the information about my drug allergies. Then they entered a false order from my doctor to give me the very drug I'm allergic to. Morphine sulfate."

He shrugged. "All that requires is an unguarded hospital terminal. That's a problem with personnel or hospital procedure, not with the software."

"But you have an investigator's license, too."

"Only so I can maintain a confidential relationship with my corporate clients." He leaned forward in his seat and braced an elbow across the steering wheel. "Lily, you don't need me. What you need are the police."

"The *police* don't believe me," she said, shifting against the seat belt. "The *police* think I'm a hysterical woman who concocted a story to explain her inability to drive. What I need is a private investigator who can understand a Zectronix 6200C system, accessed by forty-two in-house terminals and over two hundred external terminals located in three states." She rattled the numbers off with the voice of a seasoned professional.

Sam raised an eyebrow, wondering how a so-called "expert" could make such an obvious error. "Zectronix is still working on their third generation of 6200s. The 6200C hasn't been released yet."

Lily's gray eyes deepened to the color of steel, and a small smile tugged at her mouth. "Yes, it has. Bradley Pharm has had the C on-line since September. We're their test market."

"Test market? I didn't know Anthony Zechter was going to allow it out this soon."

"We've always been the test market for the new Zecs." Some of the color returned to her face. "Tony says—"

"You know Tony Zechter?" he interrupted.

"Sure." She flushed slightly. "We went to school together, kept each other awake during Pascal class."

Sam started the car. Anybody on the inside track with the elusive Tony Zechter had a distinct advantage, whether they worked directly in the business of computers or on the periphery as she did. Business scuttlebutt said the man valued brains as well as loyalty. Evidently she possessed both. "So. Tell me about the next generation of Zecs."

Their conversation quickly grew animated as they found common ground. As he headed back to Birmingham, she surprised him with her obvious familiarity with computers. He realized this was a safer topic, since neither one of them seemed eager to discuss the intricacies of attempted murder. It was amazing how they could become superficially engrossed in the mundane when the lethal hovered nearby. Yet he was glad to find a common ground.

Right outside the city limits, a white and orange ambulance roared past them on the freeway, and the sirens seemed to trigger the same unpleasant memories in her as they did in him. At least it brought a merciful halt to their conversation, which had begun to falter.

Sam tried to break through the sudden gloom which descended on both of them. "Let me ask one question. What would a farm need with a system as complex as a Zec mainframe? I mean, do you really need hardware quite so sophisticated to milk a cow or feed a chicken?" Her strained laughter took him by surprise.

"Thank you." Lily wiped a stray tear from her eye. "After today, I didn't think I'd ever laugh again. It's 'pharm' as in pharmaceutical, not pigs and chickens. Have you ever heard of Bradley Pharmaceutical?"

"Out toward Irondale? I've seen the sign."

"Good, so if I start talking about narcotics, you won't assume the worst."

Sam veered onto the shoulder of the road, switched off the engine and faced her. "Narcotics? Now wait a damn—"

"Hold it!" The gleam of amusement had drained from her eyes. "I told you not to assume the worst." She met his anger with her own indignation. "'Narcotics' is not a dirty word. It's merely a type of medication."

"A dangerous type of medication."

Lily ignored his comment and continued. "Bradley Pharm is a pharmaceutical supply house. We provide prescription and nonprescription medications to drugstores in a five-state area, including—" she raised a finger and accentuated the words by stabbing the air in his direction "—legitimate narcotics distributed with the sanction and the authority of the Drug Enforcement Administration."

The tension slowly left him. *Medicine, not illegal drugs.* "Sorry. The word 'narcotics' automatically raises my hackles. So we're talking about the *legal* distribution of narcotics?" She didn't seem to notice the slight emphasis on the word 'legal.'

"Among other things. But the narcotic stock is the most likely reason why someone would steal my briefcase. I had information about our delivery routes, our inventories. One of the files contained a listing of every narc order placed with us during the past month. We don't publicize that sort of information, mainly because drugstores don't want the general public to know just how many narcotics they keep on hand. It's an invitation for robbery."

Sam restarted the engine and threaded his way back into traffic. "What about your company? Isn't it a more likely target since you keep an even larger inventory on hand?"

"We paid good money for an extensive alarm system at Bradley Pharm so we wouldn't have to worry about that." Lily stretched, discomfort showing on her face. "So anyway, I grabbed a whole handful of folders when I left work Friday. The other files were pretty mundane stuff, vacation schedules, billing information, job-share schedules. That sort of thing."

Sam let his thoughts drift back to the previous night, rerunning his mental film of the accident. "Something's been bothering me about the truck that ran you off the road last night. I didn't get the license number, but just how many dark trucks could there be in Birmingham with a shiny metallic logo on the back with three letters? RBS."

"Twenty-seven."

"What?"

"You asked how many." She sighed, catching him in a steely stare. "And it wasn't RBS, it was BPS. *Bradley Pharmaceutical Supply*. We have twenty-seven dark blue delivery trucks." She plucked at the sleeve of her oversize sweater. "I don't like how this is adding up. The files, the truck..." Her voice died away to a whisper. "Someone with access to the motor pool tried to kill me."

"Or at least get those files at whatever the cost," Sam added.

She stared blankly out the windshield, making no comment on his remark. Sam kept quiet, allowing her the time to reflect on her situation, but his silence was an uneasy one. The gallant knight wanted to charge bravely to her side, ready to protect and to defend. The pragmatic realist reminded him of broken glass and blood—two deadly reasons to turn away and leave her to her own destiny.

When they reached the city limits, he spoke, shattering the tense silence strung between them. "There's got to be someone, your family or a friend whom you trust, with whom you can stay."

Her voice lacked energy. "My parents are dead, and the only other family I have are involved in the business with me. I have friends but..." She made a weak, fluttering gesture. "The list of people I think I can trust is growing shorter by the minute." She released a ragged breath, then looked around, evidently noticing her surroundings for the first time. "Where are we going?"

How could he explain chivalry went only so far? He cleared his throat. "I'm headed home. You need a chance to rest. Then after that, you can figure out what to do from there."

"Then you'll help me? You'll take the case?"

"No." Sam regretted the finality of the word. "I mean. I wish I could help. I know some PIs. I can probably find someone who can give you a hand. Maybe I could talk to a couple of cop friends of mine."

"Thanks." She sounded disappointed. "I'll take whatever help you can give me."

You mean what little *help I can give you.*

Lily retreated into silence as he negotiated the confusing maze of streets that heralded the entrance into his neighborhood. The trees, stripped bare by winter's occasional rosts, formed a spidery canopy over the roadway that wound through the hilly neighborhood.

Sam had grown up in this area and watched its metamorphosis from a stagnant community to a revitalized one. His own generation had grown up, moved away and returned to raise their middle-class families in the large, rambling houses that dotted the area. It was one of the few neighborhoods left in Birmingham where the letter carriers still trudged up the walkways to slip letters through old-fashioned mail drops in the front doors.

As he pulled into his street, he turned to Lily, hoping to break the uneasy silence between them. *I've got to say something....* He glanced at his sleeping passenger. *No, I guess I don't.*

LILY FLINCHED AWAKE, straining to identify the rumbling sound filling the air. She relaxed when she focused on the garage-door transmitter in Sam's hand.

"We're here." He switched off the engine. "Would you mind staying here in the car for a sec? I need to check to see how much junk I left out."

"Sure." She watched him disappear into the house. Scanning the garage, Lily eyed the organized workbench with its parade of tools neatly displayed on pegboards, the shelves with their labeled boxes.

The dashboard clock marked ten minutes, and she climbed out of the car, fearing he'd forgotten her. Lily moved toward the door, eased it open and took one look at the litter-covered floor. She turned her gaze from the mess and glanced back at the organized garage. *Something's very wrong here.*

Surrendering to her anxiety, Lily searched the car for the gun Sam had flashed at her earlier. She found the weapon tucked in a box which had been tossed carelessly onto the back seat. When her shaky fingers tightened around its shiny silver barrel, she realized Sam Markstrom had bluffed her with a very realistic, very *plastic* pistol.

Lily shoved the toy back into the box; she needed another means of defense. After examining the collection of tools, she picked out a large pipe wrench and slipped it in the back of her waistband. After tugging her sweater down to hide her weapon, Lily headed for the house. Beside the door, a yellowed baseball bat hung from a beat-up wooden plaque emblazoned with a Cub Scout logo. After a moment's hesitation, she reached for the bat and moved cautiously into the devastated house.

Away at school, Lily had once watched a tornado skip over her college. It cleared a wide path through town, bounced once, missing the entire campus, then landed on the other side, continuing its devastation. Spared from harm, she learned firsthand that weekend about total and capricious destruction.

Wandering around the house, Lily realized the calculated chaos there bore only a superficial resemblance to the twister's random demolition. Someone had torn up each room, not with meaningless malevolence but with cunning deliberation. Questions flooded her mind. *Who? Why?*

And with a sudden chill, *Where's Sam?*

Chapter Four

Lily stepped cautiously over a shattered picture, a family portrait of a policeman with a sweet-faced woman and two smiling children. She bent down to rescue the photograph but froze when she heard a noise through the floor vent. Although she couldn't understand the words, she recognized a sense of anger in the tone. She followed the sounds through a door and down some carpeted stairs. Instinct told her to remain quiet as she inched down the padded treads. The words became more distinct at the foot of the staircase.

"Damn it! Where could they be?" She realized the distorted voice didn't belong to Sam. "Wake up, stupid. I didn't hit you that hard!"

Lily heard a moan, then a splintery crash. Her breath caught in her throat.

The concrete-block walls of the basement absorbed much of the rage in the voice, leaving it harsh and flat. "You're a tricky bastard, aren't you? Well, you're not going anywhere until you tell me where those damn files are! You hear me?"

She gripped the stair railing with a shaky hand, flinching at the sound of a muted thud, then a groan. Squatting by the doorframe, she tried to become the smallest target possible as she stole a quick glance into the room.

The intruder stood by a file cabinet, hunched over the bottom drawer. Luckily he seemed unaware of her presence. But when Lily spotted Sam, she pulled back from the doorway, fighting a sudden wave of debilitating panic. He lay in the shadows on the floor with his arms tied around the back of a toppled chair. A small amount of blood puddled on the tile beneath his head. Lily crouched down again and hid in the darkness near the doorframe, again peering cautiously into the room.

The intruder wheeled around, but instead of lunging toward her, the man stood over Sam, raising a threatening fist. The puckered edges of a drawstring hood hid his face. "You've got five minutes before I torch the place, Markstrom. With you in it. Five minutes. Tell me where they are!" The intruder's voice was cold and hard, just as the stained floor must feel beneath Sam's cheek.

With a heart thundering loudly enough to be heard in the next county, Lily scrambled up the carpeted stairs, trying to find a safe balance between speed and silence. Once she reached the top, fear swelled within her, shutting down her thought process for a few precious seconds. She couldn't shake free of panic's choking grasp until a noise from downstairs reactivated her conscience.

Do something. Now!

Lily took a quick inventory of her options. She had a bat, a wrench, and—and— She looked around, desperate to find a way to help Sam. Inspiration flared through her mind. *The phone!* She nearly tripped, lunging for the telephone, but her sudden swell of courage deflated when she discovered the knot of colorful wires dangling from the receiver.

What next? Another burst of inspiration. *The car phone!*

As she battled her way through the scattered books and broken glass heading toward the garage, she chanted 9-1-1 to herself like a mantra. One miscalculated step made her lose her balance and hit a wobbly coffee table. A resounding crash betrayed her presence. Lily instinctively knew the intruder would come upstairs and investigate the sound.

Surveying the room for a place to hide, she took uninspired refuge behind a set of heavy drapes.

She tried not to shiver and give herself away. Her imagination provided a gloved hand to rip aside the curtain and a masked face to laugh at her feeble attempts to hide. Something pricked her back, and she shifted slightly to the side, revealing a keypad control panel. A glaring red light impatiently announced the home security system's inactive state.

Logic galloped at breakneck speed. If a little noise got his attention, then a lot of noise just might scare him off. Lily brushed a fingertip over the panel, reading the labels on each small button. Rather than digest the entire process, she dealt with her confusion by pushing every button on the panel. If it didn't scare the intruder, she prayed an alarm would, at least, bring help.

The dissonant howl of a siren pierced the air. Lily pushed back from the sound, feeling the uncomfortably cold glass of the window behind her. When she heard a noise outside, her insatiable curiosity compelled her to look through the window behind her. A lone figure appeared one story below her, coming out of the aboveground basement at a run. The man stumbled down a well-beaten path between two stands of trees, and, to her great relief, never turned back to see whether he was being observed. Twin brake lights flared briefly, then vanished as his car escaped along a back alley, speeding away from the house.

The siren died out, leaving its lingering echo ringing in Lily's ears. For a moment, she didn't know what to do, then she steeled her shattered nerves and resolved to go downstairs. And to pray.

Stepping from her hiding place, she tiptoed down the stairs, her heartbeat outpacing her slow, deliberate movements. Once at the bottom of the stairs, she sent up one more hurried prayer, then grasped the bat with a shaky but classic Little League grip. When she stepped into the room, a sudden burst of courage made her feel she *was* indeed ready to swing out at any threat.

But no threat remained to test her new fortitude.

Lily threaded her way through the debris and slammed the basement door, twisting the dead bolt into place. When she noticed the neat circle of glass cut from the door's lowest pane of glass, she grabbed a chair and rammed it beneath the doorknob for added safety. After she fumbled with a wall switch, the basement was flooded with bright fluorescent light. She turned, fearing what she would see.

Sam lay motionless on the floor.

Guilt surged through her, seizing her heart and lungs in an iron fist. A thousand accusing voices joined the lingering echo of the siren ringing in her ears. Her chest hurt; her knees and eyes both grew watery. If anything had happened to him...

Then he moved.

Lily threw herself to her knees behind the overturned chair, keeping the bat within reach. "Sam?" A knot of fear tightened in her stomach as her numb fingers battled the tape that circled his wrists. "Oh, please...wake up! Talk to me." *Please be all right.*

"I'm awake." His voice cracked and he coughed.

She watched his hands draw up into whitened fists as he groaned, and she released her pent-up breath. Abandoning his wrists, she moved around the red puddle on the floor. The harsh overhead light made the blood look artificial, like a cheap effect in a bad movie. Sam groaned again, reminding her of the reality of the scene. Real blood, real pain. Real danger.

Her hands trembled when she touched the blindfold tightened around his eyes. When she pulled the black cloth loose, he shied away from the sudden glare, blinking at the brightness. A thin line of blood trailed down the side of his face. His healthy tan seemed only a thin veneer over the pallor of his skin. In the absence of his accusations, her conscience supplied a pointing finger. *You did this to him.*

Her hand shook as she brushed the hair from his fore-head. "Sam, you're hurt. How bad?"

"Not that b—" He coughed again. "Scissors in the drawer." He grunted, then nodded toward a desk in the corner.

Lily blinked, then scrambled to the desk where she found the scissors beneath the mess. Returning, she inched the blades through layers of tape. "It's going to hurt when I pull this," she warned him.

"I won't notice," he quipped between labored breaths.

She shoved the scissors in her back pocket and winced in sympathy as she tugged the adhesive away from his skin. "I'm sorry, Sam." Hadn't she hurt him enough already?

He pushed himself to a sitting position, then rubbed the angry red welts left by the tape. "That's okay. Not your fault." He braced himself against the overturned chair, rising shakily.

"Careful!" She tried to steady him, very conscious of the arm he wrapped around her waist. He was supporting her as much as she was him.

"Good job," he muttered. He straightened and drew in a painful gasp. "It was a smart idea, using the alarm to frighten him away."

She felt her own knees weaken. "It was the only th-thing I could think of." She eyed his awkward posture critically, wishing she knew the extent of his injuries.

"We've got to get out of here." Sam grabbed her hand and lurched toward the stairs.

Lily tried to hold her ground, mainly because her legs wouldn't function properly. "Just wait a little. He—who-ever he was—drove off. I think you need to catch your breath." A vision haunted her, one of an anonymous en-emy returning to finish what had been left undone. "At least for a few minutes." She retrieved the bat from the floor, wondering why it suddenly seemed so heavy and hard to hold in her shaky hands.

Sam dabbed the corner of his mouth with the back of his hand. "That's great advice coming from a person who released herself from the hospital. Against common sense, I may add. C'mon, Lily." He grabbed her hand, then paused to give her fingers a slight squeeze. "Even if he isn't upstairs, we'll have an inquisition waiting for us soon enough."

"Who?"

"Concerned neighbors, one in particular. Maybe the police." Sam led the way up the stairs, leaning heavily against the handrail. Near the top stair, he whispered, "But just to be safe..." He held out his hand. "Bat."

Lily handed it to him, then stared at her empty hands. With necessity demanding inspiration, she reached back and pulled the scissors from her pocket, deciding they made a formidable enough weapon. Sam raised one dark eyebrow at her rearming procedure, but nodded in silent approval. They crept into the chaos upstairs, wary of hidden danger, human or otherwise. He led the way into every room, scanning each quickly, then moving on. They made a complete circuit of the house, securing the doors and windows and surveying the damage.

Once they'd finished, Sam eyed the desecration in the den with a critical scowl. He bent down to retrieve a pillow from the floor but drew in a raspy breath and reached out quickly to brace himself against the wall with one hand. He raised his other hand to wave off Lily's help, but rewarded her with a quick grin that dissipated some of the tension bottled inside her. "Thanks." He straightened up slowly. "If you ever need a recommendation for a job as a P.I., let me know. I can give you a great one."

"Does the job include my own plastic gun?" She cocked her head, feeling suddenly giddy about their temporary safety. "You know, you really had me going there for a while with your toy revolver."

"Sorry." He closed his eyes for a moment and drew another evidently painful breath. "It was a gamble. And it worked." When he reopened his eyes, they contained a glint of amusement. "Like you and your scissors."

"My scissors and I decline your job offer, if you don't mind." Lily glanced at the sharp blades, hefted the scissors one last time, then placed them on an empty bookshelf. "I don't want to live in a Nancy Drew world. I'd rather read my suspense than live it."

Sam splayed one hand across his lower chest, supporting his hesitant laughter, which turned too quickly into a coughing spell. He reached out, and Lily stepped closer, doing her best to brace him. As he caught his breath, he tightened his grasp on her, turning the movement into a quick hug and providing her with a sudden and pleasant sense of comfort. At the moment, she didn't care whether it was a gesture of convenience or of promise; it felt damned good.

She turned her head, trying to get a good look at him as his laughter survived his coughing attack. During the course of their brief liaison, she'd watched his expressive face reflect compassion, pain, confusion and determination—but never a smile. She ached to see how it transformed his features, but he released her all too quickly when his fingers found the pipe wrench, hidden beneath her sweater.

He pulled it out and hefted it in his hand. "What's this, 'Nancy,' my dear?"

She gulped, having forgotten about her secondary weapon. "Uh...latest thing in personal protection...and home plumbing repair?"

His grin captivated her. It lit his solemn face with a flash of brilliance as if he'd been released from a heavy burden. As quickly as she acknowledged the effect of his smile and appreciated its warmth, it faded away.

Sam reached past her and fingered the photograph Lily had rescued earlier, his face suddenly pensive. He brushed away the tiny shards of glass which coated the surface of the snapshot. "I'm glad my parents aren't here to see this." He stared into the picture. "I almost expect my father to reach out, shake his fist and yell at me about the mess."

Lily looked into the eyes of the two-dimensional figure who had placed one hand on his son's shoulder and beamed into the camera lens. She recognized the smile of paternal pride; it reminded her of a similar portrait, sitting on her own coffee table. A sudden mist blurred her vision, then passed like a fleeting memory. Concentrating on his stiff movements, she watched him place the broken frame on the bookshelf with gentle reverence.

"I was...worried when you left me out there for so long."

Sam shrugged, then winced. "When I drove up, I realized I hadn't turned on the alarm this morning. All I wanted to do was take a quick look through the house. I didn't expect to find anyone." Sam glanced around the room, grimacing at the destruction. "He jumped me as soon as I came in the door. Before I had time for all this to register." He rubbed at the dried red flakes that clung to his cheek.

"Don't do that. Let me wash it off." Lily prodded him toward the kitchen, which had escaped with only minor damage. She found a clean dish towel, dampened it and began to swab his face.

He propped both elbows on the kitchen counter. "It's evident someone—ow! Be careful, that hurts! Someone has discovered my connection with your case."

She rinsed the rag under the faucet. "But how?"

"Easy. He could have gone through my wallet after he slugged me at the accident site. Or checked the hospital records or even the police accident report." He took the towel from her and rubbed it along the back of his neck. "It was my mistake. I didn't think your attacker would be quite so thorough." Sam dropped the cloth on the counter, shifting with discomfort and covering his pain with a frown.

Lily folded the towel and replaced it on the counter. "I'm sorry I got you involved in this mess." She looked through the doorway toward the ransacked den and shook her head. "This sort of violence is frightening, knowing someone can enter your own home and—" The sound of a doorbell interrupted her, and she flinched.

Before Sam could move toward the entry hall, someone pounded on the door. "Sam, honey?" It was a woman's voice. "Are you there? What's going on, Sam? If you don't answer this door, I'll use my key!"

Lily watched some of the tension leave his face, but she found herself suddenly hit with a brief and unexpected jolt of emotion. Was this Sam's girlfriend? And why did her hands clench at the thought?

"It's okay. It's just a neighbor. Let me go talk to her."

Lily shifted out of sight as he answered the door. Although she couldn't see the woman, Lily could overhear the conversation. "You took your sweet time getting to the door, young man. I heard your alarm go off, and I figured he's tripped that silly switch again. But I got worried when you didn't call like usual...." The voice faltered. "What in heaven's name happened to your face?"

When Lily recognized the woman's air of commandeering gentility, she allowed herself a smile and willed her hands to relax. Without actually seeing the woman, Lily knew the neighbor was a member of the blue-haired legion that presided over the garden clubs and literary groups of the Deep South. The woman certainly wasn't a rival for Sam's affections.

Affections? Lily stopped for a moment, stunned by the intensity of her own feelings. Was it jealousy? Territorial instincts gone awry? Whatever it was, it was strong, unlike anything she'd ever felt before. Both unsettling and just a bit enthralling at the same time.

"Sorry, Mrs. Kay." Sam's voice echoed through the hall. "I, uh, opened the basement door and set off the alarm. When I ran upstairs to turn it off, I tripped and fell on the stairs. I guess I forgot to call you because the fall shook me up a little. I hope I didn't scare you or Mr. Kay."

Sam's apologies reminded Lily of an inventive but respectful boy trying to spin a tale satisfying enough to end his mother's probing questions. The woman's voice softened, and Lily could only hear him answer "Yes, ma'am" several times with a few "Thank-yous" thrown in, evidently for good measure.

As Sam closed the door, the woman's voice rose again. "And don't forget to put some ice on that lip!"

He returned to the den, his face reflecting a new discomfort. "It was my next-door neighbor. Everything's okay."

Lily studied his face, unable to ignore his swollen lip but even more mesmerized by the contrast of his dark hair against his pale skin. She realized the hooded distress in his eyes wasn't a side effect of his physical woes, but one reflecting his mental pain. "You didn't like lying to her, did you?"

He shrugged. "No, not really." He hesitated for a moment. "It's probably the first time I've lied to her with any success. Mrs. Kay was my fourth grade teacher, and she was always able to see through any tall tale I tried to put together. I guess I still expect her to see through my lies as an adult, too."

Lies.

It was a blunt but accurate assessment. *Too many lies,* Lily thought. *And I started it all. Well, I can end all the lies, too.* "I've reconsidered things and . . . I mean, if you'll just tell me how much I owe you . . ."

"Owe me?"

"For services rendered. And for the damages." She glanced around the room, sickened by the visible signs of unleashed violence. "I never meant for any of this to happen."

Concern etched a furrow in his forehead. "How could you have known?"

"You were right when you told me I needed the police."

"And I was right when I told you that you have no evidence to back your claims. If you go to the cops now with suggestions of a mysterious adversary, you'd better have some concrete proof. Right now, nothing's substantiated.

There's nothing to show them, nothing to connect this—''
he pointed through the door at the ransacked room beyond
''—with you. The police will pat your hand and send you
away. And then where will you be?''

''Back where I started. But this time I won't drag anybody else into it. No one else will get hurt.''

''That sounds great in theory, but it really stinks in practice.''

''Please. Sam.'' The violence heaped on his broad shoulders seemed even more pointless when contrasted with the
attraction she felt for him. No one should have to suffer on
her account. She looked at the splotches of color which
marred a face she suddenly found handsome. ''I don't want
to hire you.''

''You're a little too late.''

''But—''

''Hold it just a minute.'' He reached for her shoulder as
if his grasp would help persuade her to accept his interpre-
tation of events. ''Your adversary, whoever he is, has discovered our connection. I'm involved now. Just because you
decide to sever our brief business relationship doesn't mean
he won't go after me again. In fact—'' Sam stopped.

For a long moment, Lily thought he was going to kiss her.
What shocked her more was the revelation that it was exactly what she wanted him to do. When he released her
shoulder, the impression of his hand remained, tingling,
teasing her. He reached up, but instead of caressing her
cheek, he brushed the hair off her forehead and gently
touched the small bandage there.

''Now both of us have a personal reason to want to solve
this problem.''

Lily suddenly became aware of the slight aroma of his
after-shave. It was the same spicy scent she had concentrated on while pinned in the car. It sent a warm, reassuring
memory to soothe her pain. And fuel some new need deep
inside of her.

''Right?'' he prompted.

Pushing back extraneous thoughts of a more erotic nature, she yielded to his irrefutable logic. Her enemy, whoever he was, had declared open warfare. Innocent victims were in as much danger as intended targets. "We'll work together."

"It's the best way."

Lily sighed, taking a step away from him and wished it was a bit easier to step back emotionally. "Then what do we do next? You can't stay here, and I certainly can't go home. I'm supposed to be dead, remember?"

"You need to find a safe place to stay. Maybe with your family?"

She shook her head. "They're all involved in the business. And since the missing company files seem to be the source of my problem..." Her voice trailed off.

"I understand. How about friends?"

"Sure, there are a couple of people I'd feel comfortable enough imposing on, but... It would be the first place someone who knew me would look. Whoever ran me off the road wasn't following me. They knew exactly where I would be, what road and what time. Whoever it is, he or she knows me well."

"He. Definitely a he," Sam said, rubbing the back of his head.

She shivered at the thought of the intruder grilling one of her friends with the same ruthlessness he'd shown Sam. "Anyway, I won't have any of my friends sacrificed on my account." She glanced around at the mess which had once been Sam Markstrom's orderly life. "I suppose I could check into a hotel under an assumed name."

Sam ran one finger back and forth along the arm of the couch, obviously deep in thought. "No, I have a better idea." The shadows in his face lightened a little, bringing color to his blanched features. "I know the right place. We can stay with a friend of mine. He has plenty of space but few people know about it."

Together? "Aren't you afraid someone will trace us to your friend's house?"

"It's not exactly a house, but it's the closest thing we can get to a fortress around here. Right now, protection is a higher priority than comfort and facilities."

Lily studied the fabric of the couch with feigned concentration. "I don't have many options." She felt torn between taking charge of the situation and following Sam's suggestions. She'd been raised to be a leader, an heir apparent to the business. It was a role she truly enjoyed. But now, she was out of her league. Someone had changed the rules and neglected to tell her.

She eyed the man with the swollen lip. As an investigator, he'd been unwilling to help her until he'd been irrevocably pulled into the mess. His sense of self-preservation *might* be his only incentive, but it all boiled down to a matter of trust. Did she trust his instincts? Did she trust *him?*

The leader in her rose to the surface, reminding her that she was a good judge of character. For all his shortcomings, Chip had taken the time to speak to hospital staff who confirmed that Sam Markstrom was on the payroll as their computer consultant. The administrator himself had vouched for the man's talents.

What else can I do? Where can I go?

She glanced across the room at the family portrait, zeroing in on the fresh-faced boy with the open smile.

Who else can I trust?

Lily drew a deep breath and expelled it in a loud sigh. "I make it a rule—if you're stuck in a situation you can't figure out or fix, hire an expert." His intense gaze interrupted her thoughts for a moment. She breathed deeply again. "Then . . . then you follow his advice. You're my expert, so lead on."

He nodded. "Good. Let me get a few things together, and we'll get out of here."

After he disappeared down the hallway leading to the bedrooms, Lily played out the last vestiges of her adrenaline rush by returning some of the scattered books to the bookshelf. As her nervous energies faded and a dizzy weariness returned, Sam reappeared, wearing a fresh shirt and carrying a small gym bag.

He walked past her without saying a word and headed toward the kitchen. Lily followed. He batted at an amateurish still life which hung over the sink. The frame swung out like a door. Lily moved behind his right shoulder and watched him open the well-hidden safe. He shifted several files of papers onto the counter, then reached into the darkness, removed three small boxes and placed them on top of the papers. After he pulled out a tangled leather belt, he turned and handed it to Lily.

"Here, hold this." From the bowels of the safe, he next produced a gun. He handled it with a practiced wariness, examining the cylinder, then snapping it closed. He packed the dark metal revolver into the gym bag, along with the three boxes of ammunition. Lily struggled to untangle the leather, belatedly realizing it was a shoulder holster. A small medallion dropped out of the gun sling. Sam interrupted her examination of the bronze and ribbon decoration by plucking it from her palm. He dropped it back into the safe along with the files. She had seen the medal just long enough to read the engraved words on the front: Meritorious Service.

Sam stuffed the holster into the bag, then readjusted the framed picture to cover the safe door. "Ready?"

She eyed the gym bag. It wasn't that she disapproved of guns. Actually, she wasn't a bad shot herself of necessity, since she'd grown up in a family of hunters. But the thought of a gun made the danger a harsh reality for her.

"Are you ready?" he repeated.

Lily nodded, wishing she could ask him about the gun. About the citation. As they passed through the den, she paused at the bookcase, glancing again at the family portrait where his father wore a similar medal. The elder Markstrom also wore a guarded smile which mirrored that of the grown-up son.

Like father, like son?

"C'mon," Sam urged.

Lily caught up with him, knowing they had no time now to deal with mere curiosity; she would save her questions for another moment. Before they reached the garage, he pushed the curtain aside and punched a few buttons on the alarm panel. The result was a healthy green glow from a series of small lights.

After he helped her into the car, he placed the gym bag at her feet. As they pulled away down the quiet street, Lily marveled that, from the front, the pretty red brick house showed no signs of the devastation which had taken place inside.

Point of view, she thought to herself, watching in the side mirror as the house disappeared. *I guess it all depends on our point of view.*

SAM ATTACKED the familiar curves, using techniques he'd perfected in high school. It was a passage to manhood every boy in the neighborhood knew he would face one day. Few managed to "go all the way" at the age of sixteen, but Sam still held the record as the youngest guy in the area to make it. Matching the skill he demonstrated years earlier in his father's '67 Impala, Sam emerged from the neighborhood in thirty-two seconds flat, beating his own high school record by a full three seconds.

Despite the brief victory, Sam couldn't outrun his fear. He rammed the gears through their paces, slowing only when the streets widened to four lanes. At the first traffic signal, he sped through the intersection, ignoring the yellow light. When he glanced in the rearview mirror, he watched a black Camaro hurry through the red signal behind them.

Don't jump to conclusions. It could be a coincidence. . . .

He punched the accelerator, and the Saab shot forward.

Lily clutched the handle in the door. "What's wrong?"

Sam gripped the wheel more tightly and forced himself to speak calmly. "Behind us." The careless driver made two

successful lane changes, each time keeping three or four car
lengths directly behind them.

She wrenched the rearview mirror around. "Slow down."

"What?" He readjusted the mirror so that the image of
the Camaro loomed into sight again. "Are you crazy?"

"No!" She batted his hand from the mirror and commandeered it again. "I want to see who's driving."

Fighting another judgment that screamed for flight, Sam
decelerated. "Okay, but keep down. I don't want him to
know you're in the car."

Her face tightened. "He slowed, too."

Sam appropriated the mirror again. "We can't ID the car
unless it gets in front of us. But then he could see you. I'd
rather not chance it. Here...use this instead." He indicated the remote switch which adjusted the right side mirror.

She fiddled with the control, staring out the side window. "You can lose the tail."

It was a statement rather than a question, demonstrating
the trust she was placing in him. A trust he couldn't place in
himself. But something about her faith made him think.
Rusty thoughts creaked into motion, and he began to formulate a plan.

Sam inspected the rearview mirror again. "Yeah. Yeah,
I can," he said, his resolution building. He reached into the
pocket of the car door and tossed a small leather notebook
into her lap. "The first step is to find the work number for
Joshua Ingalls."

Lily thumbed through the pages and recited the numbers
which Sam punched into the telephone keypad.

A female voice answered. "Tidal Wave."

"Yes, may I speak to Mr. Ingalls?"

After a few clicks, his friend answered. "Ingalls here."

"Hi, Josh, it's Sam. Need a little help."

"Help? How?"

"Remember that discussion we had a couple of weeks
ago? The car wash trade-off?"

"Yeah?"

"I want to try it."

"For real?"

Sam glanced at his passenger. "For real. Can you handle it?"

"Sure. When?"

Sam glanced at his watch. "In about fifteen minutes."

"That soon? Well . . . okay. You need another vehicle?"

"Just transportation. And a substitute driver for my car."

Josh paused for a moment. "Will Douglass do?"

"Douglass." Sam tried to sound enthusiastic, but Josh's younger brother had been known as "Hell on Wheels" from his tricycle days. "Yeah . . . I guess he'll do. Thanks, buddy." Sam hung up the phone and glanced at his passenger. "Is he still back there?"

Lily nodded. "Keeping a respectful distance. Could this possibly involve another of your cases?"

"I doubt it."

"Oh."

"Traffic's getting thick. You keep an eye on our 'friend' and let me know if he starts to get closer."

"Okay."

They rode in silence as he negotiated the heavier traffic congregated around the buildings that formed the U.A.B. Medical Center. He passed under the freeway bridge, then turned into the driveway of an upscale car wash. They pulled up behind an expensive car, proudly bearing a caduceus on its license tag. Sam hesitated at the curb, allowing two or three cars to enter the driveway before finally following the expensive car to join the queue.

Josh Ingalls waddled over to Sam's car with a ticket book in his hand. "What'll ya have?" He winked conspiratorially at Sam and leered at Lily.

"Ready to test the theory?"

"Go for it, pal." Josh stuck his big paw into the car. "It's $15.50 for the wash, wax included."

"Good grief, Josh. That's twice as much as usual." Sam fumbled with his back pocket, trying to pull out his wallet.

"You're paying for two deluxe washes, remember?"

Sam stared at the meager contents of his wallet—a five-dollar bill. "So, is my credit good today?"

Josh made a face. "Can't pay the water bills with your good name. Well, shoot! Go ahead." The large man waved him ahead and rambled back to the long brick building. Sam rolled up the window and headed toward the car-wash entrance.

"When we get inside, just follow my lead, okay?" He gave Lily a quick glance.

She stared at him for a moment, then shrugged. "You're the boss."

The cars inched forward in line, heading for the entrance of the car wash. The car with the caduceus pulled onto the wash track, and Sam followed suit. He watched in the rearview mirror as the attendant had the Camaro back up and attempt to drive onto the track two different times. The black car finally entered the building just before the soap began to spill down the rear glass of Sam's vehicle.

Two large brushes began rotating at the front bumper and moved slowly down either side of Sam's car. He reached down by Lily's feet and pulled the small gym bag over the stick shift, leaning it against the steering wheel. "When I count to three, open your door and stay in front of the brush."

"What?"

"One, two, *three!*"

Chapter Five

Sam watched Lily hold her nose as if she was preparing to dive into the deep end of a swimming pool. Once she threw open the door, she skidded along the slippery floor, trying to brace herself against the soapy car hood for balance. Sam skated around the front of the car, grabbed her elbow and pulled her behind the camouflage of the rotating brush.

As soon as the soap blanketed the Camaro's windshield, blinding the driver for a moment, Sam led her to the side of the building and tugged her down to hide behind a small concrete-block wall. He raised a silencing finger to his lips, then motioned for her to keep down.

He tried to ignore the sudden resurgence of pain in his ribs while he pulled on a red and white jacket that hung on a nearby peg. After running a hand through his damp hair, he jammed an "Ingalls' Tidal Wave" cap on his head. Sam gave Lily a quick salute, coupled with a wink. "Stay here, okay?" Without waiting for an answer, he stepped over the low wall and headed toward the car-wash exit.

To blend in with a group of similarly dressed workers drying cars, Sam grabbed a rag and began to rub the hood of his own car. He nodded at its new driver, Josh's younger brother, Douglass. A young girl sat in the passenger seat, staring wistfully at her companion.

Douglass rolled down the window. "Just call me Bond. James Bond."

Sam snapped the damp cloth in his friend's face. "I'll call you 'mud' if you put a single scratch on my car."

Josh appeared at Sam's elbow, moving with surprising grace for such a large man. "Here comes the Camaro," he muttered. Sam plucked the sunglasses from the big man's nose and shoved them on his own face. Towel in hand, Sam moved over to the black car and began to dry the brake light centered in the upturned lip of the spoiler. He knelt, trying to get a better view of the driver through the rear louvers. A sticky spot of adhesive residue on the Camaro's rear bumper captured his attention. Sam stared at the vaguely familiar shape while Josh planted his enormous bulk in front of the car, polishing the wet, sloping hood. He ignored the protests of the agitated driver who waved furiously for Josh to move.

Douglass pulled the Saab slowly out of the driveway, keeping his face turned away from the black car. Sam moved alongside the Camaro, trying to look through the thin slits of darkly tinted glass and identify the amateur shadow. The driver blew the horn and gunned the engine. Josh shifted out of the way seconds before the Camaro left a trail of rubber tread marks on the driveway, speeding away in pursuit of Sam's car.

"Damn!" Sam threw the rag to the wet pavement in disgust. "I didn't get a look at the driver."

"I didn't, either."

Sam pivoted at the sound of the familiar feminine voice. He watched Lily pull off a red car-wash cap, and her long dark hair tumbled from its hiding place. His shock transformed quickly into indignation. "You were supposed to wait back there!"

She combed her fingers through the dark, tangled curls. "And let you have all the fun? No way."

Sam started to speak, but Josh interrupted him. "Weren't much to look at. Glasses, cheap mustache and hair combed down in his face." The big man stepped forward, hastily wiping his hand across his shirt and extending it toward her. "The name's Ingalls, Joshua L. Ingalls."

Lily shot Sam a hooded glance, then offered Josh a small smile. "Pleased to meet you, Mr. Ingalls. I'm Lily."

Josh finally let go of Lily's hand, then fished around in his shirt pocket, selecting a pen and a slightly damp pad of paper. He wrote down a series of letters and numbers and handed the paper to Sam. "Here."

Sam recognized the sequence: a vehicle identification number. Joshua was probably the only man in the city who could instantly memorize a string of numbers that long at a single glance. Sam nodded his thanks. "Good work, buddy. The license plate isn't going to help us, but this will."

Lily unzipped the red-and-white jacket. "Why not? Can't you trace the tag through the DMV? I'm sure we could hack into the system—"

He raised a hand to gesture her to stop. "We don't have to hack into the system. First, I'm authorized to access the DMV computer, and second, the plate was stolen."

"How do you know that?"

Sam helped her out of the jacket. "The idiot stole it off a truck. You can tell by the numbers."

Josh nodded enthusiastically. "And he didn't even bother to tighten the bolts down all the way. Did you notice the gummy stuff on the bumper? I recognized the shape—it was a rental car." Josh paused and stared over Sam's shoulder, raising a beefy hand and waving to someone. "Uh…here's your ride."

Sam pivoted, then swallowed hard. A television-channel logo decorated the side of the white van parked at the edge of the driveway. He watched the figure step out of the driver's side.

Micki.

His sister moved briskly toward them, her long coppery curls pulled into a loose braid, which bounced as she walked. She favored them with a sunny smile, indicating they'd caught her in a good mood. "Hi, Josh." Micki gave the big man an affectionate squeeze, then punched Sam in the arm. She looked critically at her brother's pale face and swollen lip, and lost her smile. "What the heck happened to you, Spence?"

Josh's enormous belly began to shake with laughter. "Yeah, *Spencer,* what is this all about?"

Sam loaded his best retort and fired. "Shut up, Lafayette."

The big man's face registered his shock with a rapid flush of color. Josh squeezed the rag in his hand so tightly that water dribbled on the size thirteen high-top sneakers. Sam found a puerile satisfaction in making the man squirm. "I'm going to kill Douglass for spilling that," Josh growled.

Sam shrugged. "Don't blame your brother. He didn't tell me your real name. I stumbled over your birth certificate at the county courthouse one day while I was working on their computer system." He pretended to appraise the large man's girth with a critical eye and fired the second round. "You know, I never would've guessed you only weighed five pounds when you were born."

Joshua's embarrassed face darkened from red to maroon.

"Would you two quit picking on each other and tell me what's going on?" Micki ignored Josh's inflamed face and glared at her brother, then at his companion. "Aren't you going to introduce us?"

Before he could speak, Lily stepped forward. "I'm Lily. You're Michelle Marks, the sportscaster, aren't you?"

Micki nodded. "Also known as Micki, Spence's big sister."

Sam turned away from his sister's mocking smile, instead noticing the dark circles beneath Lily's eyes, virtually the only color in her stark, pale face. Concern flooded him, undermining the brief thrill of success.

"Lily, are you all right?" He reached out for her, closing his hand around her trembling fingers.

Her glance held his for a moment until she returned a wan imitation of Micki's smile. "I'm fine. Don't worry about me." Lily gently pulled away from him, wrapping her arms around herself. She was unable to hide the shiver which coursed through her.

He glanced down at the jacket slung over his arm and held it out for her. "You look like hell. Here."

Lily shoved her arms through the sleeves with the same weary smile. "Thanks."

Sam turned back to his friend. "We'll get the jacket back to you later, Josh." He placed a protective arm around Lily's shoulders and led the way to Micki's van.

His sister followed them, uncharacteristically quiet. When they reached the vehicle, Micki paused at the sliding door as he and Lily climbed in. "She's not the only one who looks like hell. What did you do, Spence?"

He tried a disarming smile. "Tried to break up a dog fight."

"Yeah," she muttered, "between a Greyhound bus and a Mack truck." She slammed the sliding door, circled the front of the vehicle and climbed into the driver's seat. "Are you going to tell me what happened or am I going to have to pump *her* for the details?" Micki gestured over her shoulder toward Lily.

"You'll get name, rank and serial number. That's all, Micki."

His sister adjusted the rearview mirror so that Sam could see the disgruntled light in her eyes. "I knew I should have sold you to the ice-cream man when I had a chance."

Lily tried to smile. "You know, you two don't look anything alike. I'd never guess you were siblings."

Sam glanced at his sister. It was true; they looked nothing alike. Recessive genes had combined to provide her with red hair whereas he'd inherited his parents' dark coloring. He always wondered whether her fiery temper was merely a by-product of the merciless teasing she endured as one of the few redheaded kids in the neighborhood. Or was her hair a literal red flag to warn the uninitiated of her irascible nature?

"Mick's our genetic throwback. I tried to make her believe she was adopted when we were younger, but I couldn't convince her."

"Don't listen to him, Lily. He's just jealous." Micki rubbed her hands briskly in front of the heat vent. "By the way, you know you could at least tell me your last name."

Lily took a moment before she answered. "Brad—"

Sam leaned forward. "—ford, Lily Bradford. Sorry I didn't handle the introductions, Mick."

"Bradford?" Micki turned around to face them, revealing the slight furrow creasing her forehead. "No..." She drummed her fingers on the seat back. "I've met you before. Somewhere. You're...you're Vance Bradley's sister, aren't you?"

Sam released an exasperated sigh and pushed back in the seat. Lily stalled for time by fumbling with her lap belt. She gave him a hooded glance, and he nodded at her. "We had no chance—she knows everybody."

"Not his sister," Lily explained. "I'm his aunt. Although you'd never hear him admit it. It cramps his style to have an aunt my age."

"I can imagine. I went out with him a few times. He's certainly committed to maintaining his style." Micki grinned, and her entire face lit up with a mischievous, animated beauty, erasing the look of wariness she'd worn earlier.

"That's our Vance." Lily nodded as if they both knew a big secret. "He *does* love playing the field."

Sam stared at his sister, wondering what joke she was sharing with his client. "You went out with her nephew? Jeez, Micki, wasn't he a little young for you?"

Lily merely smiled, evidently unable to find enough energy to actively join Micki's enthusiastic laughter.

"You know I don't go for the high school set, Spence."
The smile faded. "And I haven't forgotten the fake name
you two were trying to foist on me. What gives?"

Sam stole a glance at Lily. "Nothing."

Lily shrugged. "Nothing, really."

Micki threw a harsh glare into the mirror in Sam's direction. "Spencer Andrew Markstrom, you know I'll find out.
Eventually."

Lily seemed uncomfortable, and her effort to defuse the
tension was transparent. "Spencer? I thought maybe Sam
was short for Samuel. I didn't realize it stood for your initials."

"Spencer was my mother's maiden name. I always hated
it." He stole a glance at his sister, who sighed theatrically
and turned around. "So when I went to high school, I
changed it to Sam."

"Why? I think Spencer is a nice name."

"Thanks." He felt an odd heat at his collar and covered
his reaction by turning sideways so he could keep an eye on
the flow of traffic behind them. The van rode higher than a
car, giving him a better vantage point to watch for the
Camaro. "I guess I worried about being typecast. You
know...a computer science major named Spencer who
wears glasses and a plastic pocket protector? Sam sounded
so much more mainstream. At least, it did at the time. Now,
as an adult, I wonder if I shouldn't change back to Spencer. I'd like to sound a little more like an executive than a
character out of a Dashiell Hammett novel."

"Tell her the truth, shweetheart." His sister's disruptive
voice rang out from the front seat.

Lily glanced at him, commanding his total attention with
merely a curious gaze. "What truth?"

He lowered his voice, hoping to forestall Micki's un-
wanted comments. "I've spent my entire investigative career smiling at people who thought calling me Sam Spade
was the height of humor."

Lily nodded with a sigh. "I have the same problem. I'm named Elizabeth after my mother, and most people assume I was nicknamed Lily because everyone called her Rose. Sort of a floral theme."

"So why do they call you Lily?"

She grimaced. "My father nicknamed me after a pharmaceutical business. He merely dropped the extra *L* from Lilly as in Eli Lilly and Company."

Sam laughed in spite of his efforts not to.

Stopped by a red light, Micki turned around to face her passengers. "Spence, you never told me why you needed a ride."

"We had someone following us who we didn't want to deal with."

"Following?"

Lily jumped in. "Sam's helping me with a little business problem."

"Business?" Micki raised an eyebrow. "That's why my brother looks like he's gone a couple rounds in the heavyweight championship of the world?"

Sam took a deep breath, then let it out slowly. "If you'll just drive, I'll explain everything." *Half of everything.*

"Drive to where?"

"Bean's Place."

"Oh, good grief." She made a face and gunned the engine impatiently.

Lily wore a perplexed look. "Bean's Place? I've heard of that. It's a bar."

"For the lack of a better word." Sam crossed his arms. "Bean likes to think of it as a 'variable concept public house.'"

"In other words," Micki supplied from the front seat, "a bar."

BEAN'S PLACE straddled the top of Red Mountain in an area local residents had nicknamed No Man's Land. In the early days of surveying, officials from Birmingham had marked the southernmost city limits just shy of the mountain's northern summit. On the southern side of Red Mountain, small communities grew and eventually incorporated up the side of the mountain, but their boundaries failed to include the top ridge. Later, officials admitted they had believed the land couldn't be developed due to the steep, rocky terrain. Bean's great-uncle had proven all of them wrong.

The original Bean had built a honky-tonk bar on the site, unhampered by city building codes, restrictions and zoning. He'd even included a small apartment that connected to the bar by a secret passageway. Budding country music stars played Bean's Place long before they hit Nashville and the Grand Ol' Opry. When the present Bean inherited the business and the area's nickname, his dislike for "nasal and twang" music drove him to change the format of the bar. But he couldn't make up his mind what type of establishment he wanted Bean's to be. His indecision became his inspiration.

Every three or four months, Bean changed the bar from top to bottom. The continual theme changes attracted an otherwise fickle bar crowd, who tended to drift to a new location when the old one became too familiar and comfortable.

Bean combined an acute business sense with a flair for the theatrical to revamp the bar using meager resources and his enormous talents as a stage-set designer. The last incarnation Sam had seen was The Cactus Bar and Grill whose southwestern theme featured Mexican beers and jalapeño appetizers, accompanied by a group of cowboys singing about life on the range. From past experience, Sam knew not to expect to find the bar looking anything like the previous visit.

Micki handled the winding private road like a pro. Sam knew the height of the spray of gravel she kicked up was her wordless comment on his watered-down explanation of Lily's problem.

Micki flipped her hair back with one free hand. "I don't see why you can't stay with m—"

He interrupted her. "Micki, you live in a one-bedroom condo. No space, no security. It's the first place someone would look for me."

They slid to a halt in the parking lot. "But—"

"But nothing. And you don't tell anybody where we are. *Anybody.* Understand?"

Her only answer was a frown. Sam helped Lily out of the van and headed across a short redwood bridge to the bar's side entrance. He stabbed the intercom button by the door-frame. "Morning, Bean. Rise and shine. You've got company."

A few moments later, a gruff voice answered, "No deliveries before four. Read the sign, stupid."

"Bean. It's Sam. Open up."

The voice remained brusque. "You've got some nerve, Markstrom, waking me up at this time of day. What in the hell do you want?"

"Watch it, Bean. There are ladies present."

Micki leaned toward the speaker grill. "Hi, Beano. Long time, no see."

"Micki, is that you?" The voice suddenly changed, the rough drawl turning into clipped, eager tones. "Just a minute, guys. I'll be right there. Just wait, okay?"

She smirked at her brother, then turned to Lily. "Bean keeps different hours than us normal folks, due to the bar. It's early morning to—" Micki stopped. "Lily, you don't look so good." Micki placed a hand under the woman's elbow.

Sam glanced into his client's drained face.

Lily tried to smile. "I'm not surprised. I don't feel so well...." Her knees buckled, and she pitched forward. Sam concentrated past the pain in his ribs to swing Lily's limp body into his arms.

Micki pounded on the door. "Hurry, Bean!"

The door opened, and Bean shielded his eyes from the obtrusive glare of the sun. "To what do I owe—"

"I'll explain later," Micki interrupted, using him to wedge the door open.

He ran a hand through his tousled white hair, then tightened the belt on his bathrobe. "What's going on? Who's she?" He nodded at Lily's inert form.

Sam turned sideways to carry his burden through the doorway. "Just don't stand there. Give me a hand!"

Stunned into silence, Bean helped Sam carry Lily through the hall and into the office. After they lowered her onto the leather couch, Sam knelt awkwardly beside her and began to check her pulse. "I think she just fainted."

Bean shifted from one foot to the other. "Sam, I keep a supply of ammonia caps in the bar. Want me to get one?"

"Good idea."

"No, try this." Micki handed her brother a damp bar towel.

Sam draped the wet cloth over Lily's forehead, and she began to stir. Her initial gaze was unfocused, but it grew sharper as she struggled to get up.

"No, stay here." Sam reached out to place a restraining hand on her shoulder, finding the gesture to be strangely intimate. Their gazes locked for a brief moment. "I'll... we'll get you some help."

"Don't." She continued to look only at him. The strength in her voice belied any weakness on her face. "I'll be all right. Just give me a minute." Her eyes closed briefly, then popped back open as if she had lost her concentration for a second. "I—I didn't get much sleep last night."

Micki leaned over Sam's shoulder and glared at the woman on the couch. "Lily, when was the last time you had something to eat?"

Lily's smoky eyes glazed over in thought, then quickly came back to life. "Yesterday, lunch—no, I worked through lunch. Breakfast, I guess."

Micki pushed Sam aside, ignoring his grimace of pain.
"You need to eat something. Bean!" Bean and Sam flinched
simultaneously, both recognizing the familiar I'm-taking-
charge tone in her voice.

"Yes, ma'am?"

"Get her something to eat. Some tea and crackers. And
Bean—" she pointed at Sam and sighed in exasperation
"—take him with you."

Knowing the better part of valor was sometimes surrender, Sam, trying to hide the flare of pain, pushed to his feet
and escaped. Bean led him to the kitchen, pulled out a bar
stool by the long metal worktable and shoved a bottle under his friend's nose. "Beer, the universal antidote for
whatever ails you."

Nursing the beer silently, Sam watched his friend follow
Micki's orders and load hot tea and various innocuous
foods onto a tray.

"Duty calls," Bean announced as he balanced the tray in
one hand. He disappeared into the hall.

When Sam raised the beer to drain it, a ruthless pain shot
up his side. The bottle fell to the metal surface with a loud
clatter but without shattering. Discarding his jacket, he began to unbutton his shirt. He winced when he discovered the
angry bruise mottling his skin. Probing the swelling carefully, he was unaware of his friend's return.

Bean whistled. "Damn, that must hurt!" Sam grabbed at
his shirt to cover the discoloration, but Bean shook his head.
"Too late. I already saw it. What in the hell happened to
you?"

Sam drew a deep, painful breath and began to recount the
events which had occurred within the last twenty-four hours,
describing Lily's accident, the second attempt, her untimely "demise" and the intruder.

"And the guy jumped you in your own house?"

Sam nodded. "All I did was walk into the house. I didn't
expect anyone to be there. When I saw the mess, it stopped
me cold."

"Then the guy finished the job by knocking you *out* cold." Bean pointed to Sam's side. "And how did you get that?"

Sam fingered the edge of the angry bruise. "If you look closely, you'll probably find it's basically the shape of a shoe."

Bean recoiled with a sympathetic wince. "Sorry I asked. I can see how much damage he did to you. How much did he do to the house?"

"Yeah, Spence, how much damage?"

Sam caught his breath at the sound of his sister's voice from the doorway. As she approached, he buttoned his shirt, praying she hadn't seen his injury. He felt much too lousy to put up with her surrogate maternal advice and no-discussion ultimatums.

Her freckles faded into a red flush staining her cheeks. "What a crock of lies you told me. Do you realize that woman in there thinks someone is trying to kill her?"

"How is she?" Sam caught Bean's departure out of the corner of his eye. "You didn't put her through the third degree, did you? She's had a rough day."

"I didn't grill her. She...volunteered the basics." Micki tapped her foot impatiently. "So, what do you plan to do about her?"

"Help her." Up to the point he spoke the words, he hadn't decided what to do. He'd been acting on sheer instinct, seeking higher ground. Before he made any decision, he wanted to sit down and examine the logic of the situation. After all, he intended to approach Lily's problem as he would any programming project. Determine the constraints and set up a flowchart as a guide.

But Lily couldn't be reduced to a set of variables, couldn't be controlled like strings of numbers to be pushed and pulled through a mathematical wringer until they conformed. He needed to deal with her fears, her strengths. Her ability to blot out his logic and cognitive reasoning with a mere touch.

Or a smile.

Or—

"And just how do you expect to help her?" Micki prodded.

He looked up startled, and realized he was still in the middle of a conversation—an argument—with his sister. "I'm not sure."

Micki lost the flush of color and looked suddenly drained. She jammed her hands into her pockets. "I don't get it. You've worked long and hard to get where you are. I don't understand why you'd be willing to throw it all away to play private eye."

"I'm not throwing anything away, Micki."

"It sounds like you've thrown your common sense away. That woman—"

"—has a name. Lily. Lily Bradley."

Micki ignored him and continued. "*That* woman is facing a threat that can't be reduced to a simple diagram. Don't you remember your lecture to me about the human variable? Why you prefer not to work with the one thing that can't be translated into binary code?" She paused for a minute, her face filling with something beyond anger. "Why you, Spence? Why not 'Joe Blow, Private Investigator' from the yellow pages?"

Sam stared at her, wondering if she'd ever understand. Whether she could or couldn't, he still had to try to explain. "Micki, you have to realize if I walk out right now and say, 'Sorry, I won't take the case,' there's this little problem. The guy broke into *my* house because he thinks *I'm* involved. And I'm pretty sure the next time I run into him, he's going to act first, ask questions later. I *have* to help her now. For my own good."

An uncomfortable silence settled in the room like a heavy fog. After a few tense moments, Micki broke the stillness. "Spence, I'm sorry I blew up, but you're all I have left." The anger in her voice had dissolved, leaving an emptiness to echo in her words. "I lost Mom and Dad, and I can't bear the thought of losing you, too."

The painful memory of their parents' deaths had faded very little with the passage of time. But mentioning them now was a cheap shot, a Micki Markstrom specialty. The deep breath he took caught in his throat, making his voice grow hoarse. "Don't be so damned selfish. They were my parents, too. God knows I understand the pain and fear of wondering if or when it will happen again." Sam grabbed the empty beer bottle and rolled the smooth, cold cylinder of brown glass between his two palms.

"I'm not the selfish one, Spence, you are. You're forcing me to sit and watch you dive headfirst into a situation that could be more than you can handle."

Sam recognized the shaky timbre of her voice. Tears were a rare emotion for his tough sister, a survivor in the male-dominated world of sports broadcasting. "I'm not forcing you to do anything."

Her voice broke. "I d-don't know how to deal with the fear of something happening to you."

Sam couldn't turn and look at her. He couldn't make himself acknowledge her pain by the act of witnessing it. Gripping the cold metal table in front of him, he faced the window, waiting for that one last parting shot. Instead he heard the soft rhythm of her feet crossing the room.

"Do what you have to do. And call me if you need me." Weary resignation filled her words. He looked up, seeing her reflection in the window as she paused in the doorway. "Sam, you know I love you, and I'll be there."

Before he could speak, acknowledge her act of reconciliation, she disappeared into the hall. Seconds later, he heard the door slam.

Sam remained on the bar stool, taking stock of his wounds, physical and mental. He equated an argument with Micki to the act of juggling knives. Once the blades began to spin in the air, you realized you had no idea how to stop the performance without drawing blood. Early on he'd learned to step back and let the knives drop, making sure his own toes were out of the way. But this was the first time in recorded history that Micki had stepped back first.

It was deceptively easy to push away thoughts of Micki and her patented redheaded temper and remember Lily's dark curls. While she'd tended his cuts, he'd been mesmerized by her hair, which danced against her shoulders as she moved. He'd yearned to reach up and capture one strand, to run it between his fingers.

Sam probed his swollen lip, remembering the gentleness of her touch, the quick glance they shared before more pressing issues commanded their collective attention. She was a remarkable woman, certainly beautiful, obviously compassionate. Smart. Yes, very smart, *and* savvy. She'd approached some unsettling situations with inventive reactions, confronting—even surviving—the terrors facing her so far.

He never expected to find any terror in his career. Intrigue, yes. Mystery, sure. But fear? Not really. Not in the career he'd planned for himself. Of course, he never counted on losing the federal grant and, therefore, his job.

The golden age of computers brought enlightenment to the masses. It also challenged another segment of the population; network technology begot computer crime. And computer crime begot a need for computer system protection.

Sam learned early on that computer theft was intrinsically a crime of intelligence. The brains behind the misdeeds correctly anticipated that the local police wouldn't have the means to catch them. Their crimes were not on a grand enough scale to warrant direct federal intervention. But the government responded indirectly by providing a grant to cover the expenses of setting up and maintaining a Computer Crime Division as an independent organization aligned with local law enforcement.

Sam was desperate to dredge up a good memory to replace the sour taste in his mouth left by his fight with Micki.

He couldn't help but think of the CCD. He was content in those days, matching wits with a criminal element whose victims shed sweat and tears but seldom blood.

His six years as head of the division brought many successes and only a few frustrations. He liked his job and the people he worked with, but because he was a civilian, he was only an outsider, on the fringes looking in. It was a hard position for the son of a cop to be in. When the funding dried up, he suddenly had no position, and it seemed the CCD was destined to be nothing more than a fond memory. That is, until the chief made his offer: Restart the unit from within the police department.

The catch?

Become a cop. Make it through the Academy, the rookie year and pass the examination for detective. Then the CCD could be reincarnated as a separate division.

The chief asked for the world. And Sam was ready to comply.

Too bad it didn't work out. Sam pushed back the irony, refusing to acknowledge the sequence of events that changed his life forever. *Concentrate on the here, the now.*

He rested his chin on his tented fingers, mulling over the first stages of his investigation. Suddenly he noticed Lily's scent lingering on his hand. *Peaches. I love peaches.*

Sam stood, ignoring the tightness in his chest. He needed to see her, to make sure she was all right. He walked stiffly down the hall, trying not to groan as he batted open the door leading to the apartment attached to the bar. It wasn't merely a door, but a bookcase which effectively shielded the private areas from the public ones. He met Bean in the hallway outside the master bedroom.

"Shh, she's asleep," his friend cautioned.

"I just wanted to make sure..." Sam slipped past Bean and stepped into the room.

Lily was curled up in Bean's bed, an irritating fact that didn't escape Sam's attention. Pitch-black hair spilled across the pillowcase in crimped waves, framing her pallid but serene face. No matter what demons chased her in reality, they evidently hadn't followed her into her dreams. But Sam noticed how she clutched the second pillow to her chest, looking just like a child clinging to a love-worn teddy bear.

"Are you sure—" She shifted at the sound of his voice, then nestled back into the pillow with a sleepy sigh. Sam stepped out of the room and closed the door gently. "Are you sure she's going to be all right?"

His friend shrugged. "Both she and Micki thought some food and a little sleep was all she needed. You look like you could use the same. You know where the guest room is." Bean gestured over his shoulder.

"Yeah." Sam felt his throat tighten a bit. "I noticed Lily got the master suite."

Bean merely smiled. "My momma always taught me to give my seat to a lady."

"I don't think she meant to include beds in that."

"Maybe not." Bean graced his friend with a big grin. "By the way, Douglass just returned your car. He's at the bar."

"Thanks."

Bean lagged behind as Sam headed down the hallway. Sam stopped in the wide doorway leading to the bar. Douglass sat at the long, polished counter, but Sam stared beyond his friend, at the spectacle that demanded his attention.

Bean had changed the bar. Again.

The cactus plants, which had decorated the southwestern-theme bar, were now blue and placed against an elaborately detailed backdrop of an alien night sky with twin moons. The bandstand had been redone as a transporter room with "control panels" that beeped and flashed around the large room with irritating irregularity.

Sam felt as if he had walked onto the set of a Grade Z science fiction movie. "Oh, shi—"

"Welcome to the 'Somewhere in the Distant Future' Bar." Bean stepped forward and made a grand sweeping motion with his arm.

Douglass laughed while he savored the last dollop of white foam that slid down the upturned mug.

Bean continued, ignoring the suppressed giggles from his patron. "This month, the specialty of the house is Denebian Brandy."

Sam took his time to scan the room, soaking in the futuristic atmosphere. "You've been threatening to do this ever since you saw *Star Wars*. I can't believe you finally broke down and did it!"

"It helps to find a couple of electrical engineering students who'll work for peanuts—and beer." Bean glanced proudly at the panels of pulsating lights. "They did a good job, didn't they?"

"Great, Bean. Really great." Sam shifted his attention to the young man on the bar stool. "Douglass, tell me you didn't burn out my clutch trying to power shift, and you didn't get any moving violations. I don't have time to fix any tickets today. Capische? And if I find any long-distance calls to Tahiti on my phone—"

"Not to worry, Mr. Spade. I pretended I was you and drove like a li'l ol' lady. Never got above thirty-five, not once! Not even on the interstate! At least, *after* I lost the guy who was tailing your car." Douglass smirked and nudged the empty mug toward Bean, who nodded as he retrieved it. The younger man's grin faded when the glass disappeared beneath the counter and didn't return.

"No more for you. Josh called. He wants you back at work. Pronto." Bean shrugged at Douglass, then added a wink. "When you come to the Mardi Gras party Sunday night, remind me to fix you one of my special hurricane drinks. Okay?"

"Deal." Douglass tossed the keys at Sam, and they walked out the door together. Sam watched in amusement as the young man climbed into an old, ramshackle pickup truck. A young lady sat in the middle of the faded bench seat, favoring Douglass with adoring looks. When the spray of gravel from the truck's tires flew uncomfortably close to his dusty car, Sam winced.

The soft-sided case seemed just a little heavier than he remembered, and he had to struggle to lift it out of the trunk. Trudging back to the office, he shifted the weight from one hand to the other, trying to relieve the aggravating tension in his ribs. Once he got back to the office, Sam unpacked his system and reassembled it on Bean's desk. He commandeered the phone line, plugging it into the computer's modem. Two code words later, he was tied into his home computer and had instant access to his extensive information banks.

Sam smoothed the creases from the piece of paper on which Josh had written the Camaro's V.I.N. *Whoever you are, your first mistake was hitting me.* He stared at the string of numbers. *And this was your second mistake.*

"Well?"

The man peeled off his hooded sweatshirt and threw it on the folding chair. He'd plunged past irritation long ago and now an uncontrollable rage filled him. "Nothing."

"What?"

Picking up the metal chair, he hurled it across the room where it slammed into the wall with a satisfying crash. "Nothing! I was interrupted."

His partner grew quickly subdued. "You mean the guy caught you?"

He lunged toward the other man and grabbed a double handful of oxford shirt. "You idiot, if he caught me, would I be here right now?" Revelation hit him full force; this was one fool he'd suffer neither long nor gladly. As soon as they dealt with the incriminating files, his partner would learn how truly dispensable he was.

"Wh-what do we d-do now?"

He released the stuttering man, pushing him backward. "Markstrom will be on guard from this point on. He'll go into hiding and take the files with him. Only thing we can do now is discredit the data.''

''How?''

''That's your job. But first, call your friend and make sure he keeps his part of the deal. I don't want Lily's autopsy to show anything suspicious at all.''

His partner paled and answered a bit too quickly, ''Uh, sure. I'll do that right now.'' Then he trotted off toward the kitchen, looking back once and coughing nervously.

He's hiding something.

And I want to know what it is.

Chapter Six

Where am I?

Lily scanned the unfamiliar room. The decor was definitely masculine, all dark plaids and rich wood paneling. She could smell a man's fragrance on the pillow, but it wasn't a familiar aroma. Sore and stiff, she struggled to sit. The room didn't spin, but an irritating buzz filled her ears. When the sound faded, she slowly stood up and wandered into the hall. A bookcase filled one end of the corridor, and Lily headed in the opposite direction. When she discovered the dead end, she backtracked to the bedroom door.

How do I get out of here? Lily examined the bookcase again, realizing belatedly that it didn't sit flush to the wall. When she touched it, it swung out easily. With curiosity piqued by the hidden door, she stepped cautiously through the opening and found herself dwarfed by an enormous kitchen.

Restaurant-size appliances and a long metal counter filled the room, but it was the large picture window that drew her attention. It was an unusual feature for a professionally equipped kitchen, but she appreciated the reason why.

Beyond the window, a brilliant sunset cast shadows across the valley of downtown Birmingham. Mirrored buildings in the valley reflected the orange-amber rays. As the sun sank deeper, the top levels of the tallest office towers were bathed in a faint golden light. In the distance, cars formed two thin trails of lights, one white and the other red. For a brief moment, it reminded Lily of a string of Christmas lights. She squinted to make the lights blur and complete the fantasy of an innocent childhood.

"You shouldn't be out of bed so soon."

The voice was quiet, not intrusive, but it snapped her attention back to the present. She could see the silhouette of a man perched on a stool in front of a window. His hands were wrapped around a mug, and the steam rose into his face. He shifted stiffly to his feet.

He was handsome; there was no doubt about it. Dark hair, equally dark, even riveting eyes. His bottom lip showed the signs of the indignities he'd faced on her behalf. When Lily stepped closer, she could see the edges of the bruise hiding behind a curl of hair that fell over his forehead. She shivered in spite of herself.

Forcing herself to look away from him, she stepped up to the window. Stars popped out in the navy fabric of the sky. The effect was unsettling, reminding her she was merely a minor player on an immense stage. "It looks so..."

"Peaceful?" Sam supplied.

"Hardly. More like a jungle at nightfall." Lily tried to focus past her own faint reflection in the window. "Where Beast hides behind the camouflage of Beauty, waiting to strike." She turned away from the expanse of glass. "Damn it. It's not like me to be so cynical...or so eloquent."

He released a sigh. "I suspect after what you've gone through, you're allowed to express yourself any way you want."

"Thanks."

"You want some tea? Or coffee?" He took a sip from his cup.

"Thanks, no."

"Here, have a seat." As he reached over to pull out another stool for her, a spasm of pain crossed his face.

A rush of heat made her cheeks sting. She tried to tell herself it was a side effect of her injuries, but she knew what it was. Embarrassment. Guilt.

The man had suffered because of her. She watched his pained expression fade beneath his self-control. "Are any ribs broken?"

"I don't know. Probably just bruised." He wrapped one arm around his lower chest, then managed a strained smile. "I'm okay, as long as I don't have to sneeze."

Lily nodded, wincing at the thought. Instead of sitting in the seat he offered, she moved between the stool and the window. Chilled air from the cold panes of glass penetrated the loose knit of the sweater Chip had provided. "Sam, you need to go to the hospital and get those ribs X-rayed."

He caught her in a disconcerting, intense gaze. "It doesn't hurt too much."

She barely knew her rescuer, her protector, yet her instincts flagged his bravado as a lie. A boldness flowed through her, springing from an unknown source. Her hands remained remarkably steady when she touched the first button of his shirt. She kept her head down, not daring to make eye contact with him. Her resolve began to evaporate during the trip from one button to the next.

"Stand up."

He stood.

She could feel the heat from his bare chest which rose with each rhythmic breath. Trying to adopt a clinical air, Lily pulled open his shirt to reveal the bruised skin. Her fingers didn't betray her by shaking as she probed his ribs cautiously. "Does it hurt here?" She heard him sigh, and she automatically looked up to read what she feared would be his expression of pain.

He'd been watching her, but shifted his glance. "Not really."

She knew he was lying. "Here?"

"No."

She shifted to the center of the vivid discoloration. "Here?"

His face remained impassive, but his hands clenched and his posture changed. "Yes," he whispered.

Sympathy made her stomach lurch. As a kid, she'd spent enough time around riding stables to recognize the obvious signs. "You've cracked a rib. Maybe two."

He raised a dark eyebrow. "I didn't realize you had a medical degree."

Lily ducked her head for a moment, remembering the hours she'd spent drilling Chip during his med-school years. "You pick up useful information here and there."

"I know what you mean." Critically, Sam fingered the edge of the bruise with a flinch.

"I'll say it again," she offered, reading his expression of discomfort. "You really need to go to the hospital."

Sam shook his head. "No doctors, no hospitals. A little tape and I'll be back in business. Stay here and I'll go find some."

After he left the room, Lily sagged against the stool. She felt a raw pulse throbbing through her body, making her tremble. Her thin veneer of courage had almost splintered halfway through the unbuttoning process. When she accidentally brushed against his chest, the action evaporated her strength and left her drained, embarrassed by her giddy schoolgirl attitude. She stared out the window.

Who had the right to turn her life upside down and destroy her well-ordered existence? What had she done to justify an attempt on her life? Could she cope with the unfamiliar role she found herself pushed into? And on top of everything else, she found herself experiencing giggly adolescent feelings about Sam. Why should the threat of danger destroy her ability to reason or react?

He returned, destroying even this train of thought. He placed a handful of first-aid paraphernalia on the kitchen counter and finished removing his shirt. She fought the rising color that threatened to stain her cheeks and stood as he began to fumble with a white metal spool. She took the adhesive roll from his hands and picked at the tape until she had a small corner pulled up.

"I think you can reach me better from here."

Lily looked up and found Sam sitting on the metal counter, his broad, muscled chest unavoidably placed at eye level. She prayed her hands wouldn't reveal her sudden case of nerves as she strapped his ribs with lengths of white tape and wound an elastic bandage around his lower chest. When she reached behind him to pass the roll from one hand to the other, her cheek brushed against the hair of his chest. Irrational "what ifs" invaded her attempts to keep her mind centered on survival, not pleasure.

Unsettled by wild thoughts and Sam's unavoidable proximity, she forgot her own problems. Looking up, she stopped, mesmerized by the intensity of his gaze. His fingers grazed her cheek, and the intensity grew, becoming almost unbearable for Lily. Lost in a flush of anticipation, she felt the reel of tape tumble from her hand. When she automatically reached down to retrieve it, her own injuries screamed for recognition. Groaning, she grabbed the edge of the counter for support. Her vision narrowed to a single shaft of light as pain darkened the room.

Sam tested the effectiveness of her first-aid ability by sliding off the counter and lowering himself to one knee beside her. "Lily, are you all right?"

She struggled to push back the rising tide of panic and draw her breath. Unable to speak, she gestured for Sam to wait until she could inhale without seeing shooting stars. As he helped her stand, her sweater sleeve slipped up, revealing the cotton gauze that swathed her left forearm. When she looked up, at first she thought she saw revulsion on his face. Then she realized it was shock.

He lifted the side of her sweater high enough to reveal the massive bruises that mottled her skin. "Good God," he whispered. "We can't let the bastard get away with this."

His determination took her by surprise, and the word "we" quickened her pulse. Was he proposing a partnership? A relationship?

Sam sighed, then allowed the fabric to drop back into place. "The first thing we need to do is get *you* back to the hospital."

"It looks worse than it feels. Really." She wanted to give him a reassuring smile but couldn't.

He shook his head. "I don't believe you. Your doctor must realize he had no business letting you out of the hospital." Sam reached for the telephone.

"Stop!"

Much to Lily's surprise, he obeyed her panicked command and hung up. But when he faced her, she felt the somber scrutiny of his dark gaze. A sudden tremor made her gesture to stop seem feeble. Lily stuffed her trembling hands into her pockets. "I know what I'm doing. My doctor and I discussed all the pros and cons about leaving the hospital. He did suggest I stay, but he also admitted my general health was in no danger if I left prematurely."

Lily braced herself for more arguments, hoping she could counter Sam's logic with her own reasoning. She hadn't had a chance to formulate and test any disagreements against Chip, because he'd surprised her with his encouragement to flee.

She'd really expected her ex-fiancé to storm around the room, ranting and raving, ignoring her reasoning and refusing to discuss anything. But it was Chip who eventually came up with the plan, convincing Lily that the best way to stay alive was to pretend to be dead.

Lily lifted her gaze from the floor and waited to be trapped by the brunt of Sam's reprimands and arguments.

Instead he placed the tips of his fingers under her chin and tilted her face to meet his. For a moment, she lost track of her thoughts as the tender touch sent a sudden shock through her. His hands were gentle, but one look into his eyes revealed the return of the intensity they'd shared earlier.

She leaned forward to meet him, anticipating the fierce fury of his kiss, but his gentleness caught her by surprise, offering passion without demanding it. The kiss he gave her was sweet, simple and all too brief for Lily's likes.

The second kiss was at her instigation—a longer, harder one that ignited a scorching wave of desire in Lily nearly knocking her off her feet. Sam tightened the arm he'd placed around her waist, which served to further fan the flames. The frozen lump of fear perched on the edge of her consciousness melted under their newly fulfilled longing. After a moment, they broke apart.

Lily stared at him, marveling how instinct and trust had bridged the gaps in her logic. Logic shouted there was no time for romance to grow in the midst of anarchy. Instinct whispered a simple question: couldn't love blossom like a rose in the middle of the battlefield?

Sam touched her cheek, and his gaze locked with hers. "Are you sure?"

"Sure of what?" Somehow, she'd forgotten the question.

"Of yourself."

Was he talking about the kiss? "Of myself?"

"That you can do this? Stand the consequences of finding out who's tried to kill you?"

There was only one possible response. "Yes, I'm sure."

It was the type of simple answer that would have driven Chip Hazelwood crazy, yet Sam Markstrom didn't seem to be put off by her certitude. Lily had considered her decision to be an emotional crossroad that only she could face. Her perspective might be skewed, but it was the only perspective she had.

She waited for Sam's reaction, but there were no screams, no wild gestures, no predictions of unparalleled doom. His quiet acceptance caught her off guard. Chip had seldom understood or accepted her opinions when they involved business or education or... anything. That was why he was a part of her past but not her future.

Whatever future a "dead" woman can have... Lily shivered and pushed away her morbid thoughts. She began to concentrate on Sam's words.

"...pulled up everything I could on your family business, but facts and figures can't tell me much about personalities." He began to button his shirt over the bandages. "Let's use Bean's office, and you can tell me about the skeletons in the family closet."

Lily wished they were discussing the weather, a good book, anything but the family business. *I want to sit and talk as if nothing extraordinary has happened. I'm scared, I'm tired, I'm sore...* "I'm hungry!" To her embarrassment, the last thought slipped out aloud.

Sam nodded. "I'm hungry, too. How about raiding the fridge before we start our investigation?"

"Did I hear someone say something about raiding my refrigerator?"

Lily stared at the white-haired man who spoke from the doorway. As the lanky figure stepped out of the shadows, she was surprised by his remarkably youthful appearance.

Sam beckoned to the man. "You two haven't been properly introduced, have you? Lily Bradley, this is Bean Emerson, our host."

She tried to give him a hearty smile but found her energy waning. "Please to meet you, sir, er, Mr. Emerson."

"It's just Bean," he reassured her with an infectious laugh in his youthful voice.

"I'm sorry I couldn't introduce myself earlier." When he came closer with his hand outstretched, she realized the man wasn't old, certainly not old enough to have earned his white hair the hard way. As a contemporary in age, he didn't require the deferential "sir."

He warmed her cold fingers between his warm hands. "You were slightly under the weather. I hope you're feeling better."

"Yes, thank you." She smiled tentatively in response to his comment and his comforting presence.

Sam did everything but shoulder his way between them. "Excuse me. Lily, why don't you sit down?" He pulled the stool toward her and held her elbow as she reclaimed the seat. "It's been a long day. Let me get you something to eat."

Bean straightened his shoulders, taking advantage of the difference between their heights. "No way, Markstrom. It's my home. I'll fix the lady a meal." Although his words sounded gruff, Lily spotted a gleam of challenge and humor in his eyes.

"We don't want to put you out, Bean. I'll be glad to—"

Bean bristled, shaking his head. "Not in my kitchen, you don't." He ignored his friend and turned to Lily. "How does an omelet sound? Or I could fix some soup."

She nodded. "An omelet sounds great. I'm so hungry I could eat cardboard right now."

Sam nodded earnestly. "Then you're in luck. 'Cause that's what Bean's omelets usually taste like." He raised his hands as if to fend off a rain of imaginary blows from his friend. "Just kidding, old buddy." He hoisted himself back onto the stool and smirked. "No onion in mine, please." Sam gave Lily a smile of triumph which she tried not to duplicate in deference to her host.

Glaring at his friend, Bean tossed a large metal bowl onto the counter with a resounding clang. "I think I've been had," he remarked as he began to gather the ingredients.

Lily watched Sam relax for the first time. His serious facade dissolved, and laughter lit his eyes. Bean joined in his friend's contagious mood, and their camaraderie helped to lift Lily's spirits a little. "Have you two been friends for long?" she asked.

"Yeah." Sam jabbed a thumb toward his friend. "The Beanpole and I went to grade school together. We would've gone to the same high school if he hadn't moved up here to No Man's Land. But we did end up as college roommates."

"An experience I'll never forget," Bean supplied from the counter, gesturing with a yolk-covered whisk.

"Oh, come on, Bean. I was the perfect roommate. Clean, considerate, studious."

"And a pain in the—"

Sam raised his hands in protest. "Not in front of the client, please! I have a professional image to preserve."

"To *preserve?*" The eggs sizzled as Bean poured them into the pan. "As in preserving something in alcohol? We did do a good deal of that in college."

While they ate, the friendly sparring sparked college reminiscences and campus war stories, which helped separate Lily from her miseries, both physical and mental. She countered with anecdotes of her own, doing fine until she mentioned her family business. Suddenly the present came back in full force, knocking aside the few moments of mirth and replacing them with a pressing reality.

The silence grew oppressive until the static of the intercom intruded on the gloom. "Bean? A customer at the bar wants to talk with you."

"Okay, Charlie. Be right there." Bean excused himself and disappeared. After he left, Lily pushed her plate away, unable to finish her meal.

Sam echoed the gesture, then stood. "It's time to talk. C'mon." He led her through the bookcase doorway, past the bedroom and into an office. He waved his hand at the computer equipment covering the desktop. "I was busy while you were asleep and picked up some basic information about your family. But I'm still missing a lot."

"Like what?" She dropped gingerly to the edge of the couch.

Sam propped himself against the corner of the desk, crossing his arms. "The intangibles—things that don't end up as bits of data in someone's information system. Thoughts, impressions, likes, dislikes. I have a pretty accurate two-dimensional sketch of your family members from various sources."

"What type of sources?"

"Credit ratings, police records, the Department of Motor Vehicles, newspaper archives—any business or organization that keeps computerized records. I need your input to add color to the picture and give it depth."

Lily nodded. "I think I understand. You want to know things like why Mason has sixteen clocks in his office."

"That's a good place to start. Tell me about Mason Bradley."

"I suppose you could say my cousin loves precision. Clocks are predictable, loyal, logical. If you want to give Mason a present, you find him an unusual clock, but it had better be accurate. His favorite is one that flashes the time in binary code."

"Sounds like an interesting man. Is he a creature of habit?"

She nodded. "At nine in the morning, Mason's in his office, looking at the orders from the previous day. If it's noon, he's in the gym, doing a half-hour weight-lifting session. If it's two, he's in his office, drinking his afternoon protein shake."

"What about his position in the company?"

"Mason's the anchor, a real leader with phenomenal instincts. He never had a chance to go to college, but his experience is worth much more than a degree. He recognizes trends long before anyone else sees them, and he's anticipated several downturns in the economy which we were able to survive due to his foresight. He's been with the company for over twenty-five years, but he's only in his late forties."

The rush of memory blurred her vision. "My father brought him into the family business even before I was born. After all, Mason was his nephew. He's been there forever. In fact, everyone at the Pharm refers to Mason as the 'Old Man,' but it's actually a term of respect. Now, on the other hand, there's Vance. I'd tell you what the old-timers call Vance, but I don't use language like that. 'Uncle' Vance is a real lady-killer." She laughed. "Oh, how he hates it when I call him that."

Sam stopped taking notes long enough to glance at her. "What, a lady-killer?"

"No, he loves being known as a Great Southern Playboy. He hates being called Uncle. He's my nephew, but he's older than I am." At Sam's blank look, she elaborated. "You see, my father married twice. Vance's father, Larry, Jr. was the product of the first marriage, and I'm from the second marriage. So I'm actually Vance's aunt, or at least, his half aunt." Lily smiled inwardly at the memory of her father drawing a family tree on the blackboard in her room, trying to explain the tangled family relationships to his nine-year-old daughter.

She realized she had stopped talking and picked up her narrative again. "Vance doesn't have a clear-cut position in the company. He's a sort of jack-of-all-trades, doing a little of this and a little of that. The employees find he's much more approachable than Mason. He's a people's man, willing to give someone an extra day of vacation, letting the pharmaceutical reps take him to lunch and talk his ear off."

"Is he married?"

"Divorced, years ago. I barely knew his wife, JoEllen. Vance enjoys pursuing women much more than having women. He's definitely learned to watch out for the ones with a matrimonial gleam in their eyes."

"What's his educational background?"

"He finished with a pre-med degree, but he dropped out of medical school in his second year. He doesn't talk much about it, but I'm pretty sure he didn't leave because of his grades. Rumor has it that Vance was working on...shall we say, some extracurricular activities with his anatomy professor's wife."

"Who else could we consider as suspects?" Sam prompted.

"Suspects." The word tasted bad to her. "That makes them all sound guilty."

"At this point, it's safer to consider that they're all guilty until proven innocent. Now, who else?"

She shrugged. "A handful of cousins work in the warehouse. Two are salesmen, and then there's the switchboard operator." She leaned back on the couch. "I wish B.J. was here. She could probably give you chapter and verse on everybody in the entire company."

"Is she a student of human nature?"

Lily managed a small laugh. "Not really. Barbara Jean Bradley is the world's biggest snoop. She's the only person I know who can listen in on fifteen different telephone lines and keep all the conversations straight. At least, she used to eavesdrop. She's been awfully depressed lately."

"How come?"

"Her fiancé died." Lily thought back to her last conversation with her cousin. Actually it wasn't much of a conversation. Two weeks ago, B.J. bounced between inconsolable grief and uncontrollable rage, railing at the world for his unjust death. They talked together; they cried together. But the past week, B.J. had changed, her emotional outbursts subsiding to a terse word or two spoken between clenched teeth.

"Anybody else?"

Lily shook her head. "No. I suppose you could say those are the reigning personalities at the Pharm."

"Any other Bradleys?"

She didn't like how he asked the question. "A couple of far-removed relatives and one guy named Bradley who's not even kin to us."

"Hmm..."

Somehow she knew his hooded expression meant something was bothering him. "This is no time for secrets. What is it, Sam?"

She had to give him credit; he didn't hedge or try to soften the blow with useless platitudes.

He stood and shoved his hands into his pockets. "While you were asleep, I ran the Camaro's V.I.N. through the Department of Motor Vehicles. I found out it was a rental car, charged by credit card to Bradley Pharmaceutical Supply.''

She couldn't look at him and, instead, turned away.

"Lily, the charge slip was signed by Vance E. Bradley."

Her mind went blank, unable to accept the down spiral of implications the simple revelation had started. She bounced from accusation to defense and back again, unable to decide which line of thought to follow. After a long pause for frantic speculation, she pulled together enough strength to pivot and face Sam. "Vance?" she whispered. "Why Vance? Why would he want to follow you? Wh-why would he want to kill me?"

Sam sat at the desk again. "Don't jump to conclusions, Lily. Someone might have merely used his name when they rented the car."

Abandoning the couch, she moved to the window and leaned her forehead against the cold glass. The chill numbed her skin, and she wished it could deaden the ache in her heart, as well. When she pulled away, she could see Sam's reflection in the glass, his solemn features mirrored in the window. For a brief, wild moment, she wondered if he would try to comfort her with more than words.

And she wondered what she would do if he tried.

His voice was low. "Can you think of any reason he might want you out of the picture?"

Lily drew a deep breath, then exhaled, watching it mist the window and fog his image. "I'm no threat to anyone. I don't control vast amounts of money or power or influence. And Vance is definitely not what you'd call an overly ambitious person." The lights of the city blurred into fuzzy, overlapping circles, looming in and out of focus. "What could he—or, for that matter, anyone—gain by killing me?"

"You shouldn't think of it as a desire to kill. Some people see murder as the only way to protect themselves."

"That's not very reassuring."

"I don't suppose it is." Sam stationed himself behind her shoulder. "Self-preservation is a strong enough motive to cause an ordinary person to react in an extraordinary manner. Someone—maybe Vance, maybe not—someone wanted the files in your car. They could steal the files, but what if you'd seen the contents? The only sure way to cover their tracks would be to eliminate you, then steal the files. Blow up the car, and they've removed every shred of evidence. No files, no bullet hole. No questions.''

Questions. The word bothered Lily. There shouldn't have been any questions. But someone *had* asked a question. She tried to recall the intruder's exact words. The muffled voice echoed in her memory. *"Tell me where those damn files are!"*

"Sam, there's something I don't understand. If someone attacked you at the wreck in order to steal the briefcase, then why did they show up later at your place, looking for the same files? Right before the intruder—'' The memory became suddenly painful. "B-before he kicked you, he demanded to know where the files were.'' She turned around and watched Sam's face crease in thought. "If he doesn't have the briefcase, then *who does?*''

Sam returned to the desk and leaned against it, stroking his chin slowly. "That bothers me, too. Maybe you've been caught in the middle of a crime partnership gone sour—two crooks looking for the same incriminating papers. The important thing to remember is that someone thinks I have the files, and they're not likely to take my word that I don't have them. If we could only understand why the files were so important....'' Sam's voice trailed off as he became mired in thought.

"Bradley Pharm,'' Lily supplied with a sense of finality. "We go back to the computer room and reconstruct the data. No one will be there, and we'll have plenty of time to straighten out this entire mess before anything else happens.''

He eyed her critically. "Are you feeling well enough to do something like that?''

"Don't worry about me." She straightened her shoulders. "I'll have time to recuperate *after* we figure this mess out."

He stuck his hands into his pockets and pulled out keys which he dangled from outstretched fingers. Suddenly he tossed the key ring up and caught it, shoving it back into his pocket. Lily was afraid the gesture betrayed his reluctance. He raised an eyebrow. "Let's wait until dark."

She nodded, echoing his words. "Until dark."

Chapter Seven

Sam concentrated the beam of the small flashlight directly on the keypad while Lily punched in a series of numbers. He held his breath as the door swung open to reveal Bradley Pharm's reception area. *No alarms. Good.*

He shadowed her dark form through a second set of doors. "What would you have done if they had changed the code lock?" he whispered.

"They couldn't have. Outside of the installer, I'm the only one who knows how to change it. And that guy *never* works on Saturday." She headed down a dark hallway and approached another doorway with a telephone-style keypad. Her fingers flew over the buttons, and the heavy door in front of them clicked and swung open without effort. They stepped in. When the door closed behind them, the room flooded with bright light.

"Watch out!" He pivoted, trying to find the wall switch and douse the revealing illumination.

"Don't worry. No windows."

Sam scanned the room. The walls were lined either with file cabinets or banks of machines. Two desks occupied the center of the room. Lily hit a main switch, and the equipment came to life. Terminals grew bright, and printers clicked and beeped as they reset. She sat at the largest desk and began to type on the keyboard. Eyeing the equipment,

Sam began to get an idea of the complexity of Lily's position and responsibilities.

"When's your birthday?" Lily called over one shoulder.

"March 2. Why?"

"From now on that's the code for the computer room. MARTWO, 627896. No one enters the room except you and me. Now we have the time and the security to figure out this entire mess." She turned back to the terminal and began to type. "I'm going to go back and reconstruct the stolen files. Maybe some sort of glaring error will show up."

"Before you do that, what about the code lock?" He pointed back toward the front of the building.

"What about it?"

"Can you wipe out the record of our entrance?"

Her forehead creased. "Damn! I didn't think about that."

"Boot up the security system diagnostic program."

"But—"

"Just do it. I'll show you a little trick that Avery Security Systems hasn't cleared up in their programming."

She stared blankly at him. "How did you know we used Avery?"

"I saw their decal on the door when we walked in. I've worked with them a few times and know my way around their software." At the prompt, he typed a command that allowed him access to the diagnostic's internal programming.

Lily stared over his shoulder, watching the screen. "An infinite loop?"

He nodded. "Instead of making a new record for each entrance and exit, it'll just rewrite over the old data. We can go in and out as many times as we want and leave no record." He nudged the keyboard toward her. "Now, what about the security guards?"

She glanced at her watch. "The guards made a full check a half hour ago at ten o'clock, and they'll do a perimeter check at one. They won't actually try to enter the building again until three. So if we clear out before then, we'll be fine." She tapped the keyboard nervously. "I guess we'd better get to work."

Sam watched the monitor, understanding and sometimes even anticipating the commands she typed. She started out hesitantly but built up speed until her fingers literally flew over the keys. Finally she pushed back into the seat, laced her fingers in front of her and stretched. Paper began to spill out of the nearest printer.

She pivoted in the chair. "Every Friday, we print out several reports: payroll, scheduling, inventory figures, a few others. Usually I don't need to take paperwork home with me over a weekend, but it'd been a tough week, and I didn't get all my work finished by Friday."

"Which reports did you finish?"

Lily punched a few keys, and a new display flashed on. She ran a finger down the screen. "I had the personnel schedule and part of the inventory left to check. Let's see. Wait a minute." Lily tapped the monitor with one finger. "Not only did I have the narcotic orders for the past month with me, I had our own narcotic inventory!" She rested her elbow on the desk and massaged her forehead. "How could I be so dense?" She keyed in another command that made the printer come to life again.

"We make an informal check of the narcotic inventory every Friday." The printout spilled slowly into the basket. "The Drug Enforcement Administration makes us accountable for every single milligram of each controlled substance we have in stock."

"That seems a little extreme."

"Not really. I'm personally liable for the entire inventory since my name is registered with the DEA as an officer of Bradley Pharm. I refuse to take any chances."

Sam watched the print head glide smoothly across the paper. After a few moments of uneasy silence, he turned to her. "What happens now that you're dead?"

Lily stared at him. His blunt question evidently revealed a point she hadn't considered. "Well," she began slowly, "first, the company has to find someone to replace me as the DEA registrant and handle all the red tape. Then, they have to do a complete audit of the narcotic inventory. Normally we do one every two years. In fact—" her voice lowered "—I'm supposed to start the next inventory on March 1. In less than two weeks."

The printer fell silent at the same moment that Lily finished her explanation. The silence hung in the room like a thick fog.

Realization flooded her stunned features. "Sam, I didn't have time to make the weekly narcotic-inventory check yesterday. I was going to come in today and do it." Lily gathered the papers, tore the last sheet free of the printer and shoved the stack into Sam's hands. Grabbing a key from the lap drawer, she surprised him with her nimble move toward the exit. He followed her into a cavernous warehouse.

Their flashlights revealed an acre of metal shelves lined up in neat rows, each shelf laden with boxes. A roller conveyer dominated a center aisle, then split at a T-intersection with the top part of the T stretched along a loading dock. A high chain link fence enclosed one set of shelves on the far side of the building. Lily led him to the padlocked gate.

While Sam juggled his flashlight and the printouts, her beam highlighted a large metal cubicle with a vault-style door within the fence. Lily swore under her breath and fumbled with the key and padlock. The chain link door banged loudly as she pushed it back out of her way and crossed between two tall wooden worktables toward the vault. She punched another code into the small keypad and swung open the thick, riveted door. Light flooded the interior of the vault after she reached inside.

Boxes filled the vault shelves, and Lily let out a long ragged breath when she saw them. "I almost expected the vault to be empty." She pointed at the first page of the printout. "I'll read the contents, and you check them off. Everything's in alphabetical order."

She reached for the first box on the top shelf. "Alpha-prodine hydrochloride, injectable solution, 10 ml vials... sixteen boxes, each containing twenty-four vials." Sam searched through the list, found the items and read the corresponding quantities. "Good. Next."

They stayed in the vault for nearly two hours until Lily seemed satisfied the narcotic inventory was completely accounted for. Sam pulled himself from the cold concrete floor, and his taped ribs sent up a painful protest. Neither of them spoke until they returned to the computer room.

"Disappointed?" Sam watched her punch the MAR-TWO entrance code into the computer-room entrance.

Lily dropped into her chair, cradling her temples in the palms of her hands. "I guess. I'm glad the inventory checks out, but still it would've been a convenient solution. No, not a solution... a symptom of my problem. That's it, a symptom. If the inventory hasn't been compromised, what file was he looking for? Why would Van—er, someone want it so badly they'd kill for it?"

Sam recognized the signs of her exhaustion. Her hands were shaking and she was verbalizing her string of thoughts into a monologue. She was working on pure adrenaline, which would soon play out if he didn't do something to calm her down.

"It's hard to accept, but there are seamy types in this world who'd kill without a second thought if it meant making a big score." He rubbed his hands briskly. "What we have to do is determine if Vance is the who, then figure out the how." He couldn't stop the chill that danced across his shoulders. "Boy, I could use some hot tea right now."

Lily's solemn face lifted into a small, trembling smile. "Good idea." She opened a metal storage closet to reveal a coffeemaker and all the paraphernalia for making tea. The watercooler glugged a few times as she filled the glass pot with water. After she prepared the coffeemaker, she filled a paper cone with water, drank part of it, then dabbed the rest on her face.

"Hot?" he asked.

"No. Just frustrated." She crumpled the paper and returned to the computer, making the impatient cursor skid across the screen. "I'm still not satisfied." She thumped one foot against the side of the desk, creating an uneasy rhythm. "Something's bothering me, and I don't know what it is."

Sam knew the feeling of having an irritating thought lurk just beyond the reach of consciousness. Lily was too close to the problem to see the source, but he wasn't. "Lily, what happens if your family discovers you're dead?"

She looked puzzled. "They won't. Chip said he'd screw up the paperwork and keep them from finding out."

"Chip?"

"Dr. Hazelwood."

Sam nodded. "Oh. Are you afraid he's going to mess up?"

"No." She paused, then sighed. "Yes. I'm still amazed he came up with the idea to begin with."

Sam shot her a wary glance. "It was *his* idea?"

Lily nodded. "It's an inventive lie. That kind of creativity is, I suppose, really one of his strong points. I just hope he can pull it off. The last thing I want to do is let my family mourn me when I'm not really dead."

"So he's supposed to lose your 'death certificate' in a bureaucratic maze so they won't be notified?"

She nodded. "We initially thought the lack of publicity about my death might draw out the...k-killer. But at that time, we hadn't considered the possibility that someone from the family might *be* the chief suspect."

Sam nudged his chair closer to hers and sat. "I don't see how we can undo what's already been done. Since our main objective is to protect you while figuring out who's behind all this, your fake death may be the only way to truly shield you."

"A sudden resurrection wouldn't be very feasible, would it?" She crossed her arms and released a sigh. "I just wish I didn't have to lie to everybody else."

"Lily." He reached over to brush a curl of hair away from her forehead, catching a whiff of her peach fragrance. For a split second, his concentration wavered. "Sometimes you have to lie to the people you love. For their own good." A flash of memory made his brows furrow for a moment. *I should know. I've done it before....*

Her expression grew harder, mimicking his. She drummed her fingers on the keyboard. "Well, I don't like it."

"You're not supposed to." Sam reached over and covered her hand with his own. "But sometimes you have to... to protect them." He could feel her fingers tremble beneath his, so he tightened his grasp, lifting her hand to his lips for a quick kiss.

She gave him a rueful smile. "I thought the old saying was 'and the truth shall make you free.'"

"'Loose lips sink ships,'" he countered.

Her smile lost its tentative quality. "So we're going to play dueling platitudes?"

"No, I'm just trying to make a point. I said it yesterday. Everybody's guilty until proven innocent. And—" he raised a hand to cut off her next remark "—don't tell me that's not how it works in a court of law. In real life, you seldom have a chance to appeal a death sentence. In real life, execution is immediate."

It was the wrong thing to say. He realized it the moment the words tumbled out of him. The bantering air dissolved along with her smile. "Lily...come here." He pulled her into his arms, ashamed that he'd destroyed her brief and fragile moment of respite.

She buried her face in his shoulder, and he felt his shirt grow damp with her tears. After a minute or so, she straightened, pulling away from him and drying her face with her sleeve. He gently wiped away a stray tear. "It was the wrong thing to say. I'm sorry."

"Don't be, Sam. You were telling the truth."

He reached for her hand, but she pulled away, turning to the computer, suddenly giving the monitor her total attention. "The answer has to be in here, somewhere."

Logic told Sam not to take her rebuff to heart, that it was her defense mechanism kicking in. But emotion perceived her sudden distance as a setback in their growing relationship.

Remembering his own need for distraction during rough times, Sam sighed, shifted his chair closer to the desk. "Okay. Let's approach this theft from a different direction. Assuming the problem has something to do with narcotics, how would you steal them from the company without anyone knowing?"

Lily sat back in the chair, staring at the monitor. Then she leaned forward and began to type.

"What are you doing?" Sam looked over her shoulder, staring at the screen.

"Just what you suggested. I'm trying to figure out how I can steal narcotics by playing around with the system, bypassing a few checks and balances. I don't see how it's possible, though. I designed this program myself with several security checks to eliminate the possibility of errors."

"But we're not talking about errors. We're talking about a deliberate action, a planned theft." Sam eyed the coffeemaker as it sputtered steam, then emitted a thin stream of hot water. "Did you write your program to prevent intentional misuse?"

"No." She sighed. "It's a family business. I didn't think in terms of internal theft. I was merely programming an accurate system of record-keeping to avoid mistakes." She peered at the screen and began to type. "If it's at all possible to sidestep the system, we should be able to figure it out."

For a brief moment, Sam felt an odd wave of heat pass over his face when he realized she had included him as part of her "we." She hunched over the keyboard, then stopped to give him a glance from beneath dark lashes. When their gazes locked, he watched her look of determination transform into something deeper, something akin to... desire?

He forced himself to draw in a steadying breath. *Don't read in what's not there, Markstrom. You may be today's hero but not necessarily tomorrow's.*

"Why are you helping me, Sam?" Lily asked in a low voice which made him straighten in his chair.

"Because..." He stopped, finding no definitive answer to give her. Or himself.

"Don't tell me it's to protect yourself," she continued. "Self-preservation usually means you get as far away from trouble as possible. And I don't think you're here to get retribution for the attack. You don't strike me as a man who lives for revenge."

Revenge? No. But then, why had he stayed? He wasn't sure he knew the answer himself. He could merely have taken a vacation until the whole thing blew over. Stayed away until Lily Bradley was arrested for narcotics theft. Or was really dead.

He turned away from her, unable to acknowledge her insistent look. "Because I have to," he admitted in a low voice. "I can't let them..." He stopped, unable to finish. "I have to," he repeated.

"Thank you." Lily turned away and centered her attention on the screen. Trembling hands belied her calm expression. The computer beeped as she hit the wrong keys. The tremors in her fingers increased until Sam knew he had to divert her attention and help her reclaim her control.

"Well." He performed a theatrical stretch, but the groan of discomfort accompanying it was real. "From my point of view, I'd say you could use a break. You sit there—I'll fix the tea." Sam searched through the cabinet and found two cups, which he filled with hot water from the coffeemaker. The tea steeped quickly, and after one taste, he ripped open a couple of sugar packets and dumped the contents into his mug. It tasted marginally better.

He handed the second mug to her. "Here. Drink this, but only if you're brave. Yuck!" He tossed a couple of sugars toward her. He drank his own tea as fast as possible, hoping the hot liquid would warm him.

Lily stared at the thick ceramic cup decorated with flow-chart symbols and the words "Beware of Computer Programmers. We Byte!" She turned her head, trying to hide her tears.

Sam lowered his empty mug to the desk and watched as her body began to shake with each muffled sob. He fought a suffocating sense of helplessness. "I'm sorry. I don't know what I said to..."

She covered her face with her hands and shook her head, unable to speak. He moved next to her and touched her shoulder. "Lily?" His voice dropped unconsciously to a whisper. The dam had broken, and although he had expected it to, the sudden flood of emotion still caught him off guard. He wondered which source of her pain was stronger—the physical or the mental.

"I'm...okay." She squeezed out the words between sniffs. Taking a deep breath, she faced him with tears clinging to her dark lashes. He wanted to wipe away the droplets from her blanched cheek, but he hesitated.

Her breath shuddered. "Three weeks ago, Lamarr Moody, my assistant, was killed. That—that was his favorite cup." After a long pause, her despondency suddenly turned to anger. She banged a fist on the desk. "Damn it! I don't have time for this."

Giving in to his first impulse, he reached over and brushed away the tears which clung to her cheek. "There's nothing wrong with grieving. It's a natural reaction."

She nodded. "I know." Tears continued to trickle down her face. After a few moments, she sniffed and straightened up.

"Better?" he asked.

She nodded, wiping the last of the tears on her sweater sleeve. Sam reached up and tucked a stray strand of hair behind her ear and, in doing so, uncovered a small bruise he'd never noticed before. He stared at the small discolored spot, feeling a flush of indignation. How many other hidden injuries did she have?

He realized he was staring. "Uh . . . was his death sudden?"

"Lamarr died in an airplane crash." Her answer was flat, lacking emotion.

Suspicion made the hairs rise on the back of Sam's neck. "An accident?"

"A real one, not like my so-called accident." She pressed her palms over her temples, resting her elbows on the desk. "The pilot of the commuter plane tried to land during a thunderstorm. Fourteen people died. No survivors." She shivered. "I've had the responsibilities both from his job and mine for the past couple of weeks. That's why I was taking work home last night. To catch up during the weekend."

Her explanation did little to allay his skepticism. "It's too coincidental." *Two key personnel in the computer department are killed within a few weeks of each other?* His mind began to race ahead, seeing substance in place of conjecture. He glanced at his watch. "Look, it's almost one o'clock. When did you say the guards checked back?"

She cleared her throat and hastily tidied her hair. "Th-three. Three o'clock for a premises sweep," she said, regaining some of her composure.

"Then we'd better keep going. Tell me your procedures on handling the narcotics."

She straightened and pulled the chair in front of the computer. "Schedule II narcotics require a special three-part order form, supplied only by the DEA. One copy of the form goes back to the pharmacy, we retain the second copy, and we send the third to the DEA regional headquarters at the end of each month."

"Show me," Sam commanded, pointing to the screen.

She nodded and punched the keys. "When I input an order, the computer asks for the pharmacy's registration number. If I type a fake number, the computer will reject it. If I put in a real number, the computer recognizes it and completes the order. But at the end of the month, when we compare the records against the actual inventory and they don't agree, then all sorts of alarms will go off."

"The same alarms would cover simple theft, too, right?"

She nodded. "When we go through the inventory, we check it three different ways."

Sam tried to split his attention between what she was saying and how she was saying it. Her rapid-fire delivery and pale face bothered him. He spoke with slow deliberation, hoping she would unconsciously follow the tempo he set. "Maybe the person who is responsible for the monthly inventory has ignored—"

"Hold it." Lily raised a hand to stop him. "Before you finish that statement, *I* do the monthly inventory." Her voice rose with emotion. "My assistant performed an informal inventory on Fridays, but I always did the official end-of-the-month report." She stiffened. "And it always checked out."

Sam offered a gesture of surrender. "I'm sorry. I didn't mean to imply—"

She interrupted him with a shake of her head. "No, I'm the one who's sorry. I'm glad you're here." She breathed a sigh of relief. "You can see things from a different vantage point. You might be able to catch the things I miss." Her emotional outburst faded, and she turned back to the monitor. "We check the narcotic inventory against what the computer *says* we should have. What if the computer is wrong? If I had stolen narcotics and didn't want anybody to know, I'd make damn sure the computer records were changed to match the actual inventory."

Sam nodded, watching the color return to her face. "Makes sense to me. A system is only as accurate as the numbers that go into it. Can you reconstruct the inventory levels from a different direction?''

''Yes.'' Lily began to type. ''I'll pull up the end-of-month figures for December, then subtract the January orders plus add in January's shipments from the manufacturers. The result is the January end-of-month inventory. I'll do the same with the February decreases and additions. It should generate the same to date figures we have on the weekly inventory.''

They both waited impatiently for the computer to calculate, then print out the results. Draping the long strips of paper over her desk, Lily ran her finger down the column of figures. She compared each set to the inventory sheet they had checked off in the vault.

''Sam, these figures aren't the same,'' she announced in a hushed voice. She rummaged through her desk and pulled out a pile of dog-eared and smudged papers. ''Usually I don't keep my working copy of the end-of-month inventory report, but I never got around to throwing January's away.'' She spread the paper out next to the newer report, then stepped back. ''Look. The amounts are different. Someone went into the computer and changed the inventory figures.'' She slapped the desk with an open palm, and the sound echoed through the room. ''That's how they did it!''

Sam studied the printouts. ''You're right.''

''And the way it's been structured, the false orders would make the end of the month appear to be correct.'' She landed in her chair with a thud and an expression of discomfort. ''But it doesn't make sense. I would've found the discrepancies during the two-year audit. When I reported the loss to the DEA, they would have closed us down and begun an extensive investigation.''

''But the thief has had an opportunity to steal from the company for as long as two years without being caught. After a two-year spree, he could retire with a very nice bank account. When we find out who arranged this little scam, we find out who tried to kill you."

"Sam, we're ignoring one thing. The weekly inventories must have been wrong, but Lamarr never reported any problem."

It all became uncomfortably clear to Sam. "That's because he was a part of the rip-off! Look, it all makes sense. An inside man fixes the computer to hide the losses, and the outside man removes the merchandise and fences it. It's a classic warehouse scam. When Lamarr was killed, it put a big kink in the plans. Without his ability to cover up the thefts, the lid would blow off this scheme. Whoever stole those files bought some time for himself. Your 'death' will probably throw the company into such an uproar, the thefts might not be discovered for some time. Otherwise you would've found out about the discrepancies in less than two weeks."

Lily shivered, then turned to the terminal and switched it off. "Vance and Lamarr—partners in crime? This is too much for me to deal with all at once. Can we go back to Bean's? I'll be able to think better in the morning."

"I agree." Although she seemed to have survived her emotional outburst, Sam realized her energy levels were at a dangerous low. While she folded the printouts and returned the computer room to normal, he took care of their mugs.

Afterward he performed a histrionic yawn that became real halfway through the act. "I'm ready to hit the sack, too. It's been a long day." He glanced at his watch. One-forty. "Bean's Place should be emptying out about the time we get there. Bars get pretty noisy on Saturday nights, and neither of us could have gotten much sleep until now, anyway. Come on, let's go." He slipped his arm around her shoulders, and they left the computer room in darkness.

As they stepped into the main office, Lily paused. "Sam, we still have some time before the guards get here. Why don't we go through Vance's desk?"

"What do you expect to find?"

She shrugged. "I don't know. But it wouldn't hurt to check."

"Okay." He followed her as she headed to Vance's desk where she began to go through the lap drawer. Soon her fingers were trembling, this time due to the cold, not nerves. She wrapped her arms around herself.

"You cold?" Sam asked quietly. Before she could answer, he stripped off his jacket. "Here."

Lily thanked him and pulled on the oversize coat, which swallowed her arms in its long dangling sleeves. The jacket still carried the heat from his body, and she wrapped it tightly around her, comforted by its warmth. If only she could do something about the chunk of ice that surrounded her heart...

She stared vacantly at the drawer. What did she really expect to find? A signed confession?

Sam placed a palm on the desk and leaned down. "What's that?" He pointed to a shiny object reflecting in his flashlight's small beam.

Lily fished out a gold pen engraved with the initials V.E.B. "It's just Vance's pen." She glanced up at Sam, noticing the beads of moisture glistening on his forehead. *He's sweating. Why? It's not hot.* "Sam, are you all right?"

His grin caught her by surprise. It revealed a single dimple she had never noticed before. He added a throaty, almost carefree laugh. Features she had thought to be merely handsome became undeniably sexy.

He straightened up. "Sure, just a little warm, that's all."

Lily stood and placed a hand against his flushed cheek, and was startled by the heat he radiated. "Sam, you're burning up."

"I feel fine." He pushed her hand away from his face.

"You feel like a furnace."

"I'm fine. When we get back to my place, I'll take a couple of aspirin and drink some ice water. I'll be better in no time." He rubbed one eye with his fingers, and his smile faded. He started toward the door.

"Sam, stop!"

He pivoted in midstep. The smile was gone, replaced by a blank expression. "What?" He stumbled into a desk, knocked over a chair, then recoiled with a lurch.

Lily maneuvered around the overturned chair and grabbed his arm. "Just hold on, Sam."

"What do you want?" He latched onto her fingers, trying to pull her hand from his sleeve. He glared in her direction, but his eyes seemed strangely vacant. "Let's just go back to my place. I'll feel better there."

"Sam, stop and think. We can't go to your place. We're staying with Bean—at the bar."

He stared distantly through the window, then shook off his apparent reverie. "Yeah, I forgot. No big deal." He relaxed his tight grip and ran his hand through his hair.

Lily watched him closely as suspicion became a terrible certainty. "Do you remember saying the tea tasted different?"

"Yeah. It was bad. T-terrible."

"Did you drink all of it, anyway?"

"Yeah. I thought I'd need the caffeine to help me stay awake on the drive home. I was right. Jeez, I'm tired." His words began to slur.

"Come on." She began to pull him toward the computer room.

"What are you doing?" He spoke slowly as if he had to think in order to articulate each word. "Let's just head home." He fished in his pocket and pulled out a set of keys.

"Sam, you're in no condition to drive." She snatched the keys from him and stuffed them into her own pocket.

He shrugged but allowed her to guide him across the darkened office. "Lily, how can you stand that herbal tea you drink?" Sam stumbled, steadying himself with one hand against a desk.

"It was *supposed* to be just plain tea. Describe the taste."

"Different. Not bitter, just different." He shifted slightly, then shook his head. "I added more..." He seemed to struggle for the word. "More s-sugar, so I could finish it." He sagged into the nearest chair.

"Come on, Sam. We've got to get back into the computer room, and I can't carry you. Wake up!"

He slumped forward, knocking the telephone from the desk.

"Sam, you've been drugged. Try to stay awake." She attempted to pull him away from the desk, but he resisted, his head lolling back, his eyes closed. His only communication was a grunt.

Lily squeezed her eyes shut for a moment. With a sigh of regret, she drew back her hand. The sound of her slap echoed through the quiet office like a rifle shot.

Chapter Eight

Sam's eyes snapped open and flared with an intensity that matched his fever. A large red welt appeared on his cheek. He lurched out of the chair and fell against the edge of the desk, striking his ribs in the process. Lily flinched, expecting his pain to be unbearable, but it barely shook him out of his drugged lethargy. He looked around and seemed to recognize the office.

"Gotta get to the car, go to a hospital," he managed to say between clenched teeth.

"We're sitting on top of the state's largest collection of antidotes. All we have to do is figure out what drug you've been given." *And how you were given it,* she added to herself. Lily helped him up and guided him down the hallway leading to the computer room. Her hands shook as she inputted the code.

The door didn't respond.

Her heart began to race, and panic filled her chest. "Sam, I can't get the door open."

He leaned against her heavily and reached for the keypad, slowly punching in the new birthday code she had forgotten in her anxiety. "Hap-py birth-day to me..." he warbled in an unsteady voice. The door clicked and swung open.

He staggered toward a chair while Lily searched for the mugs. Her stomach tightened when she found them—turned upside down and drying on a towel. Sam's conscientious act had ruined any chance of analyzing the dregs.

The drug had to be in the tea. But how? Examining her supplies, she discovered each tea bag was sealed in its original paper envelope, showing no signs of tampering. The sugar packets appeared untouched, as well, with no needle marks or discolorations on the paper. "Damn! If it wasn't in the tea or the sugar, then how did it get into you? Sam, help me think!"

He ran a hand through his damp hair. His eyes closed, then flew back open again. His first attempt to speak was unintelligible. His face contorted as he leaned toward her. She realized he was putting deliberate pressure on his taped ribs, knowing the pain would keep him conscious for a little while longer. His words became momentarily coherent. "Wasn't in the water. You drank some. No reactions. Maybe in the coffeemaker. Check the—" he paused and looked at her in numbed confusion "—f-filter. Check the filter."

She dismantled the coffeemaker, ripping out the basket that normally held the paper filter. Examining the brown plastic filter basket, she discovered a suspicious clump of damp powder clinging to the bottom of it.

Lily understood the implications. "You're right. It was in the filter holder. But there's not enough left to tell what kind of medication it was." She overturned the trash can in the middle of the floor and began to scramble through the refuse, looking for a discarded package.

Sam slumped toward the wall and took a shaky breath. "It's different now. I'm not s-sleepy," he slurred. "Dizzy. Hard to concentrate. Head hurts... bad."

Lily tore through the can's contents, examining each suspicious piece of paper. She snatched at a piece of metallic foil hiding between some old printouts, discovering three discarded blister packs, each designed to hold a single capsule. She held them up to the light, trying to read the tiny print in the glare of the fluorescent light. She found the medication name and dosage on the torn foil backing.

"Sam, I found it! Morphine sulfate tablets." She palmed the main computer power control, then sat at one of the terminals. The keys clicked at a furious rate. "Come on...come on. Make a connection, damn you. Hurry...all right, we're in!" Her fingers danced over the keyboard, and the monitor flashed in response.

"Whatcha doing?" Sam pushed himself upright in the chair. Lily saw his eyes widen at the sight of her discovery, and she hoped his renewed interest would help him remain alert.

"I've got a modem connection to a national drug diagnostic center that will give us information about overdoses and drug interactions. Here we go. Morphine sulfate, 60 mg dose. Usual dosage...30 mg." *Oh, God—double the dose!* She tried to keep her voice from shaking. "Sam, are you taking any other medications?"

"Took a couple of aspirin before you wrapped my ribs. That's all." He stared blankly at the screen.

She sped through the readout. "You've been given a strong dose of morphine, more than usually prescribed."

"L-lethal?" His breathing grew labored.

Lily lost herself in mental calculations, trying to dredge up vague memories of morphine overdoses as well as read the file.

"Lily..." His voice trailed off for a moment. "T-tell me."

"I don't know. I mean, I'm not sure. Wait—" She scrolled through the file. "It looks like you're having a reaction to the drug, as well. Your symptoms fit the possible adverse reactions." She ran a finger down the screen. "Light-headedness, dizziness, sedation, sweating..." She stopped reading aloud when she found the words *respiratory and cardiac arrest.*

"Oh, great." He balanced his elbows on his knees and held his head between both hands. "Not only will the morphine knock me out, but it'll make me miserable along the way."

She searched through the file until she found the suggested treatment. Turning away from the screen, she slid her chair toward him and grabbed his wrist, monitoring his unusually slow pulse. "Sam, if you can stay awake just a little while longer, I know what to do to help."

"I'm awake," he growled, pressing against his temples. She placed a cool hand on the back of his neck, startled by the heat and the electricity pulsing through her fingers.

Lily realized she had no time for fear when she ran out the door. She knew exactly what she wanted and where it was kept. When she returned with the supplies clutched in her fists, a wave of uncertainty hit her.

Part of being raised a Bradley was the required education in pharmacology. A confirmed independent in a family of conformists, she'd been considered unorthodox to major in business and computers. It was understandable she'd picked up a working knowledge of medicine through osmosis; it was unusual to apply that unofficial education in an emergency situation. And extremely illegal, to boot.

She stared at the items she'd retrieved from the warehouse: a small brown bottle and a prefilled hypodermic. Sam's life just might depend on her actions. At the moment, he didn't look as if he could make it to the door, much less to the car for a trip to the hospital. The time they spent waiting for the paramedics might make a big difference in his fight for life.

"What is that stuff?" He leaned forward, his face contorted in pain.

"Sam..." She hesitated. "I don't... I mean, I think... Oh, hell! I'm not a pharmacist, much less a doctor. I'm positive we've identified the drug, and I know this is the recommended treatment, but—"

"But what?"

"I've never done anything like this before." She showed him the syringe.

His feeble grin did little to overcome her doubts. "That makes two of us."

"Sam, what if I'm wrong?"

"If you're right, what will happen?"

"It'll counteract the narcotic that's already in your system."

"If you're wrong?"

"I don't—"

"Will it kill me?" He lifted a sweat-drenched face and stared at her.

"No," she whispered. "It won't. And I made sure this hypo came from a box with all seals intact. According to the diagnostic center—"

"Just do it, Lily." His voice seemed artificially serene.

She uncapped the syringe while he awkwardly pushed up his shirtsleeve. Holding the hypodermic like a pencil, she swallowed hard, then plunged the needle into his upper arm. He didn't flinch, but the muscles in his neck betrayed her painful lack of skill. When she withdrew the needle, her hand began to shake.

Sam rubbed at the injection site. "I've had worse. What is that stuff?"

Lily tried to drop the empty syringe into the trash can but her shaky aim made her miss. "It's a narcotic antagonist. It'll help counteract the morphine already in your bloodstream." She stooped and retrieved the errant syringe.

"How long will it take?" A violent shudder seized him.

"I'm not sure."

He reached over and picked up the brown bottle she had dropped to the desk. "Ipecac, too?"

"I thought you might be able to get rid of the undigested medicine."

He contemplated the bottle with a sour look on his face, then reacted with a shaky speed, which took Lily by surprise. Before she could stop him, he stripped off the seal on the bottle, opened it and downed the contents.

"No!" She grabbed at the container. But by the time her fingers curled around it, he'd emptied it. She stared at the bottle. "No," she repeated in quiet dread.

Sam wiped his hand over his face. "What's wrong? This way, the stuff will get out of my system quicker."

She grabbed his arm. "But it can be dangerous. If the morphine kicks in and you pass out—"

He pushed her hand away, struggling to his feet. "I feel too miserable to pass out right now." He lunged toward the door.

"Sam, where are you going?"

"Where I can get a little privacy." Sam fumbled with the door, opened it, then headed into the hallway. He walked an admirably straight path to the men's-room door.

She tried to keep the panic out of her voice. "You shouldn't be in there by yourself."

Sam leaned his head against the door. "Just like you shouldn't be out of the hospital?"

Lily ignored his comparison. "I'd feel better if—"

"I wouldn't. I'd rather be by myself right now."

She hesitated, then shrugged. "Okay, but I'll be right outside the door if you need me."

"That's reassuring." Sam disappeared into the bathroom, and the door swung shut behind him.

Fifteen minutes later, he opened the door. Wiping his pallid face with a damp paper towel, he smiled wanly at Lily and leaned against the wall.

She touched his back gently. "Everything all right?"

Sam slowly nodded. "Yes and no. It worked. But I still feel sort of dopey."

Lily slipped her arm around his waist. Although he didn't seem to require her support, Sam made no effort to move away from her. "Why don't you try to rest? The diagnostic report said something about rest making the patient feel better. There's a couch in the conference room, and it's pretty comfortable."

Sam squinted at his watch. "What time is it?"

"Almost two. We have to be out before the guards get here at three. But I think you need as much rest as possible."

He nodded and they began to move down the hallway toward the office area. Halfway to the conference room, he began to lean more heavily on her. Entering the door, Lily dropped the flashlight, and they stumbled and fell to the couch together.

"Sam, let me get—" She heard a soft snore, and his head sagged against her shoulder. Lily squirmed under the burden of Sam's limp body, trying to roll him off her and on to the couch. She finally slipped out from beneath the bulk of his weight, ending up with only his head cradled in her lap. When she tried to slide out from beneath him, he groaned in what she prayed was merely a deep sleep. Guilt grabbed her and intensified when she felt the hard lump on the side of his head.

The pale glow of the security lights illuminated Sam's drained face. He had strong features: a straight nose, a wide forehead covered by an errant curl or two of dark hair. He seemed a solemn man for the most part, having displayed merely a tempered smile when he described his college high jinks with Bean.

Asleep, a telltale shadow indicated where his single dimple had appeared earlier when he shot her his disarming, drug-induced grin. The expression had warmed her, offering a glimpse at a side of him she hadn't seen before. She suspected the morphine must have loosened the tight reins he normally held on his emotions.

Lily ran her fingers over the stubble beginning to darken his cheeks, relieved to see that the mark of her slap had faded away. His chest rose and fell with a steady motion. Placing two fingers against his neck, she measured his now-stronger pulse and noted with relief his normal temperature. *Maybe he'll be all right....*

Guilt tugged at her. *"You did this to him."* She swallowed hard, pushing back the accusations. *"If he hadn't been here trying to help, he never would've gotten the drug meant for you.''*

With his eyes closed and his face relaxed, he appeared much younger asleep than awake. She brushed one curl off his forehead, revealing a raw, blood-encrusted cut that disappeared into his hairline. Without thinking, Lily caressed his cheek with the tips of her fingers and placed a kiss on Sam's unresponsive lips. She meant it as a gesture of friendship, of concern, but the quickening of her pulse betrayed a deeper meaning.

Was she confusing the rescue with the rescuer?

Sam roused slightly, shifted uncomfortably, then drew in a long, shuddering breath. When he turned his head, she saw him wince with pain even as he slept.

Guilt struck another blow, and Lily felt his pain as strongly as if it were her own. Overwhelmed by her own burden of blame, she sought retreat. She slipped out from beneath him and gently repositioned a pillow under his head.

What can I do now? Lily glanced through the door into the dark central office. *I can either sit here and vegetate or I can do something to end all this stupidity.* Retrieving her flashlight, she padded across the carpet, temporarily abandoning Sam and her confusing emotions in the conference room. She started a systematic search of the offices.

She began where she left off—with Vance's desk. Without a clear idea of what to look for, she riffled through the files in her nephew's desk drawers, searching for anything that might appear to be odd or out of place. When the file drawer yielded nothing of importance, she moved to the side drawer, then to the piles of material scattered on the top of the desk.

Finally, she worked her way down to the green blotter which covered his desk. Jotted notes marred its surface, referring to obscure people and places. Doodles filled the rest of the area. His favorite seemed to be a series of boxes filled with circles. In the lower right corner of the blotter, she found her initials and an odd notation. *LB LB LB Why? Why not?*

When she pulled the blotter closer in order to decipher another doodle, two file folders hidden beneath the flat surface dropped to the floor. As soon as she touched the folders, something inside her sounded a prophetic, silent warning. An irritating bead of sweat trickled down her forehead.

The first file contained a copy of the monthly narcotic inventory report in which some figures had been crossed out and new totals penciled in. The handwritten values were hauntingly familiar; the new figures corresponded with the altered report for January.

Numb with the realization, Lily sat back in Vance's chair and stared blankly at the implicating papers. With a sudden fury, she shoved the report into the file and pushed the folder to the edge of the desk, as far from her as she could reach. The chair, *his* chair became an unbearable place to sit. Lily jumped to her feet, edging away from his desk.

It took a little while before she could bring herself to touch the second file folder. Spreading it open on the green blotter, she discovered the folder contained a single sheet of paper, detailing the medical profile of one Elizabeth J. Bradley. The section marked "Known Allergies" was circled in red.

It galled her to know that a research project of her own design had been used against her. A hospital had asked Bradley Pharm to design a patient pharmaceutical profile, and Lily had used office personnel as the test cases, creating a sample data base to demonstrate the system. Of course, she had included her own medical profile, showing how medical allergies could be flagged to warn of sensitivity reactions. She examined the printout; the smudged circle captured the words "Morphine sulfate."

Why had Vance put the drug in her coffeemaker?

That's a stupid question. With his medical background, Vance had to realize how it would affect me. And he knows

I usually fix a cup of tea to drink on the way home. Her stomach churned as she imagined how the drug would have slowed her reactions during the car crash.

Why didn't I make tea on Friday? She thought back to her flight from Mason's fury at the end of the day. He'd been raging about Vance's latest antics, and Lily had been too busy and too upset to complete her usual evening ritual.

In her mind's eye, she viewed clips from a series of mental home movies. Vance teaching her how to hold a bat. Mason letting her sit on his desk and make a sculpture out of paper clips. Vance arguing with Mason to give her a summer job. Sitting in the back-porch swing between the two men, discussing boys and dating. Mason hugging her after her high school graduation. Vance holding her hand at her father's funeral.

Lily fingered the sterling silver frame perched on the corner of Vance's desk. It was a photograph from her father's retirement bash. He had his arms around the other two men in her life, and they all wore the same familial grin. The frame toppled from her shaking hand, and she collapsed to the chair. Her tears formed dark circular blotches on the offending blotter.

When she heard Sam's groan, she hastily wiped her eyes on her sleeve and returned to the conference room. He shifted restlessly in his sleep, throwing one arm over his head. His shirt gapped where one button had popped open, and Lily could see the bandage underneath. With hesitant fingers, she unbuttoned his shirt, revealing the ugly discoloration only partially covered by the tape and gauze. She ran a finger lightly over one piece of tape that had begun to pull away from his skin. Her hand brushed across the dark curls on his chest. Embarrassed by the shock wave traveling through her fingers, she shifted her hand to his forehead, which had cooled perceptibly.

I was so concerned with my own problems. Why did it take me so long to realize he was hurt? Lily buttoned up his shirt again and settled into the soft chair next to the couch.

THE EDITOR'S "THANK YOU" FREE GIFTS INCLUDE:
▶ Four BRAND-NEW romance novels
▶ A pewter-finish Victorian picture frame

PLACE
FREE GIFT
SEAL
HERE

YES!
I have placed my Editor's "thank you" seal in the space provided above. Please send me 4 free books and a Victorian picture frame. I understand I am under no obligation to purchase any books, as explained on the back and on the opposite page.

181 CIH ANCT (U-H-I-02/94)

_____

NAME

_____

ADDRESS   APT.

_____

CITY   STATE   ZIP

Thank you!

THE HARLEQUIN READER SERVICE®: HERE'S HOW IT WORKS

Accepting free books puts you under no obligation to buy anything. You may keep the books and gift and return the shipping statement marked "cancel." If you do not cancel, about a month later we will send you 4 additional novels, and bill you just $2.49 each plus 25¢ delivery and applicable sales tax, if any.* That's the complete price, and—compared to cover prices of $2.99 each—quite a bargain! You may cancel at any time, but if you choose to continue, every month we'll send you 4 more books, which you may either purchase at the discount price...or return at our expense and cancel your subscription.

*Terms and prices subject to change without notice. Sales tax applicable in N.Y.

Her mind flooded with more thoughts and accusations. Her own aches and discomforts from the wreck diminished in importance compared to the multiple indignities Sam had suffered. She drew her knees up and wrapped her arms around them, rocking slightly back and forth, waiting for her hero to rouse.

A soft electronic beep from Sam's watch jerked her from her reverie. She glanced at her own watch: five minutes to three. She returned to the couch and kneeled beside the quietly sleeping man. "Sam, you've got to wake up." She gingerly shook his shoulder. When he rolled over and groggily smiled at her, the single dimple made another appearance. "Sam . . ."

He answered her by running one hand behind her neck and pulling her closer. "I like how you say my name."

"Come on, Sam."

His smile deepened. "Do you know what you do to me, woman?" His lips met hers with sharp, hard passion, taking her by surprise.

For a brief moment, she didn't care whether or not his mind was befuddled by the drug remaining in his system. She took pleasure in the compelling contact until the insidious reality of guilt stopped her. Lily pulled away, still feeling the heat of his kiss color her cheeks and ignite a forgotten ember of desire inside her. "Sam?" The huskiness of her own voice startled her.

"I've been waiting a long time to do that." He sighed and closed his eyes. The hand behind her neck loosened and fell limply. His single dimple melted away as his face relaxed in sleep.

His lack of response dampened the small flame of desire that burned deep within her. Passion and hope were extinguished in her flood of logic, leaving only a sense of disappointment to gnaw at her.

He wasn't awake. I could have been anybody.

After taking a calming breath to collect her thoughts, Lily tugged at his collar. "Sam, wake up. We have to leave." She glanced down at her watch again; the security crew would be arriving at any minute. "We have to get out of here!"

When he failed to respond, her next actions became painfully necessary. She raised a hand, prepared to wake him the only way she knew how. As her open palm arced toward his face, his eyes opened. He intercepted her slap with lightning reflexes. "I'm awake." Sam held her wrist firmly. He struggled to a sitting position, then shakily stood. "Dizzy, but awake." He enunciated each word with deliberation. "I understand. We have to go."

She tucked the incriminating folders under her arm and walked with him to the door. When they stepped outside, the cold air woke him completely. He fished in his pocket. "Where are my keys?"

She dangled them from her hand as she walked around to the driver's side. "If you think I'm going to let you drive, you're crazy."

As they drove through the silent streets, Sam realized Lily was watching him as much as she was watching the road. "You don't have to keep checking on me. I'm all right."

She slipped him another quick glance, accompanied by a tight smile. "I'm just worried. I've never prescribed any medications before."

Sam squirmed in his seat, trying to find a comfortable position. For all its faults, at least the morphine had dulled the constant ache of his ribs. But now the positive side effects were wearing off, as well. "I was worried, too. But it's over now."

"No, it's not." He could see her grip on the steering wheel tighten, and her knuckles whiten. She continued. "Someone meant the morphine for me."

It was good to know the obvious hadn't escaped her attention. "I realized that." He watched her concentrate much too hard on the straight, empty stretch of highway. Something else was bothering her. "There's more, isn't there?"

She gave him a sharp glance. "What makes you say that?"

"Your face." A flicker of telltale emotion lit her eyes for a moment. "Come on, Lily. What is it?"

"I... You..." Whatever it was, she couldn't bring herself to say it. He waited patiently. "Sam, I... I found something...." After the false starts, she renewed her death grip on the steering wheel. "Damn! Just take a look at the files on the back seat. They explain everything."

Sam reached between their seats and retrieved the manila folders. She didn't wait for him to finish reading the files, much less digest the implications before she spoke again. "It's proof that Vance is behind the narcotics theft and the attempts on my life."

Sam studied the sheets closely, then whistled. "Where did you find this?"

"Hidden under a blotter on Vance's desk." She seemed strangely unemotional and distant. Her detachment bothered him. "Look at the next one," she prompted.

He read the pharmaceutical profile, and the words "Medical Allergies" caught his attention. He read the entry, suddenly understanding why morphine sulfate had been used twice—first in her office and the second time in the hospital. Sam reached up and rubbed his chin. "Lily, let's suppose you drank that tea. What would have happened to you?"

She steered off the interstate, taking the exit at an ambitious speed. "When I was a child, I fell and broke my arm in several places. It was... messy. The doctor gave me morphine to control the pain. That's when we discovered I was a borderline asthmatic. I had a horrible reaction to the morphine, which apparently wasn't uncommon with children suffering from asthma. Maybe the morphine wouldn't affect me like that, anymore. I haven't had an asthma attack in years, since I became an adult. But I haven't been willing or had the opportunity to test whether I would have the same reaction to morphine again." The road grade grew steeper, and she shifted the car into third, forestalling the conversation by her increase in concentration.

Sam grabbed the files before they could slide off his lap. "Even if you didn't have a bad reaction to the medication, you would've had a hard time controlling your car under the drug's influence. If your reaction time had been slowed…" The passing halo of the streetlight illuminated her drained face, and Sam regretted the bluntness of his assessment. "I'm sorry."

Her pale expression hardened. "You're right. I'm damned lucky. But you can seldom rely on luck. What I needed was proof, and now I've got it. That's what counts. It'll let me get back to my own life again." She stamped the accelerator, punctuating her remarks with the increased speed of the car. Neither one of them spoke for the next few miles.

Sam watched the blur of dark houses pass by. Forty-eight hours ago, he slept in a silent house, oblivious to the dangers awaiting him. He yearned to recapture that sense of security. He realized Lily believed the two files represented the beginning of the end to her. That was her sense of security. "Proof" she called it.

He called it conjecture.

And Lily Bradley was bright enough to know conjecture wouldn't hold up in a court of law. But she was clutching at straws, desperate to end the reign of suspicion and terror. She thought she was safe. Yet too many dangers still existed. He didn't have time to wait until she regained her perspective in the light of day. He had to make her see and understand the dangers and their consequences.

"You've jumped to the wrong conclusion with these files."

Her face betrayed no emotion. "What do you mean?"

"They don't constitute legal evidence. At best, they're only circumstantial." His words hung in the frosty air, cooled by the outside temperature as well as Lily's frozen reception.

"They're all the proof I need."

"I agree with you. It's all the proof *you* need. But the police will need more. I promise you, they won't issue a warrant on the basis of these." Sam indicated the folders in his lap.

"How would you know?"

"Because I used to be a cop."

"A cop?"

Disbelief. It was the usual reaction. "Yeah...a cop. With a uniform and a badge." There, he'd said it. A ball of fire didn't drop on him from the heavens, the earth didn't swallow him, and a flood of memories didn't wash him away in a torrent of blood.

Her only reaction to his soul-wrenching confession was a disinterested "Oh."

After several years of acquaintances who danced around the word "police" to spare his shattered feelings, her indifference was surprisingly refreshing. But he knew this was no time to rejoice in the tiny triumphs of life. If life, *her* life was to continue, he had to make her understand. Even when she didn't want to.

He glanced out the side window and watched the Bean's Place sign fade into the darkness. "You missed the turn. If you circle through that driveway up there, we can go in the back way."

The car jumped forward as she accelerated. "I'm not going there. I'm going home. You can drive yourself back to Bean's or your house or wherever, afterward."

"What?" he roared, grabbing the wheel and pulling it to the right.

Lily braked moments before they would have bounced over the raised curb of an apartment driveway. Fury colored her face. "What are you trying to do? Kill us?"

"I ought to ask you the same question. Why would you think all of a sudden it's safe to go home? That's stupid!"

She gripped the wheel and glared at him. "I have enough proof now to implicate Vance. It's over."

"Like hell it is!" Sam slammed his fist against the dash. "If he was willing to kill in order to get the other folders, what makes you think he won't do it again?"

"He doesn't know I have them." She crossed her arms, staring defiantly out the front windshield. "Anyway, I'm dead, remember?"

"Yeah. Try explaining that to the cops. They won't take your little ruse very kindly at all. It may have given you some time, but now it makes you look as guilty as hell." Sam jerked the keys out of the ignition. "Earlier you said you believed in hiring a professional, then letting him do his job. If you really meant that, then let me do my job without interference."

Ice edged her words. "Then you leave me no choice. You're fired."

Chapter Nine

Sam sat numbly in the car, watching Lily disappear into the shadow-draped sidewalk. After a stunned moment, he scrambled out of the passenger door. "Wait up." He ignored the lethargy still trying to slow him. "Take a minute to calm down. Think about what you're doing."

She stopped, wrapping her arms around herself. "I've made my decision." A cold fog swirled around their ankles. "I'm going home by myself."

His own anger took him by surprise. "Why? Are you ready to give up? Is that it?" She tried to pivot, but he stepped in her way.

"Sam, get away from me. It's dangerous to hang around me."

"Dangerous? Dangerous is walking into an empty house. Dangerous is refusing help from the one person you know you can trust."

Her frigid gaze flared white-hot for a brief moment, then turned icy again. When he spotted the tears welling in her eyes, he tightened his hands into fists. "I guess I was wrong when I thought you were a courageous person. I didn't expect you to disappoint me so soon."

A cold mask dropped into place on her face. "Don't make a stupid mistake, Mr. Markstrom. I don't measure my worth in terms of how I disappoint or satisfy your expectations. I don't do that for any man." She turned sharply and headed into the darkness.

He followed. "I'm not asking you to do that. All I want to know is why you're willing to give up." He grabbed her by the shoulder and forced her to turn around. "Lily, look at me."

When she tilted her head up, he saw the answer in her eyes, an answer of anger, desolation and sweet bitterness. If he hadn't consciously thought "love" before, he did now.

"Yes," she agreed. "Look at you." The mask of cool anger dropped away. One trembling hand touched his face. "How much more can you take, Sam? You've been bludgeoned, kicked, poisoned.... Your house has been ripped apart. How much more of this can *you* take?"

Sam closed his eyes. Here she was, worried about his safety at the hands of an unknown enemy, oblivious to the damage she was inflicting on him all by herself. "Don't worry about me. I can handle it. I can help you...if you'll let me."

Tears couldn't dampen her dignity. She straightened her shoulders. "No one fights my battles for me. No one."

He swallowed the pain of his longing, trying to force it back to where it originated. Persistent, it became a glorious ache, one he could learn to enjoy—but not at the price she was willing to pay. "Lily, is this the reason you're doing this? You're trying to save me by sacrificing yourself?"

"I don't have to sacrifice anything. I have the proof—"

"You have nothing!" His voice echoed through the night like a clap of thunder.

She jumped at the sound, making Sam regret his flash of temper. But when he reached up to touch her wet cheeks, she flinched. It hurt more than any indignity he'd suffered at the intruder's hands.

Lily wiped the droplets from her cheeks. After a moment of eerie silence, she spoke. "Damn it, Sam. It's over."

The ambiguous meaning of her words chilled him. Exactly what was over? Their business relationship? Or the potential for a personal one? He reached out, his fingertips discovering the pounding pulse in her wrist.

The heat of her tears didn't thaw the cold frost in her eyes. "Send me your bill. Better yet, I'll mail you a blank check." She struggled out of his grasp and took several steps backward until she was out of his reach.

When he lunged forward and pulled her into his arms, the strength of her opposition waned. Sam kissed her, tasting the salt of her tears. He wouldn't let her escape without a fight. "I won't let go," he whispered.

She returned his kiss with a zeal, which took him by surprise. He closed his eyes, surrendering to the fevered maelstrom of thoughts and desires she created in the frigid darkness. As they kissed, she pulled at the zipper of his coat. Chilled fingertips rested on his chest. Suddenly he hated that bandage; it represented both a physical and a mental barrier between them.

The glory of the moment lasted until she stiffened, then broke away. "I...I can't. Not now." The haze of passion clouding her eyes evaporated. "I...like you, Sam. I... Damn it, I think I could love you, given the proper place and time."

His heart thundered, filling his ears. "Love doesn't pay attention to proprieties." He reached for her again, but she neatly sidestepped him.

"And love won't protect you from danger. That's why I can't let you stay involved. I have to take care of this situation by myself." She stepped back, emotionally increasing the gulf between them.

"The hell you will!" Sam moved toward her.

"Under any other circumstance—"

"No, don't talk about circumstances. I hate that word. It's nothing more than a convenient excuse people use when they're unable to face the truth."

According to his friends, his co-workers, even the Internal Affairs officials, circumstances were responsible for his partner's death. Not a lump of lead. Not a drunken fool with a gun. And certainly not an inexperienced rookie who panicked at the first sight of danger.

Now Lily was trying to evoke the word to justify her departure. He'd be damned if he let circumstances take anything from him again. His heart pounded as he ached to feel her in his arms. He reached out for her. "All you have to do is stop and—"

"Don't touch me." Her eyes sparked with warning, and she raised one clenched fist. "You can't stop me. The men in my family have been trying to control me for my entire life. My father, my cousins. Of course, they're bright. Devious, even. They wrap up the commands in pretty packages and call them suggestions or ideas or—my personal favorite—a 'show of support.' But no matter what they called them, I knew what they were trying to do. And do you know what? It didn't work. It never does. But they don't give up. They keep trying and—"

"I'm not trying to run your life, Lily. Just save it."

"I don't need a hero. I don't need anybody at all." She lowered her fist.

Sam watched as she stepped out of the protective pool of light and faded into the darkness. He knew he couldn't counter her depth of feelings with mere logic, but he couldn't just stand there and watch her vanish out of his sight. Out of his life. "Lily," he called out.

"Go away." The shadows swallowed her angry words.

He didn't have to ask why. He knew how pride, obstinacy and determination could mix together to form a stubborn, skewed rationality. He'd suffered from the same symptoms after Walt's death. Logic faded under the pressure of fear.

"Lily. Just one more night at Bean's. Just tonight. In the morning, I'll contact a buddy in the department and run this stuff through him." He paused, then added, "I don't want to be your hero. Just your friend."

The sound of her footsteps stopped. "No." Her tired voice echoed from the darkness. "It's a dangerous thing to be my friend, Sam. Just go away."

"Fine." Sam trudged back to the car, started the engine and pulled into the street. He trailed behind her, driving slowly and keeping her highlighted in the low beams. He could see her shiver with each step. *I can't let her do this. I can't.*

Why can't he just leave me alone? Lily moved quickly, trying to keep warm in the cold, penetrating breeze. As the car crept behind her, she wished she could find her way out of the hole her own sick pride had dug for her and accept Sam's offer to drive her home. After her wild tirade against men, she was surprised he could even care what happened to her.

With each quaking step, she came closer to a decision: lose face and accept the ride. She had resigned herself to surrender when the car stopped. Lily took a few more steps, then stole a quick glance over her shoulder. Sam's head rested against the steering wheel.

"It's a trick." She voiced her thoughts aloud as if speaking the words would guarantee their validity. She continued forward, confident he couldn't hoodwink her with an obvious gambit designed to attract her sympathy and attention. After a few more yards, she realized the car hadn't moved.

Maybe it's not a trick. What if he's had a relapse? She remembered his drug-induced sleep on the couch in the conference room. An uncomfortable feeling of panic crawled up her spine. She turned and headed toward the car. Dread made her move quickly but suspicion made her hesitate when she neared the Saab.

"If this is a trick, Sam Markstrom..." Lily muttered under her breath. She approached the passenger door, figuring she could see him without being within his reach. A convenient shadow obscured his face. *Are his eyes closed?*

She knew how to call his bluff. She lifted one hand and soundly slapped the roof of the car. The jarring noise echoed through the quiet neighborhood, making her jump at the unexpected reverberations. He didn't react to the sound at all.

"Sam?" She held her breath as she moved around the front of the car and jerked open his door. Again, he didn't move. With a trembling hand, she pulled him away from the wheel. His head lolled forward, and he slumped over in the passenger seat, eyes closed and mouth gaping open.

Oh, God. He looks . . . Lily couldn't bring herself to finish her thought. She leaned into the car and bent down to place one ear to his chest. Before she could sigh in relief at the sound of his strong heartbeat, she felt him shift beneath her. Turning her head, she stared into his very alert eyes.

He had the audacity to wink before he grabbed her by the wrist and hauled her across his lap and into the car. The upholstery muffled her outrage. By the time Lily fought her way upright, Sam had the car turned around and was heading back to the entrance to Bean's Place.

"Watch your feet."

"Why, you . . ." Lily wanted to finish with a string of oaths she hoped would make the man blush all the way down to his Jockey shorts. But she didn't. All he deserved was silence.

And that's all he got.

After they pulled into the parking lot at Bean's, Sam turned to her and gave her a sheepish smile. "Let's go inside."

She refused to acknowledge him.

Sam exited and walked around to her side, opening the door for her. "Come on. You'll freeze out here." He held out his hand and offered her an apologetic smile. "I'm a lot like you. I hate when people tell me what to do. Even if they're right. *Especially* when they're right. All I want you to do is look at the files again in the morning. If you still want to call it quits and go home, I'll drive you myself. But make your decision in the morning. Not now."

Damn you, Sam Markstrom. Damn your arrogant smirk and your contemptible tricks! With each word, the pain of ignoring him increased. *Damn you for... for being right.* "Leave me alone." She turned away from him.

"You give me no choice." He sighed, then grabbed her arm, forcing her out of the car.

"Let go of me!" She emphasized her words by tightening her muscles and pulling out of his grip. In the process of shouldering him away, she caught him squarely in his taped ribs.

He groaned as he leaned against the car door, clutching his stomach. "Oh, no-o-o...." She watched him warily, waiting for the insolent wink confirming another ruse. He continued to moan.

"If this is a trick..." she began. Sam dropped to his knees. "I'm warning you, I won't stand any more."

He leaned over and vomited on the gravel.

"Oh, no-o-o...." she echoed in a tired voice. She turned her frustrations to the apartment door and pounded on it. "Bean? Bean!"

Bean opened the door and took one long look at his friend, retching in the parking lot, and his bedraggled guest, shivering with cold. He smiled. "You guys have fun tonight?"

A NIGHTMARE PUNCTUATED Lily's sleep.

She sat in the audience while Vance, the consummate salesman, made his pitch. "We've spared no effort to give you a wide range of items to choose from. First, the garrote, a French favorite. Asphyxiation is clean, neat, as well as effective. And in addition, we have the standard selection of lead pipes, brass knuckles, knives and guns.... But first—a demonstration! An excellent way to prove how well my products work. If you'll look over here..."

Vance clapped. Lights flared.

Sam sat in the middle of his basement office facing away from her. She could see the thick white ropes knotted around his wrists. Vance grasped the wooden ends of the garrote, flexed it in the air, then threw the loop over Sam's head. "It's a simple procedure, one requiring patience rather than strength. Just a little pressure..."

Sam struggled in the chair, first with violence, then with decreasing energy. Finally, his head lolled forward, and his clenched fists relaxed.

"See? Expedient, bloodless death. I thank you for your consideration." Vance bowed and the stage grew dark....

Lily woke with a start, fighting an overwhelming, suffocating sense of dread. Light filtered through the cracks around the heavy curtains draping the windows. She searched the bedside table blindly and found her watch.

Eleven-thirty. Nearly noon? She pushed herself up and found a red plaid robe placed across the foot of the bed. Stumbling out of the room into the hallway engulfed in the long robe, Lily followed the beckoning aromas to the kitchen. Bean sat on a stool at the counter, his attention captured by a newspaper.

He glanced up and broke into an engaging smile. "Mornin', Miss Lily B. Ready for a little breakfast?" He lifted the paper to reveal a plate of eggs, bacon and grits.

"Thanks, but not yet." She felt an unappetizing lump in her stomach. "Breakfast always smells better than it tastes first thing in the morning. Of course, it's almost afternoon, isn't it?" She winced as she tried to look out the window at the bright glare of day.

Bean folded the paper and placed it on the counter. "Yeah, but you have to change your timing when you own a place like this. Breakfast is around eleven, lunch at four, and dinner at ten. You can't go to bed until after the place closes at two." He dug his fork into the eggs and savored them with a smile.

"You miss some beautiful sunrises."

He shrugged. "It's the price I pay. But every once in a while, I catch a real beauty before I get to bed. How about some coffee so you can wake up and appreciate this beautiful day?"

Lily eyed a teakettle steaming on the commercial stove. Bean read her expression of greed with surprising accuracy. "Oh no, not another tea lover! You and Markstrom. He nearly bathes in the stuff." Bean slipped off the stool and returned with a thick white mug, which he placed in front of her. "When Sam and I roomed together, I learned not to speak to him until I shoved a cup of disgustingly sweet tea in his face." Bean turned with the kettle and filled the mug.

Lily climbed onto a stool and dunked the tea bag in the water, warming herself over the curls of steam.

"Help yourself to the paper." He shoved several sections of the thick Sunday paper toward her.

Drifting through the pages, she paid little attention to the headlines and "Super, Stupendous February Clearance Sale" ads. It was the picture she spotted first. Then she read the article beneath it.

Accident Claims Business Woman

Elizabeth J. Bradley, a local business owner, died Saturday morning from injuries she received in an automobile accident, Friday night. Police say Miss Bradley lost control of her vehicle while driving on Calhan-Redmont Road.

The vehicle tumbled into a ravine, struck a tree and later exploded. An eyewitness stated Miss Bradley was forced off the road by an unidentified vehicle. No suspects are in custody at this time.

Miss Bradley was principal owner of Bradley Pharmaceutical Supply...

Lily started the article three times but couldn't finish it a single time. *A total stranger is about to be buried as me?*

Shivers ran up her arms, making the paper shake. She stared at the words and the insipid picture of her that accompanied the article. *I hate that picture. I always have.*

Bean glanced up from his breakfast. "What's wrong? You've been staring at that page so hard I'm afraid it'll burst into flames."

Lily pushed the section across the shiny metal surface toward Bean and tapped the picture of herself. "You won't believe it." She slid off the stool, her growing appetite destroyed by the uncomfortable boulder sitting in the pit of her stomach. "Is there a phone I can use?"

Bean gestured over his shoulder. "By the refrigerator." After a moment's hesitation, he gave her a hesitant smile. "If you need a little privacy, you can use the one in my office."

She almost ran into the office where she slammed the door behind her. It surprised her that the number came to her so readily, a number she'd thought she'd relegated to the dark recesses of her memory.

After four rings, a sleepy voice answered, "Hello?"

"You really screwed up this time, didn't you, Chip?"

"Lil—" He lowered his voice. "Now, Lily, before you get all bent out of shape, hear me out. It's not my fault."

"It's never your fault."

"No, really. I've been trying to find you, but you didn't tell me where you were going. I keep getting the answering machine at Markstrom's place."

"Have you seen the papers? We weren't going to let things go this far. You said you could give me until Tuesday before I 'returned' to the living."

"I can explain," he answered too quickly. "I really can. I tagged the woman with your name and buried the paperwork to keep her in the morgue until Monday night at the very least. I called in so many favors, I'll be working every Christmas and Thanksgiving for the next six years!"

"My heart bleeds for you, Chip." Her grip tightened on the receiver. "This means Mason and everybody truly think I'm dead."

"What could I do? Some resident got enthusiastic and tackled the files. Once the death certificate was filed, there was nothing I could do but play along. Luckily, I protected both of us by persuading Mason to let me handle everything... for old times' sake."

"Old times' sake?" she sputtered.

"Sure. How else was I going to cover my tracks? The AMA could have my license for misreporting a death. I bribed the mortician to insist it had to be a closed-coffin service because of the injuries to your face."

"My face..." She paused, trying to make some sense out of the garbled story. "Chip, you mean to tell me they're burying an empty casket today?"

She heard him sigh over the phone. "Uh... not exactly."

"Chip—" she felt her blood pressure creep upward "—tell me everything. And tell me now."

"Once the death certificate was filed, there was nothing I could do, Lily. I *had* to have a body because the family had already been notified, and I had to identify a body as yours. The whole burial procedure was about to begin and there was lonely ol' Jane Doe on ice. No family, no one even interested enough to visit her. What else could I do?"

"You mean they're burying that poor woman, thinking she's me?"

"Uh... yeah. After all, I know it wasn't your fault she died instead of you, but at least she deserves a decent burial."

"Oh, Chip..."

"But what else could I do, Lily?" She heard the very tone she'd learned to despise in his voice. The very reason why they broke up. She slammed down the phone. Things had gotten out of hand. She saw only one solution to her growing problems.

The truth.

When she returned to the kitchen, Bean looked at the article then back at her. "It's not every day you get to critique your own obituary. Did they get all the facts right?"

His amused face reflected a sense of whimsy Lily didn't share. "Sure, they got everything right, except for one thing. I'm not dead."

"And speaking of the undead . . ." Bean pointed beyond her toward the door.

Sam yawned and blinked, shielding his eyes from the bright sunlight that reflected from the metal counter. He wore nothing but a pair of gray sweatpants and the bandage around his torso. He stumbled to the counter and plopped himself on a stool. "Tea," he croaked in a voice still clogged with sleep, "strong, sweet, hot . . ."

"Good morning." Her hands shook, and the liquid in the cup sloshed onto the metal counter.

"Morning." He leaned too close to the cold edge of the table and recoiled quickly. "Damn, this thing's like ice!"

Bean slammed a brimming mug in front of his friend. "Then put on some clothes, stupid. You're embarrassing the lady."

"Lady . . . humph." Steam rose into Sam's face as he muttered into the teacup. "After what she did last night . . ."

"I'm not going to apologize." The muscles in her hand stiffened. "You know it was an accident. But you won't have to worry about me anymore. I'll be out of your hair soon. I have the proof I need to end this little charade. And it has to end today before someone else gets hurt." She indicated the paper with a nod of her head. "Read this."

Lily gripped the table with whitened knuckles while he scanned the article.

After an abominably long time, he looked up, wearing the same detached expression. "You have an opportunity few are given. To go to your own funeral."

She propped her elbows on the counter and held her head between her hands. "What *is* it with you? Both of you? Is this some type of crazy joke?" She reached out blindly and grabbed the first page she could find and wadded it. Ironically, it was the comics section that caught the brunt of her anger. She clutched the colorful, crumpled ball in one hand. "The plan was to delay the filing of the death certificate so we'd have time to investigate. No one was ever supposed to believe I was dead except the person who 'killed' me."

"But that doesn't make sense. How would the killer find out if your death wasn't made public?"

"Oh... I don't know. But this has all been a big mistake. And I have to correct that mistake."

"You can't do that, Lily."

His frank contradiction angered her. "What do you mean, I can't? I can... and I will."

"No. Because the damage is already done. If Vance had any suspicions that your murder was botched, he doesn't now. We have to keep this a secret."

"But he saw me—alive—in your car."

"No," Sam objected. "He saw a woman. I'm not so sure he could tell it was you. And I think we did a good job of faking him out at the car wash."

Lily tried to massage away the pounding pressure in her temples. After a moment, she gathered enough courage to look at Sam's emotionless face. "I can't stand this anymore. I'm going to turn over my information to the police."

Sam crossed to the window and took one sip of his tea as he stared outside. "So you'll just wander into the police station and say 'Hi, there. I'm not really dead, only pretending.' You hand them some papers that show *someone* with expert knowledge of the company computers has been screwing around with the inventory levels and presumably stealing beaucoup bucks' worth of narcotics. And you *say* you found your evidence in Vance's desk, but I'm not able to corroborate your story because I wasn't awake at the time. Who's to say you didn't drug my tea?"

She gaped at him. "Surely you don't think—"

"We're not talking about what I think. All that matters now is what the police think." Sam drained his tea and pushed the empty cup away. "You're the only person around with the capability to outfox your own computer system. You're the sole party responsible for tracking the inventory. And here's the kicker. Your assistant can't substantiate your claims of innocence or dispute your accusations of his guilt. He's conveniently dead!"

Sam began to count the possible charges on his fingers. "Embezzlement, possession of controlled substances, possible insurance fraud." Emotion crept into his expression. "Hell, they might even go back and exhume your assistant in order to look for evidence of foul play."

He stalked back to the counter and faced her. "You'll have the local police plus the Feds breathing down your neck, putting together a case for the prosecution you'll never beat." He turned away and headed for the door. "Although you're no longer my client, I won't charge you for that bit of professional advice. You and Bean can figure out the room and board details between yourselves." Sam disappeared into the hallway.

Lily felt the blood rush to her face. Her head throbbed, and she fought the overwhelming urge to throw the ceramic mug across the room. Instead she forced herself to finish her tea. "Bean, he's right. I do owe you more than just my thanks for putting me up. Whatever you think is—"

Bean stopped her with a shake of his head. "Lily, shut up before you say something you'll regret. There's something Sam hasn't told you."

"What?"

"Not many people are aware of the fact that Sam was a cop for a while."

"I know. He told me."

"I'm not talking about the years he spent heading up the computer division. I'm talking about being a real cop with a gun and a badge."

"He told me about that, too."

Bean contemplated his coffee for a moment. "I suppose it really shouldn't surprise me. Did he tell you why he quit?"

She shook her head. "No."

He shrugged. "Normally I'd say it wasn't my business to tell tales out of school, but this isn't a normal situation. There are some things I think you need to know." He gave her a quick look then focused on his coffee cup.

"Sam's dad was a cop who didn't have a chance to die in the line of duty. While Sam was growing up, I can remember his dad always talking about his son following in his old man's footsteps, but Sam really didn't want to be a cop. He was always interested in science and computers."

Bean managed a half grin. "We always gave him a hard time about turning into Spencer Markstrom, computer geek." The expression faded. "Eventually he combined both his ambitions and those of his father by working in the police department's computer section on a government grant. When the grant ended, Sam liked the work so much, he decided to join the department as a cop."

Bean stopped to take a sip of his coffee, then continued. "He was just about through with his rookie year when he and his partner, Walt, were called out to a bar to investigate a 'disturbing the peace' call. It turned out—"

"It's my story," said a voice from the doorway. "You ought to at least have the decency to let me tell it when I'm ready to." Sam stood in the doorway with his hands clenched into white-knuckled fists.

Bean stiffened. "If you don't tell her, I will."

"Bean..."

"I'm not kidding, Sam. You do it...or I will."

Sam's posture changed perceptibly, his hands slowly relaxing and hanging loose by his side. He gazed in their direction, not quite focusing on either of them. "We got the call in the wee hours. To a sleazy dive near the freight yards.

"It was the usual complaint. Some guy had drunk up his paycheck and wasn't ready for his Saturday night to end. When we drove up, the guy was standing with his back to us, and we couldn't see his .357 or the sawed-off shotgun. Walt, my partner, knew something was wrong. Instincts, I guess. He was reaching for the shotgun when our windshield exploded. The shot took out most of his face.'' Sam's rigid stare hardened.

"I slid down in my seat, trying to take the only cover I could behind the car's engine block. I was next and I knew it. Walt... Walt...''

He faltered for the first time, and Lily felt hot tears of empathy pool in her eyes.

"Walt was dead." Sam's expressionless mask remained intact. "Blood and glass were everywhere. No matter how much training I had, no matter how much procedure had become reflex action to me, I wasn't ready. My partner, my friend, was dead. For the first time in my life, outside of target practice, I pulled my gun and ordered the perp to stop.'' Sam paused. Then he sighed and added, ''He didn't. So I blew the bastard away.''

Lily stared at him, watching his face crease with remembered pain.

"I emptied my service revolver into him and would have used the shotgun if—'' He stopped, his hands tightening into fists again.

When he drew a deep, raspy breath, Lily wrapped her arms around herself, as if trying to hold together the two halves of a heart torn apart by compassion.

The slightest tremor colored his voice, the first sign of emotion to creep into his words. "Walt wouldn't let me have the gun. Even though he was dead, he wouldn't let me pull the shotgun out of his hands." Just as it seemed he might react to the memory, composure from some hidden reserve washed away any expression from his face.

"When the backup unit got there, they couldn't tell if there were two bodies or three. I was covered in blood, all Walt's. Not a single drop of my own. My partner was dead, and I didn't have a scratch on me.''

For the first time, he focused in their direction. Lily realized he was looking at her. "I relived the incident a thousand times before we got to the emergency room. Technicolor memories in slow motion, a movie I played forward and backward in my mind. It was so simple. Walt was protecting the rookie, and it slowed him down. So simple but so unfair."

He paused for a moment, his gaze directed somewhere over Lily's head. "It took me a while to accept the injustice of life. I did a lot of listening for the next couple of months. To doctors, cops, friends, enemies. When I tried to tell someone what happened, the movie would start up in my head again. So I didn't talk. A simple answer but not a very effective one. But with help—" he looked in Bean's direction for a few seconds before turning away "—I was eventually able to accept the facts and start over again."

He stared stone-faced in her direction, but Lily knew he didn't see her. He drew a deep breath, pivoted and disappeared into the hallway. She wiped a tear from the corner of her eye, then covered her face.

"Lily."

She turned toward the voice. Profound sadness commanded Bean's features. "Do you understand now?"

"I . . . I suppose. It's as complicated as he is."

Bean stared at her for an inordinately long time before he spoke again. "You're right. But the real story only starts with the shooting. Sam didn't mention what happened at the hospital."

He raised one finger to silence their conversation, then walked to the door and glanced down the hallway. He turned back to Lily, keeping his voice at a low, conspiratorial level. "What with the blame that some of Walt's friends placed on him and the guilt he placed on himself, Sam went off the deep end." Bean swallowed with obvious pain. "It took a year for him to find his way back."

Lily watched his face closely. "Then the bit about not talking . . ."

He nodded. "Some people turn to booze or drugs. Sam turned inward. He didn't speak for three months. Not to me or to the doctors or to anyone."

"What about his sister?" Lily couldn't identify the emotion that crept over Bean's face. "Didn't he at least talk to Micki about it?"

He sighed. "She's the last person he'd confide in. Most of what Micki knows about it even now is more fiction than fact."

"Why?"

He shrugged. "Who knows? She'd just moved cross-country to Seattle with a new job. They sort of lost contact during that time. Micki was busy with new broadcasting responsibilities and was on the road every week. I think their answering machines had a more involved relationship than they did. Then, after the incident, I think he didn't want to intrude on her new life."

"Intrude? But she's his sister!"

"My thoughts exactly. But he made me promise not to tell her. And I didn't. He told her a sanitized version two years later about how Walt's death had upset him and how he talked a few times with the police psychologist to work it all out. But he never told her he'd actually joined the force and had become Walt's partner. In fact, doesn't know to this day that he was a cop."

"But why didn't he tell her?"

"Who knows?" he said again. "All I could do was stay out of it. It's between the two of them. I don't volunteer any information. And if Micki asks too many questions, I change the subject. He'll tell her everything someday." Bean hesitated. "I hope."

"I hope so, too," Lily added. Brought up an only child, she began to think the dynamics between siblings was beyond her comprehension.

Bean glanced again toward the hallway. "Lily, go after him. Talk to him. Do anything you have to, but get him back on the case working with you."

"But—"

Bean stiffened, drawing up to his full height, nearly filling the doorway. "I don't know you very well at all, and you certainly don't know me. But I do know Sam. He'll be a loose cannon and keep on sticking his nose into your business whether you want him to or not."

"Then what am I supposed to do?"

He shrugged. "Keep him from getting himself killed."

Lily glanced at the grainy black-and-white photo of herself in the newspaper. "I don't know how effective I can be, Bean. They've already killed *me*."

Chapter Ten

The sun looked deceptively warm until Lily stepped out onto the porch. She tightened the robe belt, trying to stave off the uncomfortable breeze that whistled around her bare legs. She said nothing as she mimicked Sam's stance at the rail, leaning on the wooden beam with fingers clasped. A thin gray cloud hung over the downtown skyscrapers, marring an otherwise clear sky.

She cleared her throat before she spoke. "I can remember when the pollution used to be much worse than this."

"Back in the days when Birmingham really was the Steel City." His voice sounded rusty.

"I guess those days are gone."

He shrugged. "Is that what you came out here to discuss? The glory days of blast furnaces and pig iron?"

"No. I wanted to talk to you."

"So... talk."

A violent shiver betrayed the image of control she wanted to project. "Do you think we can do it inside? I'm freezing."

He abandoned the railing, headed across the porch and held open the door for her. After nodding her thanks, she chose a table by the window and slipped into a sun-warmed seat.

She glanced up, noting his unnaturally stiff posture. "Sit down. Please? I'll get a crick in my neck if I have to stare up at you."

Sam selected the seat on the opposite side of the table. His distant expression didn't surprise her. She cleared her throat. "I want to apologize. For last night. For what I said. For what I did." He remained silent, his gaze not quite meeting hers. "I panicked last night, Sam. And I got mad at the wrong person—you. I'm sorry. I truly am."

"Apology accepted." The edge to his voice disturbed her.

"You were right," she continued. "It's not over. Not by a long shot. Embezzlement, possession of controlled substances, insurance fraud. I was too close to see the implications. I never dreamed—no, I *did* dream. A terrible nightmare," she whispered, pushing back a sudden flare of distorted memory—Vance and his garrote. "I guess that's why I was afraid. Afraid my nightmares might come true."

"I know that feeling." He centered his unfocused gaze somewhere over her left shoulder.

Lily placed her upturned palm on the table. After a moment's hesitation, Sam placed his hand in hers. The simple gesture meant more than any words.

"I still need your help, Sam."

He offered no response.

"I can't do it by myself." The moment after she spoke, realization poured through the hole in her pride. She'd spent a lifetime carving a place in the family business for herself, fighting the inequalities placed on her either by convention or mere circumstance. Years of independence wouldn't crumble because she asked for Sam's help. To admit her need for his guidance didn't mean defeat. It didn't mean she was putting the control of her future into someone else's hands.

By God, she needed him. She needed his strength, his support, his—

His love? She tightened her grasp on his hand, staring into the cloudy depths of his stoic gaze. "I need—"

Sam interrupted her by leaning forward and pulling her toward him. "You need the same thing I do," he whispered, reaching up and brushing his fingertips lightly along her cheek. The tingling, teasing sensation made her draw a shaky breath.

Then he kissed her.

It was a sudden kiss, hard, passionate, filled with the emotion he couldn't or wouldn't show in his face. His clasp on her hand tightened, mirroring her own rising level of desire. For a moment, their souls locked together. She knew his hopes, his fears, and she shared her own without saying a word.

He released her fingers and shifted his chair closer to hers. He rested his hand behind her neck and buried his face in her morning-tousled curls. "I wasn't looking for someone to love, you know."

Her heart contracted; her body screamed its desire in a silent explosion. "Me, neither," she managed in a hoarse whisper. "But from what I've heard, it's supposed to happen when you least expect it."

"And *where* you least expect it. When I went down that embankment to inspect your car, I didn't expect to find the woman of my dreams. . . ." His voice trailed off.

She knew why. The woman of his dreams? Or of his nightmares? "Sam, I'm sorry—"

"No." His face was just inches from hers. "Don't say it. You haven't done anything to be sorry for." He ran another maddening finger along her lips, a simple caress, yet it was driving her crazy. After a moment, he sighed, found her hand again and gave it a little squeeze. He wore an almost sheepish grin as he tugged her to her feet. "Come on."

She envisioned a wickedly delightful excursion to the nearest bedroom, from which they would refuse to leave for a week. "Where?" she asked innocently, fiddling with the belt of her robe.

"Go get dressed."

Dressed? He'd gotten it backward.

He read the disappointment in her face and raised an eyebrow at her. "Lily. God knows, I want to. I *really* want to, but—" he glanced at his watch "—I have this idea," he explained.

Lily looked at him pensively, watching the results of his thought process show clearly on his face. It was as if, by looking in his eyes, she could read his mind. "The funeral?"

He nodded. "It starts soon."

She shivered. "I hate funerals."

"I do, too." He brought her hand to his lips for a quick kiss.

"I *really* hate funerals," she repeated. She looked down at the red plaid robe, then up, giving him her most enticing, come-hither look. "And I have nothing to wear."

He groaned and dragged a hand through his hair. "Bean can take care of that."

She kicked at the hem of the robe sweeping the floor. "How?"

Sam offered a strained but infectious grin. "Costumes."

"AND SO, WHILE I WAS putting together the set for the third act, the police appeared out of nowhere." Bean deftly steered the old pickup truck around the curves that snaked through a residential area.

Lily had tried not to gape when Bean selected the primer-coated gray truck instead of the sleek red Porsche sitting next to it in the garage. He'd only smiled at her and muttered something about the sports car having only two seats.

"Evidently," he continued, "someone had reported there were two gangs about to rumble in the alley behind the theater. I had a hard time convincing them the 'gangs' were the Sharks and Jets, practicing their blocking movements and choreography. Neither of the cops had ever seen *West Side Story.*"

She appreciated Bean's constant flow of stories, which allowed her time to consider the newest facet to her relationship with Sam. Squeezed between the two men on the faded bench seat, Lily found a great deal of satisfaction and support in Sam's mere presence. It wasn't dependence, but a shared independence.

"We're here." Bean parked in front of the theater, ignoring the yellow-painted curb. Lily climbed out of the truck behind Sam and shivered in the cold, waiting for Bean to unlock one of the large glass doors. She hesitated entering the shadowy lobby. The darkness seemed foreboding, reminiscent of the danger she'd encountered in Sam's basement.

Sam glanced at her, then slipped his fingers between hers. "You okay?"

She gulped, feeling the warm support flow between them, further opening the emotional doors they had both slammed in anger. "Better."

"You two stay put until I get the lights on." Bean faded into the darkness. A few moments later, a large chandelier sprang to life, and a series of brass and crystal sconces washed the walls with soft pools of light.

The illumination chased away the last of her uneasy ghosts, and she relaxed in the familiar atmosphere of the theater lobby. She'd never been in the room when it wasn't packed full of people, talking, laughing. The distractions of conversation had kept her from admiring the lobby's simple elegance. She didn't realize she was staring until Bean spoke. "You haven't been here before?"

She dropped her gaze from the tiered chandelier to glance at the shimmering reflections it created on the plush carpet. "I've been here many times, but I never really stopped to appreciate the beauty."

Bean crooked a finger at her. "Let me show you where the real magic takes place. It's not as impressive as the lobby, but it's twice as interesting." He led them into the theater, down a side aisle and through an inconspicuous doorway near the stage. They left behind the elegant trappings of velvet and brass and immersed themselves in the make-believe world of the theater.

Bean took them past bucolic scenery flats and papier-mâché trees, ignoring walls with doors that led nowhere. He headed for a staircase which looked no more substantial than the rest of the sets. Sam and Lily followed him down the stairs and into a large dressing area with three mirrored walls. Bean dragged them past the gleaming reflections and into a smaller room filled with racks of clothing.

"I wish we could've contacted the wardrobe mistress to do this, but I guess I'll have to muddle through myself. I'm sure we can find something in here for you to wear." Bean pawed through the racks. "I assume we're looking for something in basic black?"

Lily wrinkled her nose. "I never wear black."

"You should." Sam's appraising look made a warm shiver run down her arms. "You'd look good in it."

Bean pushed on, ignoring his friend's pointed observation. "Black will be a good camouflage, then. People won't associate the color with you."

She ended up modeling three outfits, and the final selection became a subject of debate and won with an eventual split vote. Lily held up the leading candidate, a dress more suitable for a cocktail party than a ceremony of mourning. "You two have got to be kidding. I wouldn't be caught dead in this dress." She paused as the absurdity of the statement was mirrored in their faces.

Bean stifled his laughter. "It'll be the perfect disguise. That is, with a few more touches." He rustled through a box marked Headgear and began to toss hats onto the work-table.

Lily picked up a flowered creation with one drooping feather, and perched it on her head. "A hat seems so...so..."

"Dramatic?" Sam eyed her image in the mirror and shook his head. "Uh-uh."

"It *is* a drama, though, isn't it?" Bean extricated himself from the deep recesses of the container, clutching a wide-brimmed black hat. "The whole thing's a sham, but we have to make it a believable sham. People will definitely notice the clothes. They'd be blind not to. And when they notice us, it'll be as a couple, not as two individuals. No one will connect the two of us because we never met while you were...alive." He flashed her a twinkling grin. "And that was definitely my loss."

"That's why Bean will escort you to poor Lily's funeral, not me." Sam gingerly hoisted himself onto the counter that ran beneath the mirror. "Vance is aware of the connection between us. If he spots me, he might tumble onto the fact you're still among the land of the living."

Lily sat down in a chair next to him and tried on a dark beret. She pursed her lips at the men, doing her best impression of a femme fatale. She tugged off the cap, blushing when she caught the look Sam gave her. It went beyond mere amusement.

"Here, Mlle Lily." Bean plopped a curly blond wig into her lap. "Try this on."

Lily twisted her long hair into a ponytail, pulled the wig on like a bathing cap, and tucked in a few errant dark curls. Sam drew his sunglasses from his shirt pocket and propped them on her nose. When Lily looked in the mirror, she didn't recognize her own reflection.

Bean thumbed through the racks and selected several articles of clothing. "I've got what I need. Are we ready?"

Sam slid off the counter and offered Lily a hand. "Let's go, Mata Hari. Your mourners await."

LILY HATED FUNERALS.

And attending her own was the worst torture ever devised. She watched in heartbreaking silence as some of her friends and family sat in their seats, a few crying, others wearing looks of shock. Another group stood beside the closed casket. It took all the self-control Lily could muster to keep from leaping to her feet and revealing herself. She kept her head down to hide her face under the brim of her hat and veil, suddenly uncertain of the ability of a thin piece of lace and a wig to disguise her identity.

When Lily and Bean entered the chapel and sat down, she felt as if everybody's attention was on them. Bean had combed his white hair straight back and kept his sunglasses on, even while inside the chapel. He wore a black turtleneck with a white suit, a black carnation adorning the lapel—his "concession to such a tragic loss." Lily couldn't decide whether he looked like a cinematic mob gangster or a pulp-novel spy. During their drive across town, Sam had good-naturedly dubbed him "Mike Danger, Private Eye" and declared that Bean needed to trade in his dark glasses for an eye patch. Either way, he was a surreal companion no one would ever connect with the very ordinary, and recently deceased, Elizabeth J. Bradley.

Bean reached over and gave her a reassuring squeeze. "You okay?"

"Yes," she whispered. Out of the corner of her eye, she could see her family. *No. Not really, she admitted to herself.*

Her cousin Barbara Jean sat at the end of the pew, wearing the same black dress she'd worn to Lamarr's memorial service. *Poor B.J. Two funerals in one month.* B.J. had been a wreck during Lamarr's service and Lily had taken her outside to calm down. That's when her cousin admitted she and Lamarr had planned to elope. She'd pulled the tear-stained papers out of her purse: a marriage license, insurance papers, and an itinerary for a honeymoon to Acapulco.

And now a second funeral.

This time, B.J. seemed eerily calm. She took surreptitious glances around the room as if she was looking for someone. Lily held her breath when B.J.'s gaze settled on her for a brief moment, paused longer on Bean, then skipped on down the pew.

When Lily dared raise her head again, she noticed Vance had slipped into the reserved family section. She shivered at the prospect of making unintentional eye contact with him, but she watched him nonetheless. She comforted herself with the thought that if the ever-vigilant B.J. hadn't seen through Lily's disguise, no one would.

Vance's emotions seemed diametrically opposed to the others'. He fidgeted with the buttons of the Italian suit tailored to his athletic build. Running a hand through his dark blond hair, he darted nervous glances around the room. He spent much of the time checking out the crowd, then suddenly seemed to remember to affect a look of grief.

Lily gathered enough courage to turn her head and search the chapel for Sam. When she saw him at the back of the room, she felt a sudden sense of security. He acknowledged their brief contact with the slightest nod.

Lily turned around, and Sam surveyed the crowd while the minister conducted the ceremony. The chapel was packed with dark-clothed mourners, and the solemn service was a touching tribute to a "young woman taken before her time." As the minister finished the last prayer with a hushed "Amen," Sam slipped from his seat in the rear and exited ahead of the crowd.

He cut through the cemetery to the grave site and pretended to stand in meditation at another headstone. The attendants gathered under the tent protecting the fresh grave and an ornate monument with the name Bradley chiseled in it. Balancing a camera on the headstone, he observed the crowd through the telephoto lens.

Vance Bradley. The man wore an appropriately solemn expression and hung back from the rest of the family. Sam snapped a picture of Vance just as a young lady leaned forward and made a comment, which elicited a fleeting smile from the man.

The facade had already cracked. *So much for sympathy.*

Sam turned his attention and lens toward Mason Bradley. Flanked by his wife and children, Mason headed an informal receiving line as mourners paid their respects. Between lulls in what Sam assumed was sympathetic conversation, the man reached over and comforted his wife, ruffling his son's hair and squatting to speak to his daughter.

Chip Hazelwood. The good doctor appeared a little less composed than the last time Sam had seen him. The suit was sharp, the hair styled, but the golden good looks had been smudged by dark circles beneath his eyes. The man kept his nervous gaze trained on the casket, which didn't surprise Sam in the least. If he didn't like Hazelwood before, he definitely didn't like the doctor now after seeing how badly the man had messed up.

Sam looked over the camera, trying to spot his cohorts. He found them toward the back of the group, shying away from the main gathering. Sam started to snap a picture of Bean and Lily but stopped when Bean placed an arm around her shoulders. If Sam immortalized the pose in film, he knew he'd have a permanent memento of his first flare of jealousy. The intensity of the feeling took him completely by surprise.

Pushing back the unexpected flush of emotion, Sam panned the crowd, spotting a figure in dark glasses who stood to one side of the gathering. Muffled against the cold with a scarf, hat and upturned collar, the man moved hesitantly toward the tent, then backed up as if he couldn't decide whether or not to approach the family group. Finally, he ducked his head and worked his way behind the knot of mourners who gathered around the family members.

Sam continued to shoot pictures while keeping his own attention on a small flash of white in the man's hand, presumably a piece of paper. Perhaps a note. The man disappeared for a moment behind the crowd, then reappeared, moving away from the group. Sam tracked him in the camera's viewfinder, snapping pictures every few seconds. When Sam realized the man's hands were empty, he turned the camera in time to see a piece of paper flutter to the ground in the middle of the crowd. He searched the faces of the mourners, trying to read duplicity in any of their faces. Unable to determine who had dropped the note, Sam divided his attention between the burial procedures and the piece of paper on the ground.

The graveside services ended, and the crowd slowly began to drift back to their cars. Sam knew he had to get the paper before anyone else picked it up. He tucked his camera under his arm and strolled toward the grave, patting his jacket to reassure himself that the false press credentials were still in his pocket. Walking toward the paper, Sam tried to remain inconspicuous as he dropped to one knee to adjust a shoelace. He palmed the crumpled note without being noticed and headed straight to the car.

While he waited for Bean and Lily to reappear, Sam unfolded the wrinkled paper and stared at three words: *RUN DAMN ESIA.*

"WHAT DO YOU THINK it means?" Lily peeled the wig from her head and placed it on the corner of Bean's desk. She combed her fingers through her mass of dark tangled curls.

Sam examined the scrap of paper; the printed letters were crooked as if hastily written. "It's difficult to figure where the word breaks occur. The first two words, 'RUN' and 'DAMN,' are pretty clear, but the last word is either 'ESTA' or 'ESIA.' What could 'esta' mean?"

Lily picked up the paper and examined it closely. "It looks like Spanish to me."

Bean scanned the shelves behind him and extracted a book. Thumbing through the pages, he stopped, then nodded. "She's right. *Está* is part of the verb to be or it could mean east."

Sam glanced over Lily's shoulder at the note. "Bean, look up E-S-I-A."

"You know, that looks more like one of those weird words you find in crossword puzzles." Bean returned to the bookcase and pulled out two more books. He pushed the dictionary across the desk toward Lily and tossed a small paperback to Sam.

Sam discovered the book was a crossword dictionary. He began a search for the obscure word.

"E-S-I-A isn't Spanish." Bean sighed and closed the book. "Did you find it, Sam?"

"No."

"It's not in the *Webster's.*" Lily lifted the heavy book from the desk, but it slipped through her fingers, making a loud thud as it hit the floor.

Sam reached down to retrieve the book at the same time Lily did. Their expressions of discomfort were mirror images of each other. When he realized she was trembling, he forgot about his own injuries. "What's wrong?" Sam pushed the book aside and reached for her cold hands, helping her to stand. Her eyes were filled with fear and another emotion he couldn't quite name.

"It just hit me." Lily's voice was low and shaky. "Vance's middle name is East."

Sam reacted to her despondency with a sympathetic hug, but compassion threatened to turn into passion as his senses responded to her warmth. They stood intertwined, unaware of the passage of time. When he remembered they weren't the only ones in the room, he glanced up to see Bean slipping out the door.

Lily lifted her cheek from Sam's shoulder, then scanned the room. "Where's Bean?"

"Probably changing clothes." Sam guided her to the couch and they sat down. She ducked her head, hiding her face beneath her hands and the protective draping of her hair. Sam gently lifted her chin, making the dark tendrils fall back.

She looked at him through damp lashes. "We were close, more like each other than anybody else in the family. Nearly brother and sister. I'll be the first one to admit Vance's not perfect. I might even believe he engineered the theft. But I can't believe he'd try to kill me." Her blurred gray eyes echoed the depth of emotion in her words. "Not Vance," she whispered.

Sam ran his thumb down her cheek, then pulled his hand back, surprised by the familiarity of his gesture. "Lily, we all like to think the best of people. . . ." His voice trailed off when her storm-clouded eyes made him lose all concentration. He couldn't express himself in mere words when he wanted to touch her again so badly. Sam grasped at the last shreds of his waning objectivity. "It's an admirable trait to stand behind the people who. . ." He couldn't finish; his words sounded so trite.

Lily lowered her head again.

"Please, Lily, don't hide from me." Sam moved to kneel in front of her. He took her pale face in one hand and brushed her hair back with the other. "I'm not good at sympathy. I don't know what to say."

"Don't say anything."

He didn't.

He kissed her. After a few moments of tender contact, he pulled back, wondering what magic she possessed to enchant him so thoroughly. When he dared look at her again, her eyes and her hands drew him closer.

Lily rested her forearms on his shoulders and locked her fingers behind his head. As their lips met, he felt an electrical charge radiate through his body and send a tingling sensation shooting through his arms and legs. Sam held her in his arms, content to just comfort her for a moment, feeling as if this cocoon of protection could keep all their fears and doubts at bay. When she pulled back, the tensions flooded in, replacing the sweet excitement with pangs of dread. He couldn't bear to let her leave this one brief oasis of pleasure to return to a barren place of lies and suspicion.

"It's hard to think about the future when the present looks so bleak." His voice rose barely above a whisper.

She sighed.

"Up to now," Sam continued, "I've always thought the best attitude was to expect the worst so anything better would be a pleasant surprise. But we can't do that. We can't expect the worst."

She squeezed her eyes shut, forcing out the remaining tears. "But I can't allow myself to have any false hopes."

"You're right." He stroked her cheek. "But Lily, the pain will go away, soon."

"How can you say that?"

"Because—" he ran one fingertip over her bottom lip "—I'll do my best to make it go away," he whispered. With her face only inches from his, the kiss was inevitable.

But this time, Lily surprised him with the intensity of her reaction. She drew him closer with such a tight grasp he could feel his own pulse accelerate, mimicking hers. Tenderness had given way to a deeper emotion, a passion that tugged insolently at his conscience.

He tried to tell himself to pull away, that it wasn't time to begin a new chapter in his life, but the force of an undeniable attraction steamrollered over the part of his brain that whispered caution.

He wasn't sure how long they stood there locked together, or when they moved to the couch. He wasn't aware of the moment his conscious mind surrendered to his unconscious. Years ago, he'd erected mental safeguards to protect himself against pain, regret and overwhelming guilt. At that time, it had been a matter of necessity. After a while, the barriers became permanent, blunting all emotions, making old pains bearable, diluting new pleasures.

At Lily's instigation, the self-imposed walls fell, leaving him vulnerable to old memories, old guilts. But instead of pain, he felt desire. Glorious, skyrockets-in-the-night desire. The kind of sensations that fueled young men's dreams and old men's fondest memories.

Sam had never wanted so much in his life. Wanted the chance to dream, to savor the memories, to have her in his arms, in his life. The sudden ferocity of his thoughts made him draw back for a moment, to realize the rhythm of his thundering heart matched the tempo of his fevered thoughts.

"Sam?" Lily's face was flushed, tinged with confusion and anticipation. He leaned forward, ready to seize the moment, to seize her. His heart skipped a beat as he thought about Lily in the throes of something hot and passionate and lasting forever.

A resounding crash exploded in the kitchen, the unmistakable sound of shattering glass. Sam pushed Lily down behind the desk, hoping to shield her from the possible danger.

"What—"

"Quiet," he commanded.

A moment later, the intercom crackled. "Uh, guys? That was me. Nothing to worry about. I just dropped a tray of glasses."

The tension slowly trickled out of Sam, draining the strength from his tightened fists. He released a sigh, stood and offered Lily a hand. She rose from the floor, wearing a rueful smile. "I guess we both overreacted."

He nodded. "Yeah, I guess we did."

"I suppose it's understandable," she offered.

Sam nodded again, relieved to find his thundering heartbeat subsiding to a tolerable roar. "You sure you're okay?"

Lily shrugged, rubbing her arms briskly. "I am now." A telltale tremble danced across her lips. "At l-least, I will be."

"Cold?" When she nodded, he pulled her closer, wrapping his arms around her. After a moment, he felt her shake and make a muffled noise against his shoulder. "It's okay," he whispered. "Everything's going to be all right." Her tears seeped into his shirt. "It was just Bean. Clumsy ol' Bean. Remember when he and I were talking about our college days?"

She nodded without lifting her head. "Mmm."

"Remember when he mentioned he worked in the dorm cafeteria for a while?" Lily nodded, her face still buried in his shirt. "What he failed to mention was that the job lasted two whole days. On the second day, he slipped on some wet tile and hit the glassware racks. They estimated he broke 1,328 glasses in one blow. A new school record, which I think still stands unmatched."

She shifted, lifting her head to reveal red-rimmed eyes and a bleary grin. "You mean the record hasn't been *broken* yet?"

He tightened his hold on her as they laughed. It was sweet relief from the tensions they'd experienced, but only a faded echo of the passion he had so desperately wanted to share with her. After their laughter subsided, he let out a deliberate, deep breath, knowing unfinished business stood between. *Everything has its own time.*

They shared a bittersweet smile, then she dried her eyes, reached across Bean's desk and retrieved the crumpled note. She stared at the paper, shook her head, then handed it to him. "I have no idea what this means."

"Run damn esta. Run damn east. I could understand run east, but not the damn. Maybe we'll learn more when the pictures come back. My buddy said he'll get the blowups back to us as soon as possible. Until then…" He shrugged.

Lily paced in front of the desk, then stopped to drum impatient fingers on the wooden surface. "Sam, if you were me, what would you do? Could you just sit around, waiting for other people to solve your problem?" She didn't wait for his answer. "I can't do that. I just can't," she repeated. "My company will be in chaos by the end of the week."

"Isn't the ordering system automated?"

"It could run a few days without human intervention. Everything, that is, but the narcotic orders. They have to be inputted by hand, and no one is there to do it." She paused. "If fact, no one can even get into the computer room since we changed the code lock."

Sam sat quietly at the desk, bending a paper clip back and forth until the metal warmed in his hands and broke. He threw the remains toward the trash can. A fledgling scheme hovered at the back of his mind. "Lily, did you ever consider hiring another assistant after—what was his name?"

"Lamarr Moody," she supplied, dropping slowly to the couch.

"After Moody died, were you going to replace him?"

Her expression grew softer. "I knew we needed to hire somebody, but I didn't want to turn around right after the funeral and start the interview process." She wove her fingers into a nervous knot. "I was torn between grief and the realization that life goes on. I needed to keep the computer section running at normal speed, but it seemed so callous to be looking for Lamarr's replacement."

"But eventually—"

"Eventually, I'll hire someone," she acknowledged reluctantly. "But it'll be difficult to find someone with the expertise, the experience and the ingenu—" She stopped in midword, and a suspicious look crossed her face. "Sam, you're not planning . . ."

Sam began to torture another paper clip. "Think about it, Lily. What other way can I get into the computer room and completely reconstruct the records? This way, I can track down how and when the inventory changes were made and keep tabs on Vance and the narcotics in the vault."

"I won't let you do that! If Vance was willing to run me off the road—I mean, if he thought you were in his way—who knows what could happen?" Lily twisted a strand of dark hair around her finger. "Anyway, what would you do? Just walk into the office Monday morning and say 'Lily hired me before she died'?"

"Something like that."

"Come on, Sam, be realistic. Mason would never believe that story. And what if Vance recognized you?"

Sam nodded toward the door. "We have the master thespian in the kitchen cleaning up the broken glass. If he can disguise you so that your own family don't recognize you, giving me a new identity will be a snap."

"Well, I suppose it could work."

Sam looked up from his pile of paper-clip remains. "Do you trust Mason?"

Lily hesitated before meeting his glance, then she nodded. "Yes."

"You don't sound convinced."

"What do you expect?" Her eyes reminded him of a storm cloud, ready to explode, not with rain but with bolts of lightning. "I've just found out the person closest to me, someone I grew up with and have always loved like a brother, wanted to kill me. It tends to make me think twice about trusting anyone!" She turned to the window and stared out. "I do trust Mason, though." Her voice had softened. "He and Vance never agree about anything. I've always had a hard time keeping them away from each other's throats in everyday life, so I can guarantee you they aren't partners in crime."

"Then why don't I call him and arrange a meeting? I'll tell him you hired me the day before you died."

She shook her head. "Mason wouldn't just take your word."

Sam began to smile. "But what if I had a signed letter from the dearly departed, dated Thursday or Friday, confirming my new position in the company?" He could see her mental gymnastics clearly reflected in her face.

Her doubt faded into reluctant consent. "It might work. Mason would definitely recognize my signature."

"It would serve as a binding contract with the company. Then your uncle would have to accept me as a new employee."

"My cousin, you mean," she corrected.

Sam rolled his eyes and grimaced. "I can't keep your family tree straight. Uncles who are really nephews, half brothers, cousins—and everybody's named Bradley!" He slid the phone across the desk to her. "You dial, I'll talk."

Chapter Eleven

Mason Bradley gave Sam a hard appraisal before extending a hand. Sam returned the powerful handshake, then gestured for the man to sit on the sun-warmed bench overlooking a panoramic view of the city. The cast-iron statue of Vulcan, God of the Forge, stood impassively overhead, pointing his torch toward the thin clouds dotting the late afternoon sky.

"I prefer to stand, Mr. Andrews. Now, please tell me why it was so important for me to leave my grieving family and meet you here." He waved impatiently at the area surrounding the base of the statue.

Sam glanced up, knowing Mason couldn't spot Lily's face pressed against the observation-deck window. He zipped his jacket in response to the cool breeze that created a swirl of dead leaves at their feet.

The bogus "Andrews" identity had been Sam's invention, backed by a few judicious calls to the clients he used as references. He added a false computer trail which misidentified Sam Markstrom as Spencer Andrews. He gave Mason Bradley a sympathetic smile. "It's about your niece, Lily Bradley."

"You mean my cousin." Mason's deep accent dripped with breeding and education.

"Cousin, of course. I'm sorry to intrude during your time of grief." Sam slipped into what he called his "chameleon mode"; his words and inflections precisely matched the cultured, Old South manner Mason used. "I was truly dismayed when I read the article in the paper concerning her unfortunate accident."

The man's expression appeared to be carved in the same kind of unyielding granite as Lily's headstone. "Lily's death took us all by surprise, Mr. Andrews. Although I appreciate your sympathy, I wish you'd tell me why you dragged me here."

"Miss Bradley contacted me on Friday with an offer to join your firm to be her assistant. We had discussed the position and agreed I should report to work on Monday. I didn't want to show up in the morning without giving you advance warning." Sam lowered his voice. "And of course, I didn't want to upset your family by discussing the matter in their presence, sir."

Mason continued to stand stiffly. "It's true Lily needed an assistant, but I'm afraid your word of her offer isn't sufficient. I need something concrete to confirm that Lily spoke with you and considered hiring you."

Sam reached into his jacket and removed some folded papers from an inside pocket. "Then I'm lucky this came in yesterday's mail."

Mason studied the letter, evidently paying as much attention to the signature as he did to the fake offer Sam and Lily had concocted. "And you are agreeable to these terms, Mr. Andrews?"

Sam nodded. "Although the salary is less than my standard consulting fee, it's sufficient for the short-term contract she offered me."

"We still have a problem, Mr. Andrews."

"What, sir?"

"All this contract business may be moot. Before Lily left on Friday, she changed the code lock for the computer room." The man's brief flare of anger hardened into a stony stare. "No one can get in."

"Then, sir, I suspect my services are even more critical to your company if the computer room is unmanned and inaccessible. My background is in computer security, and I have considerable experience with cipher lock controls. I'm positive I can overcome your security system and get into the room." The setting sun began to make long, cold shadows on the sidewalk, but Sam knew the chill he experienced wasn't due to the weather.

Mason's stiff posture grew even more rigid. "Yes, Mr. Andrews, I'm fully aware of your background. I certainly wouldn't have agreed to meet you if I hadn't checked you out. I must say I'm impressed by your credentials, but I am curious. Why are you willing to work at Bradley Pharm when you have your own successful career as an independent consultant?"

Sam shrugged. The man was thorough, just as Lily had said he would be. "We had a mutual acquaintance who told me about the company's problems. I thought I'd enjoy a brief challenge, acting as an intermediary assistant until Bradley Pharm could locate a more long-term associate."

The man's face reflected indecision, then begrudging acceptance. "If you are successful in gaining access to the computer room, then I should be able to confirm your employment." He offered a hesitant hand, which Sam accepted. "I certainly hope Lily's records corroborate the offer."

"I'm sure they will, as I'm sure our business relationship will be productive, sir," Sam returned with the slightest nod.

The man gave him one more appraising look, only this time a bit less scathing than before. "Indeed, Mr. Andrews, indeed. If that's all, I'll return to my family."

"Thank you, sir."

Mason nodded in acknowledgment, then followed the wide sidewalk that curved past the base of Vulcan and wound back to the parking lot. As soon as he passed out of view, Sam signaled Lily. A few minutes later, she emerged from the elevator at the base of the monument. By the time she reached him, he'd stripped off the fake mustache provided by a makeup-artist friend of Bean's and ruffled up his slicked-back hair.

"How'd it go?" she asked impatiently.

"I'm in. It wasn't easy, but I'm in."

Lily leaned her head on Sam's shoulder and released a sigh. "Boy, am I glad that's over."

"Me, too." He pulled her into a warm embrace and placed a kiss on her forehead. "Let's head back to Bean's. I need to start my homework."

"Homework? What homework?"

"You're the teacher. You're going to tell me everything you know about the entire Bradley Pharm computer operations."

"What makes you think you can learn it all in—" she intertwined her fingers in his, then pulled up his arm to expose his watch "—fifteen hours?"

He smiled. "I always try to impress the teacher."

HE STOOD IN THE SHADOWS of a large pine, watching intently, but unable to hear any of the conversation. He'd been smart to put a tap on all the Bradleys' phones. When the call from Spencer Andrews came in, it sounded damned suspicious, because he knew Lily hadn't made any effort yet to find an assistant. It was either a new twist on the old "monogrammed Bible" scam or this guy Andrews had something more sinister up his sleeve.

Either way, it's a scam that might cut into my part of the action.

He watched Mason Bradley stalk off toward his car, leaving Andrews behind. Moments later, a woman exited from the building at the base of the statue.

From a distance, there was something eerily familiar about her. Figure, posture, body language...something. She and Andrews waited there for a while, then started toward the parking lot, deeply engrossed in conversation. As they came closer, he ducked behind the tree, but he recognized her voice long before he had a chance to see her unmistakable face.

Lily!

AFTER A BRIEF but intense crash course on the inner workings of Bradley Pharm, Sam insisted Lily needed rest. Although she wanted to sleep, she sat on the bed, plagued by a tangle of thoughts and feelings she couldn't sort through.

Anger and fear weighted each end of the emotional seesaw she felt chained to. Anger screamed its outrage that anyone would put such a low price on her existence. Unadulterated fear worried that Vance might succeed in ending her tenuous existence. Would he regret killing her? Was this merely a situation of distorted self-preservation? As emotions nudged her down a spiral of depression, one shining thought became her lifeline.

Sam.

The memory of their kiss drove all the other images out of her head. Her body relived the fire of his unexpected passion, the intoxicating thrill of his touch. She closed her eyes and sighed, and her pounding heart brought a tremor to her clammy hands.

When she opened her eyes, reality flooded back, washing away the few moments of pleasure, replacing them with harsh truths about finite life. Suddenly the rapid beating of her heart had nothing to do with memories of pleasure. The walls of her room began to close in, and she barreled through the door as if she could outrun her own thoughts and leave them behind in the bedroom.

The white box in Bean's hands suffered a serious dent when Lily rushed into the hallway and crashed into him. She pulled together a small tight-lipped smile for her host. "Sorry, Bean. I guess I wasn't watching where I was going."

"You okay?"

"Yes. No. I don't know, Bean."

"Come on." He led her back to the bedroom and gestured for her to sit down.

She complied, perching on the edge of the bed. "I haven't sorted everything out yet. It's all so confusing."

"Is Sam one of those confusing things?"

Lily nodded. "I can't help but think about what's happening to him. About what he's doing now." She released a deep breath.

Bean gave her a wide smile. "It's a good thing I came to cheer you up, then." He shoved the dented box into her hands. "Here's Dr. Beaner's magic elixir. Guaranteed to put the spring back into your step and a smile on your lips!"

She eyed the box without comprehension. "What do you mean?"

He gave her an adolescent grin that belied his snowy head of hair. "When the going gets rough, the tough throw a party! Your timing is impeccable. The Mardi Gras celebrations always start with the annual King Bean Costume Ball, and that's tonight." Bean whipped off an imaginary hat and doubled up his long, lanky frame in a comical bow. "I would be pleased if you would accept my personal invitation to join the festivities."

"A party? Oh, Bean, I couldn't..." Lily tried to hand the box back to him, but he refused to take it.

"Look, Lily, I know how you feel. I don't expect you to be ready to forget all your troubles and be the life of the party. But if you try, you might be able to distract yourself. And who knows? You just might enjoy yourself, in spite of it all." He placed his palms together. "Say you'll come," he pleaded. "Please, Lily? Everyone wears a mask so your secret will be safe."

"Well..." The unwieldy box defied her attempt to balance it while trying to take a quick peek inside. She shifted her grip on the box and raised one eyebrow at the white-haired man in front of her. "I suppose this is my costume?"

"Yes, ma'am, and if you don't like it, any member of my staff will be more than pleased to provide you with a more suitable outfit." He struck another comical pose to match his grand words and gestures.

"Your staff?"

Bean ducked his head with a young boy's sheepish grin. "I suppose I could send one of the bartenders back to the theater to riffle through the racks until we found a better costume."

She shrugged. "Don't bother. If it doesn't fit, I'll borrow a sheet and make a toga, or be a ghost or something."

"That's the spirit. The party starts at eight. I'll send a suitable escort to accompany you to the ball, Cinderella." Bean contrived another exaggerated bow, then disappeared around the corner.

Lily paused, then nudged the door closed behind her. She dropped the box onto the bed and stepped back to give it a critical stare. *I hope he wasn't being literal when he mentioned Cinderella.* She had no desire to float around a roomful of strangers dressed as a fairy-tale princess, waiting to be chosen by the handsome prince. But a sudden mental image of Sam in tights flooded her thoughts, making her giggle.

Get a grip, girl! Regaining fragile control over her emotions, she took a deep breath and pried off the cardboard lid. An explosion of colors burst from the box; gold and purple geometric patterns in the smooth fabric reflected the light from the bedside lamp. Lily lifted the material, and it unfolded to reveal a glossy shirt. Beneath the shirt, she found matching pants, a cap and a riding crop.

"Jockey silks...how original!" Slipping off her sweater and jeans, she pulled on the silk pants, pleased with their fit. The diamond-patterned shirt required a little more dexterity as she gingerly pulled it over her bruises. Lily caught sight of herself in the mirror, half-dressed, and began to laugh. The gold and purple bruises matched her costume. The laughter jolted her aching ribs, but she ignored the discomfort, enjoying the emotional release the absurdity of the moment offered.

"'When the going gets rough, the tough throw a party....'" Maybe Bean's advice wasn't so bad after all.

SAM PUSHED BACK in Bean's chair, waiting for his computer to beep and signal he'd accessed his home system. After a few clicks and pops, the computer screen jumped to life. Three code words later, he was in.

The electronic morgue at the *News* only produced two articles about Lamarr Moody, Lily's late assistant. The first report described Moody as one of fourteen victims of a small commuter-airplane crash. The second article was his obituary. Neither offered much personal information about the man.

Activating his extensive data-net, Sam did a blanket search through his clients' resource bases. The DMV reported Lamarr Moody's address as an apartment, not far from Bradley Pharm. Moody drove an '87 Bronco and had received several moving violations, including one drunk-driving citation. The bank that held the lien on his truck indicated he had paid it off about a month before he died. Sam obtained the name of Moody's insurance company from the bank records and discovered the man had requested insurance on a new Corvette only ten days before the day he died. The insurance company noted there was no lien holder on the vehicle.

No lien? He paid cash?

Moody's six credit cards had been cleared recently to a zero balance. Going back several months before, Sam discovered the man had a total debt of nearly ten thousand dollars. His payment history on each account showed that he borrowed on every card nearly to the maximum credit limit, yet paid only the minimum due payment each month. That is, until the December billing cycle when every account showed it had been paid in full.

All the signs were there. The man had been living beyond his means, racking up some big debts and experiencing life courtesy of the installment plan. *Suddenly he's flush. But he's also cocky enough to think the world will go on, just as it did before. He pays his bills, makes a few fancy purchases and expects no one to be the wiser. Was he that careless? Or that sure of himself?*

Sam decided to call in a favor. He had the computer find the correct number, then dialed.

"Public Affairs. Barkley."

"Keith? Sam Markstrom."

"Mr. Spade, long time! What's shakin'?"

Sam picked up a paper clip from the desk. "Nothing much. I just want to call in a marker. A TransSouth commuter went down on January 31, in St. Clair County. What happened?"

"Lessee…oh, I remember. The pilot radioed in and said he'd lost fuel pressure. He thought he had a leak in the fuel line. He did. It blew in midair. It was pretty grisly. We were mopping up bits of plane over a ten-square-mile area. Nasty weather that day, too."

"Was there any question of foul play?"

"Nothing overt, but I have my suspicions. Mind you, most of the proof is sitting at the bottom of the deepest lake in St. Clair County." Keith paused for a moment, then lowered his voice. "I'm not convinced the leak was accidental."

"You think someone cut the line?" The paper clip fell to Bean's desk in two pieces.

"Off the record? Yes. The way I figure it, the plane dumped too much fuel too fast for a small cut. The line had to separate completely in order to imitate a Roman candle the way it did."

Sam made a face at the image Keith conjured up. "Barkley, you always had a way with words."

"It's a talent the National Transportation Safety Board doesn't really appreciate. Sam, you gonna tell me what this is all about?"

"No. But I will spring for a round at Bean's after it's over."

"You got it."

Sam hung up the phone and pushed back in his chair. *Moody threw a lot of money around without being discreet. Buying a Corvette with cash is about as conspicuous as you can get.*

His gaze strayed to the clock on Bean's desk—7:45. Fighting a twinge of panic, Sam realized he had barely enough time to take a hot shower to loosen his stiff muscles and change into his costume. Attendance was all but mandatory at the annual Mardi Gras party. In fact, no excuse short of death was tolerated. Sam tried to smile at his own brand of gallows humor but couldn't.

The perennial Lone Ranger outfit had been Bean's idea years ago. He called it occupational therapy when Sam worked in CCD. The significance of the outfit became painful the February following Walt's death. The badge and the gun evoked bitter memories Bean forced Sam to face. Each Mardi Gras, it had grown a little easier to wear the costume, and last year Sam had even resumed his authoritarian position as a bouncer.

This time Sam showered then dressed quickly, giving little thought to the associations that had troubled him through the years. Rather than concentrate on the past, he had a future to worry about. A duty to protect Lily's future. His future.

He smiled at the absurd thought of Lily as a duty. He glanced at his watch.

It was 8:01.

Lily glanced at the bedside clock as she wedged the cap over her tightly braided hair. She admired the gaudy reflection in the mirror; it was quite a sight to behold.

The Jacuzzi had relaxed her sore muscles, and the prospect of the party gave life an illusion of normalcy. For the first time in the last few days, she forgot about Bradley Pharm, her desk piled high with work, even the sight of a tree, embedding itself in the hood of her car. It was time to relax. Time to take a well-deserved break from the business of being afraid.

Lily felt a sense of self-betrayal when the sharp knock on the door caused her to jump. With her calm vision shattered, she answered with a shaky, "Yes?"

An unidentified voice answered her. "Ma'am, Bean asked me to escort you to the ball since your date hasn't arrived yet."

She surrendered to the nerves that screamed for caution. "Uh . . . that's all right. I'll wait here, if you don't mind."

"Bean thought you might say that. He sent this note." A piece of paper appeared in the crack beneath the door.

Lily retrieved it.

Okay, so you've proved yourself to be cautious. The pirate bearing this note is a rogue of the highest honor. Put on your mask and leave your fears behind to join the festivities.

Your devoted servant,
Dr. Bean of Magic Elixir fame.

Lily sighed, opened the door and stared at the blond, well-muscled pirate in the hallway. He looked as if he'd be more comfortable ruling the seas from a surfboard than a ship sailing under the Jolly Roger. He wore a flowing white shirt artfully arranged to reveal a magnificent set of pecs. *Defensive lineman,* she guessed.

He whipped off his hat and made a sweeping bow. "For you, m'lady. Were it but a rose." He held out a black mask. "It's tradition not to reveal your identity until after midnight."

After adjusting the elastic string which held the mask in place, she glanced back at the mirror. The image she saw bore no resemblance to the dearly departed Lily Bradley. She nodded and smiled at herself. The pirate offered his arm which she accepted.

"Full swing" didn't come close to describing the scene in the barroom. The "Somewhere in the Distant Future" Bar was gone, and a throne room had been constructed in its place. Bean lounged on a velvet-draped chair in the center of the dais. His elaborate plum-colored doublet had been stuffed so that his royal figure appeared on the portly side, making his legs look even longer and thinner. An ermine-trimmed cape trailed behind him, and a jeweled crown sat askew on his head. Her escort took her on stage to sit at Bean's side.

"Fair maiden, please sit with me until your knight appears to pay his respects to your loveliness." Bean replaced his comfortable Southern drawl with a clipped British accent.

"Who am I supposed to be? The royal jockey?" Lily shifted on her draped throne, discovering that, beneath the fabric, it bore a strange resemblance to a metal folding chair.

"This is Mardi Gras! You may become *anyone* you want to be." A large carrot walked past the stage, commanding their collective attention. "Or any*thing!*"

Bean's carefree chuckle warmed her, but thoughts of caution permeated the sense of merriment. "Are you sure it's safe for me to be here?"

He roared with regal laughter. "My dear, haven't you looked at yourself in a mirror? You bear no resemblance to the poor thing who swooned at my door. We will use no names, thus allowing you to be as anonymous as you wish. Many of my subjects refuse to speak, and thereby protect their identities." Bean dropped his pompous posture and affected accent and leaned toward her. "I bet Sam wouldn't recognize you."

"What kind of costume is he wearing?"

Bean leaned closer, grinning conspiratorially. "'Hi-ho
Silver! Away!'"

Lily straightened and smiled. "Very appropriate. You
picked it out, didn't you?"

He responded with a shrug and a grin. "It's just one of
our many traditions."

"Then I shall wait anxiously for the Masked Man." She
stood, faced her host and executed a small, stiff bow. "By
your leave, Your Majesty."

The crowded dance floor became an obstacle course
where she dodged the costumed couples who jerked in
rhythm to the music. Only a few people had opted for the
uninspired bed-sheet toga. Most partygoers had immersed
themselves in the spirit of the fun with elaborate and inventive costumes. A cowboy danced with Cleopatra while
Godzilla waddled away from the bar with two drinks in
claw. A Christmas tree leaned in one corner, gesturing with
green-gloved hands to no one in particular. Two playing
cards, the jack of diamonds and the queen of hearts, sat at
a small table holding hands while a jangling gypsy rattled
with each rhythmic dance step.

Two bandstands squatted at opposite ends of the building. A Dixieland jazz band held the floor at the moment,
filling the air with a sweet trilling clarinet and a driving
drum solo. Captivated by the compelling beat, Lily retreated to a corner to watch the parade of costumed couples.

The Lone Ranger strode through the doorway and
glanced around as if he was looking for someone. His outfit was identical to the one worn by the masked man of
movies and television, right down to the silver Texas Ranger's star and the gun belt loaded with silver bullets. He readjusted his black mask, then pushed his hat to the back of
his head, admiring the party atmosphere.

Intoxicated with a sense of mirth, Lily grabbed for his
hand, cutting in front of an Indian maiden who'd eyed his
well-fitting costume with obvious hunger. Lily silently

pulled him into the frenzied melee of dancers who were applauding an announcement from the bandstand. A softly muted trumpet began to wail, and couples swayed easily to the languorous tempo. Ignoring the Lone Ranger's half-hearted protests, Lily draped herself across his chest, moving to the slow cadence of the music.

Concentration became difficult as she began to appreciate the expertise of his fluid movements. Apparently, dancing was another of his talents.

"Do we know each other?" He leaned closer to her, his lips brushing her ear as he spoke. She shivered as she reacted to his teasing caress. She tried to respond with a shake of her head, the only answer she could manage, but he captured her face in his hands and kissed her.

Her words of surprise melted as their lips met. Sam slid his palms down to her shoulders, then to her arms, lightly stroking the satiny material of her costume. He spoke her name before she could open her eyes. "Lily..."

She dropped her arms and gazed at him with a dejected sigh. "I'm not Lily tonight. She has too many problems to enjoy a party like this."

Sam's broad grin caught her off guard. For a brief moment, she hated the black mask he wore; it veiled his features, diluting the effects of his unbridled response. The smile dissolved into another expression which made her heart beat faster.

In the midst of the crowded dance floor, they were alone. The only outwardly visible sign of their contact was a simple kiss. Inwardly, Lily battled the tumult of sensations that became hopelessly intertwined with her hopes, her dreams and her fears. They moved as one to the rhythm, oblivious to the end of one song and the beginning of the next. She found peace in his arms despite the confusion of voices and music swirling outside the small, private world they'd forged. Lily allowed herself a young girl's daydreams, letting her rejuvenated imagination supply a future for them.

Lily and Sam sitting in a tree...

She blushed, and he smiled again. An exuberant participant broke through the protective ring of Sam's arms. Jostled, Lily fought to ignore the pang of intrusive pain and remain in the idealistic realm they had created together. She silenced Sam's words of concern with a finger placed on his lips.

"Are you sure?" he mouthed against the wall of noise.

She smiled at him and leaned closer until her lips brushed his ear. "Right now, there's only one thing in my life I'm sure about."

His arms tightened around her. "And what would that be?"

A shiver darted up her back. "You," she whispered, leaning against his shoulder. "Me." She glanced up at his masked features. "Us, now." She felt him draw in a deep breath, his chest expanding beneath her touch.

He leaned down, placing an electrifying kiss on her exposed neck. "And later..."

They danced until thunderous applause indicated the end of the set. After scanning the room of revelers, Sam guided her to a less crowded corner. He laced his gloved fingers through hers. "Do you think it's safe to be out in the open like this?"

"As long as I don't speak to anyone, who could possibly recognize me? You didn't even realize it was me until..." Conscious of her attraction to him, she pulled away. "I don't know if I can explain how I feel. Maybe I've broken under the pressure. I'm so tired of feeling scared and hurt. All I want to do is forget this entire weekend of hell. My problems won't go away, but maybe they'll leave us alone for a little while."

Sam gave her hand a squeeze and led the way to a small table away from the undulating crowd of dancers. He pulled out the chair for her. "We can sit here and become different people for tonight. I've got a silver bullet and a mask to provide my identity. What about you? Who do you want to be tonight?"

"Funny, that's what Bean told me. I could be anybody I wanted to be." Lily glanced down at her bright costume. "I certainly don't look anything like Tonto."

Sam ran an appraising gaze down her costume. "Definitely not, *kemo sabe*. You remind me of Elizabeth Taylor in *National Velvet.*" The gloves muted the snap of his fingers. "That's it, I'll call you Velvet." He captured her hand again. "Could you stand another dance? The Cajun band is next."

Lily joined him as the second bandstand came to life, the musicians playing the hot spicy music that once had been native only to the bayous of Louisiana. Raucous zydeco tunes bounced and caromed off the walls, sending the crowd into wild gyrations. When the first song ended, the throng responded with a rousing ovation and clamor for more. Sam begged off after the second breathtaking dance, chivalrously citing his own injury as a reason to remain on the sidelines and let Lily rest.

When the set ended, the resplendent Bean advanced regally to the microphone and commanded the room's collective attention. "Ladies and gentlemen of the court, I am pleased to welcome you to the tenth annual King Bean Costume Ball. I, your beloved monarch, order you to have fun! Join in the festivities! Remember, my loyal subjects, what wondrous occasion are we celebrating?"

"Mardi Gras!" the crowd shouted in unison.

Bean waited until the applause died down before he continued. "I, your benevolent ruler, order you to eat, drink and make generous contributions to our charity, Project Homestead, by spending lots of money at our game booths." He paused, then raised the scepter over his head. "Let the festivities continue!" The jazz band broke into such an infectious tune that Bean abandoned his throne, grabbed a gypsy and commanded the center of the dance floor. Lily noticed the telltale red curls beneath the gypsy's bandanna and recognized Sam's sister beneath the gaudy makeup.

Lily had to yell to be heard above the roar. "Bean sure knows how to throw a party."

Sam nodded and grabbed her hand. "Come on, one more dance!"

The spirit of fun outlasted Lily's energy reserves. After two exhausting dances, she declined the third. "I can't get my breath," she gasped, lowering herself into a chair. Sam excused himself, then returned in a few minutes with two tall hurricane drinks. She sipped the pink concoction and noticed a conspicuous absence. "Mr. Ranger, I am over twenty-one, you know. You could have gotten me something other than a New Orleans–style Shirley Temple."

He shrugged. "That's all they're serving right now. Our host insists Mardi Gras is, and I quote, 'too intoxicating by its own nature to mix liberally with alcohol.' So the first few rounds contain no booze. The real hurricanes come out only after everyone has had a few tame glasses of fruit slush and a couple handfuls of hors d'oeuvres to line their stomachs. Then he closes up the bar about an hour before the party ends."

"I guess I shouldn't be surprised. Bean is an... unusual person."

"It's a private function. He can do whatever he wants, whether it's tradition or not." Sam flinched at the sudden whoop that pierced the air from the direction of the bandstand. "It's too loud in here to talk. You want to go outside and hit the booths, Miss Velvet?"

She rubbed a gloved hand around the back of her neck, enjoying the feel of satin against her skin. "I don't think I have the energy." She stretched, trying not to grimace when several stiff muscles sent up a protest.

Sam reached for her hand, a look of concern evident behind his mask. "You ready to call it a night?"

She shrugged. "Not really, but maybe we could take a breather. Someplace where it's quieter?"

"Tell you what." His grin was infectious. "You head back to the apartment, and I'll meet you there in a minute." He pushed the hat to the back of his head. "I think I'll mosey on over to the bar and convince that there barkeep to break out the real stuff for us. How's that sound, little lady?"

"Something slushy with a little kick?"

He nodded. "Yep."

"And you'll deliver it in person?"

"Yep."

"Sounds good to me."

His grin faded to a smoldering look, unhampered, perhaps even amplified, by the mystery of the mask. He stood, tipping his hat. "Yep."

Lily admired the view as Sam cut a zigzag path through the crowd. The fringed shirt accentuated his broad shoulders. The rakish angle of his hat combined with the fancy Western holster slung around his narrow hips made her heart take an extra beat. She pulled herself to her feet, mentally navigating the fastest route to Bean's apartment. Just the thought of her own masked man made her move faster.

The dancers moved erratically to the music, thwarting her attempts to circumnavigate the crowd. Gaps appeared then closed, frustrating Lily as she tried to make her way to the apartment. She waited impatiently as a parade of costumed revelers congoed past her. The last dancer tried to pull her into the frenzy, but she steadfastly declined. Beyond the line of dancers, Lily could see Sam's hat. He held the two drinks high over his head to avoid the gyrations of an excited dancer.

Lily threaded her way through the crowd and reached him, grabbing one drink. "Here, let me help you before they spill."

"Why, thank you, little lady. But forget the drinks. I'd rather dance with you."

Lily froze as the familiar voice made every muscle in her body tighten.

Chapter Twelve

Before she could utter a sound, Vance grabbed her hand and propelled her into an unoccupied place on the dance floor. Drawing her into a close embrace, he matched the leisurely movements of the other couples.

In one vivid flash of memory, Lily was a child again, standing on Vance's shoes and trying to learn how to dance. With unceasing patience, he'd shored up her adolescent insecurities. Thirteen was a difficult enough age without being dragged to formal adult gatherings when her father was between wives.

Vance hadn't offered overpowering praise like her father or, for that matter, Mason. To Vance, she wasn't the brightest and the best, the hope of future generations; yet her heart would soar with pride when he'd grin and say, "You're okay, kid."

Abject fear now ripped her favorite memories into a thousand pieces.

His smile, once encouraging, supportive, was now an ugly leer. "Howdy, ma'am. The name's Marshal Dillon. To whom do I have the honor of addressin'?"

His silver badge branded her shoulder, leaving a sensation as painful as the bruises from the steering wheel. She turned away from her nephew; either he didn't recognize her or he was playing some sort of sick game. She didn't know which. Either way, she refused to make eye contact with him.

"Bashful, eh?" He released a throaty laugh. "I didn't think there were any shy women left in this world." When she didn't dare respond, he pulled her more tightly into his arms. "Your perfume is—" his hot breath scorched her neck "—delicious. I'm sure I've smelled it before. Have we met somewhere?"

She managed to shake her head. Inside, her heart filled her throat. He sounded as if he was trying to pick her up. *Maybe he doesn't recognize me. Maybe it's merely a coincidence....*

"You're taking this 'masquerade to midnight' stuff to heart, aren't you? I can't blame you 'cause I love Mardi Gras, too. Of course, this doesn't hold a candle to the real thing in New Orleans. Now those people really know how to celebrate. But this isn't bad. I understand it's an annual affair. Did you come last year?"

Again, Lily shook her head to answer him. Anxiety gripped her as she stared into the sea of masked faces, searching for Sam. Coincidence or not, she wanted out of here. Now.

"I've never met this Bean guy," Vance continued, oblivious of her panicked quest. "I tagged along with a friend who had an invitation. I'm sure glad I came now." He shifted his hold on her, thrusting himself forward with deliberate provocation. "Aren't you?" Lily couldn't stop the tremor that coursed through her. To her utter relief, he didn't mistake her shiver as anticipation. "You must be cold. Here..." He draped his fringed sleeve over her shoulders. "I'll warm you up," he whispered in her ear.

Her feet responded like lead to the music. She wouldn't allow her mounting fear to control her actions and thoughts, but the difficulty lay in how to escape without arousing both his suspicions and his libido. She knew all too well that Vance enjoyed the chase as much as collecting the prize.

"You have a classic beauty like Elizabeth Taylor. You remind me of her in that movie, the one about the horses. Do you have those same magnificent violet eyes? Or are you just a shy Violet?" Vance laughed at his own joke, then moved closer.

In a gravelly voice, he began to describe the ways he might be able to help her escape the chains of shyness. As his comments became more suggestive, Lily realized she had two options, and the most satisfying of the two involved her knee and his groin. When his hand began to trace circles down her back, panic made her dig her fingers into his back. It was definitely a gesture he misunderstood.

"Why don't we step out for a breath of fresh air? Where we can get to know each other better...." His voice trailed off as if she was supposed to decide just how well acquainted they should get. Before she could react, a man dressed in a clown suit tapped Vance on the shoulder.

"Excuse me, sir. Sorry to interrupt your dance but..." The clown flashed a painted smile at Lily. "Honey, the baby-sitter just called. Jimmy, Jr.'s running a fever, and the baby's been crying all night. I'm afraid we have to leave."

Lily responded immediately, hoping she could use the mistaken identity for her own purpose. She used the most un-Lily-like, saccharinely sweet voice she could manage. "Of course, dear. Thank you very much for the dance, sir." Without so much as a glance at Vance, she grabbed the clown's arm and dragged him toward the door. Lily prayed she could get out of earshot before the man realized she wasn't his wife. Before she could explain her actions, the clown patted her on the hand.

"Good going. Sam said you'd play along, and he was right. He said he'd meet you in the apartment in a few minutes." The rescuer-clown melted away into the crowd.

She pushed her way to the kitchen and through the bookcase door to the apartment. Once she was in the hallway, the music subsided to a dull throb, signifying the party and its dangers were behind her for the time being. Instead of feeling relief, her stomach knotted in fear as she stumbled into the bedroom.

The waiting time stretched into an eternity. The oppressive silence of the room served only to weaken her resolve. Memories of Vance's suggestions made her stomach turn. The rush of blood in her ears almost drowned out the sound of a knock. She checked the impulse to hide and forced what little strength she had into her voice. "Who is it?"

"It's me. Sam." He entered the room, gazing at her with an apologetic smile. "Sorry I got held up, but I had to..." His voice trailed off and his expression faded into one of concern. "My God, Lily. What happened?"

She had intended to stand and give him a coherent answer, but her knees gave out. He got to her side before she completed her drop to the bed. "Take a deep breath."

Lily wanted to reassure him she wasn't falling apart, but the words wouldn't come. She buried her face in the fringed material of his shirt.

He wrapped his arms around her. "Don't be upset, honey. Anybody could have made the same mistake. The guy must have rented his costume from the same shop I did." He pulled back to give her a reassuring smile. "It's okay. We masked men are a dime a dozen." She stared at him, momentarily seeing danger beneath the disguise. "See, it's really me." Sam pulled off his hat and removed his mask.

"It was Vance." Her voice came out as a croak.

His smile disappeared, and he gripped her arms. "What?"

"The other cowboy—it was Vance," she repeated.

His gloved fingers tensed, crushing the brim of his hat. "Did he say anything? Threaten you? If he did anything—"

Lily raised one shaking hand to interrupt his tirade. "He didn't recognize me, but I knew it was him." She turned away from Sam, unwilling to let him witness her lack of control. "I've never felt so scared before. All I wanted to do was scream and run away."

"Lily, look at me." She hesitated before complying, but when she did glance up, Lily saw in his eyes the strength she needed to fight her fears. "I'm going to check out the situation. Lock the door behind me and stay away from the window." He released her arms. "Don't let anybody in this room except me. Understand?"

Wordless, she managed a nod.

Sam pulled on his mask and hat and headed for the door. A shiver of reminiscent fear rippled through Lily. The resounding click of the lock brought with it a sense of helplessness. At first, she waited on the bed, but it seemed unconscionable to merely sit. Rather than remain still, she paced the room, painfully aware of each second that dragged on.

The party sounds rumbling in the distance, the muted peals of laughter, the beat of music thrumming through the walls—all seemed to mock her fears. She breathed deeply trying to restore a sense of calm. Just as she thought she'd regained control over her runaway heartbeat, she heard a knock on the door. Her nerves shattered, amplifying the quiet sound to a thunderous level. She jumped, her elbow striking a glass bookend, which tumbled to the floor with an ominous crash.

"Lily!" The doorknob rattled. "Lily, it's Sam. Are you all right? Open the door!" She fumbled with the knob, stepping back in time to avoid a collision as he rushed in. He scanned the room, his hand dipping to the holster slung at his hip. "What happened? What was that noise?"

"I knocked off a b-bookend. It's okay."

Sam locked the door behind him and stalked across the room to the windows. "Vance is still on the dance floor, but Bean has the staff watching him. Tell me what he said to you."

"Nothing, really." She watched Sam savagely tug the curtains closed. "He didn't recognize me." She sat down awkwardly on the end of the bed.

"Are you sure? I mean, what are the chances he'd show up here by accident? Are you really sure he didn't see through your disguise?"

She nodded. "I'm positive. He tried to pick me up." She cringed at the memory of the crude words whispered in her ear and the hand snaking across her back. She shivered again when she looked up at the man in front of her.

The mask...

It reminded her of fear, of pain, of trust thrown to the wind like so much dust.

"Lily?" Sam knelt at her feet. "Are you all right?"

"Would you mind? The mask..."

Sam pulled off his hat, removed the mask and threw both of them toward the desk. "Sorry. I understand." He ran his gloved fingers through his dark hair. "This was all my fault, Lily. When I went to get our drinks, I ran into Douglass, the guy who returned my car from the car wash. I'd told him I'd make sure he got a special drink as a thank-you for helping us. When I saw you dancing with a man dressed like me, I figured you couldn't get away without causing a fuss. I never dreamed it was Vance." His face stiffened. "Can you forgive me?"

She lifted her hand and touched his cheek, trying to reassure him as well as herself. "How could you know? How could either of us have known?" A sudden sense of intimacy flared, then faded when fear returned. "What do we do now? Vance is here... so close."

"We get rid of him."

"How?"

"When I left, Bean was mixing him a special drink. Two sips and Vance'll be going home on the floorboard of a taxi. All we have to do is wait awhile." Sam stripped off his gloves and stuffed them into his hat, then removed the gun from its holster.

Just wait? It can't be that easy.

Lily noticed Sam's shiny toy pistol had been replaced by a real one; his sense of caution obviously belied his air of nonchalance. His hands remained steady as he exposed the cylinder and began to load the weapon with bullets from his pocket. He looked up, aware of her unwavering gaze. "It pays to be careful." Unbuckling the holster, he draped it over the back of a chair and placed the gun within reach on the desk.

The faint thunder of the drums vibrated through the walls, the rhythm reminding Lily of the costumed dancers. *Costumes. Masks. Faces hiding behind masks, hands hiding in gloves...* Lily shuddered in revulsion, remembering Vance's gloved hand snaking down her back.

"Are you cold?" Without waiting for an answer, Sam placed an arm around her shoulders. Lily jumped up, moving away from the deadly, familiar gesture.

He stiffened at her reaction until he saw her staring at his clothes. Then the revelation hit him. "My God, Lily. I didn't realize..." He finished his statement by quickly stripping out of the offending fringed shirt.

Lily eyed the bruises his bandage didn't quite cover. She stretched out a tentative hand to smooth a rolled edge of the elastic material.

Sam drew a shaky breath. Twenty-four hours ago, he'd withstood the temptation of her touch, but now things had changed. He reached out, intercepting her hand. Interlacing his fingers with hers, he pulled her closer. She tipped her head back to look into his face. Her pale eyes reflected a clear message, not blatant, not coy.

"I'm scared, Sam."

"I know." He ran the pad of his thumb across her cheek.

She closed her eyes, and her lips parted. Her voice was little more than a whisper. "Hold me."

He pulled her into his arms, feeling the silent tears make wet trails down his chest to soak into his bandage. Suddenly he realized how desperately he wanted to comfort her, to reassure her—to make love to her. He tightened his hold.

Lily sniffed, then raised her head. "You're getting wet." She ran her finger along the top edge of the damp material.

"It's okay." He kissed her forehead.

She sighed and nestled against him. After a moment, she managed a shaky smile. "I can hear your heart." Her fingers plucked at the dark hair above his bandage, a simple gesture which started a complicated spiral of desire within Sam.

She tipped her head up again, and he saw a single droplet rolling down her face. Her eyes were shining like wet steel. Lily was strong but not invulnerable. Did she need him, want him, as much as he needed her?

When he touched her cheek, he meant only to brush away the tear, but the silk of her skin was electrifying, the sensation lingering long after he withdrew his hand. When he leaned forward to place another kiss on her forehead, she tilted her head so her lips met his.

She slid her palms over the rigid muscles of his chest. "Make me forget . . . everything, Sam."

The husky way she said his name made his control weaken. Her perfume rode the wave of heat forming between them. Intoxicated, he kissed her neck, slowly working his way to the hollow of her throat. Pulling back, he raked his fingers through her thick braid, loosening the tightly woven strands into waves of crimped, ebony hair, which he fanned over her satin-clad shoulders.

She broke away, her breathy voice singeing his resolve. "Sam, I want you to—" She stopped, reaching over to pick up his hand and place a kiss in his palm. The simple gesture made him stiffen with desire.

Then she shivered as she guided his hand from her lips to the front of her jockey's shirt. He splayed his fingers around one soft breast, and her small gasp of pleasure aroused him even more. Passion built quickly and matched the rhythm of music reverberating through the walls. She arched toward him, allowing him to trail hot kisses from her throat on down. He blazed a path, meeting the challenge of each button until he reached the smooth skin above the waistband of her satiny pants. He shifted back up to capture her mouth, waiting for her invitation to go a step further.

"Let me make love to you." Her hoarse whisper cut through his control.

Lily's sudden forcefulness caught him by surprise, but the idea of her as the aggressor excited him. Her lips parted, their invitation enticing him to move closer. It was as if she had diverted all her energies from fear to desire. Smoldering thoughts within him ignited at her touch, starting a fire that intimacy could only feed, not quench. He'd just come to grips with the sudden strength of his own fervor when she stiffened and broke contact.

"Wait," she murmured.

"Don't go away. . . ." He intertwined the fingers of one hand with hers and pulled her closer. She'd captured his heart and he, her body. Who was the aggressor now?

Lily kept her balance by placing one hand against his chest, holding him at bay. Sam didn't attempt to push past her meager defenses, but when her gaze met his, he read an intensity in her eyes which matched his own. If she would only surrender to the passion he craved to share with her.

"I don't . . ." Her voice trailed to a whisper.

The harsh light of comprehension revealed the dark corner where his inadequacies lay hidden. The small voice of doubt gained strength, blaming her unwillingness on him. *She doesn't want you. . . .*

". . . have any protection."

The doubts dissipated, and he allowed himself the brief luxury of a deep, cleansing breath. He headed into the bathroom, praying he would find what he needed. He glanced back at her for a moment, feeling a bolt of yearning slice through him. She sat cross-legged in the middle of the bed, bathed by a silvery rectangle of moonlight. Her satin shirt hung open, offering him a teasing glimpse of lace and flesh.

After a few harried moments, he returned with a foil packet, stopping when he spotted the moonlight caressing bare skin. She sat in the same patch of light, wearing nothing but a pair of thin cotton panties. Sam couldn't deny, much less resist, the feelings she stirred inside him.

One moment, he stared at her; the next, they were together on the bed. He fought to rid himself of his own clothes, the barriers between them. She ran a caressing palm up the side of his bare leg to his waist, pausing before she traced the thin trail of hair leading down from his navel.

Tantalizing him, teasing him, inviting him.

He discovered how to make her writhe with the same enraptured expectancy she kindled in him. Within the span of a quicksilver heartbeat, she became the center of his desires, the center of his universe.

The tempo of their lovemaking grew to match the driving rhythm of his pulse. Pent-up emotions were released in a frenzy of sensual climaxes, melting Sam's self-control under the heat of unmatched pleasure. He hadn't expected salvation with such speed or satisfaction. "Oh, Lily..."

A fury had built up inside her, pounding against her reserve and demanding to be released. Yet it took nothing more than Sam's touch to consume her fears, and from the ashes of terror rose desire—pure, unbridled, insatiable.

The act of love became a symphony of emotions, euphonic and euphoric. His unerring combination of strength and tenderness drove her to peaks of ecstasy she never knew her body capable of experiencing. At the very moment their passions threatened to drown both of them in a flood of unsurpassed sensations, their world exploded in a pulsating finale, a climax of inconceivable pleasures, leaving Sam breathless and Lily weak with a sense of ultimate achievement.

She stretched herself against his lean, tight body, exhausted and spent. She toyed with the hair on his chest, and he grinned sleepily. Lily ran her fingertips over his single dimple. "You don't smile enough."

His expression deepened. "What do you call this? A frown?"

She ran her fingers over the enticing ridges. "You look like the Cheshire cat who swallowed the canary."

His muscles tightened, the sudden definition displaying their latent power. "You expect me to partake, then disappear?"

"No." Lily gazed into his eyes, reading his mixture of concern and amusement. "That's not the type of person you are. Me, neither."

"Damn straight." He stretched again, then pulled her closer.

In the protective circle of his arms, Lily found solace in shadows she normally would have feared. Sam succumbed to sleep, but she stayed awake, reliving the memories of his tender caresses and inspired passion. Fear might resume control of her world in the morning, but at the moment, she wanted to savor the warmth and comfort of his body.

She shifted in the crook of his elbow and rested her head on his chest, her impish fingers drawn to the dark curls. He opened his eyes, and his face reflected pleasure beyond that of a smile. Then, in a single fluid motion, he rolled over, balancing his body over hers. She ran her hands along the flexed muscles of his chest, then leaned up to brush her lips across the iron ridges. When she worked up to the hollow of his throat, he arched his back, groaned in pleasure, and lowered his body to hers.

LILY RESTED HER ELBOWS on the cold metal countertop as she sipped her tea. The early morning sun struggled to warm the kitchen by bathing it in a faint winter light. She could hear the hum of the water pipes, indicating Sam was up and showering. Bean hadn't made an appearance yet. Judging by the snores from the den, he wasn't likely to stir anytime soon.

Only a few buildings pierced the thin layer of fog that filled the valley. It robbed Lily of the scenic view she'd come to enjoy. Any pleasure she could find in Monday morning involved memories of Sunday night. And of Sam.

She'd stayed awake most of the night, admiring the lean body stretched next to her in bed. The dark of night was a time for terror, terror that traditionally grew inert in the brilliance of the sun. But it was just the opposite for her. The remnants of pleasure dissolved in the light of day, revealing the harsh reality of danger, a danger she never expected to find within the halls of her own office building. Sam would report to work that morning. He would encounter Vance. Face-to-face.

Lily had a hard time equating Vance with violence. In a family whose motto should have been Solemnity At All Times, she had found an early ally in her nephew. Their antics were legendary among their more stolid relatives, but even when maturity gave her a new vantage point, she realized their juvenile pranks were for the most part harmless. As an adult, Vance may have become involved in some shady deals, but she'd bet her life—

Her life. Her death.

A twitchy feeling kept Lily on her feet, forcing her to search for a diversion to divert nervous energy. She pawed through the leftover party food jammed into the refrigerator. Sam would need a lunch, she thought.

She felt a strange sense of achievement when she finished her self-imposed task. She didn't realize Sam had entered the room until she heard his voice.

"Well, what do you think?"

Turning, she flinched when she spotted an unfamiliar figure in the doorway. At second glance, she recognized the man with whom she had spent the better part of the night making love.

Sam wore a pair of sharply pressed trousers, held by a set of dark suspenders. His crisp white dress shirt fit him well, framing his broad shoulders and tapering to a tight waist. His red tie seemed an appropriate contrast to the dark, conservative jacket he suspended from one hand. A wonderfully realistic mustache was perched over his lip, and he wiggled it at her as he grinned. Wearing fashionable wire-rimmed glasses and with his dark curls tamed and slicked back, he bore no resemblance to her Sam.

"I barely recognized you." She moved closer to him, feeling a growing titillation at the thought of making love to this incredibly different-looking man.

His smile didn't quite reach his eyes. "That's the whole point of this disguise. I don't want Vance to recognize me. He knows what I look like from our little set-to in my basement." Sam slipped on the suit coat. "I'll try to call at least every hour. If you discover anything even the least bit suspicious while you're working from here, make sure you disguise your voice, or better yet, have Bean place the call."

"No problem. I have a private line because of B.J., my cousin, the switchboard operator. We won't have to worry about being overheard." Lily reached up and straightened his tie. She was stalling, and she knew it. Finally she forced the words out. "Sam, be careful. If Vance is willing to kill me—family—he won't think twice about eliminating a stranger." Her hand lingered near the tie, then she slowly lifted her fingers and touched his freshly shaven cheek. "I don't want anything to happen to you."

Sadness and another emotion pooled in her liquid gray eyes. He couldn't identify the combination yet he shared it all the same. He reached out and brought her hand to his lips for a quick kiss. "I promise to be careful and not trust anyone. With Mason's help, I'll get the proof we need. Don't worry."

Lily pulled him closer and surprised him with the possessive passion of her embrace. They held each other tightly for a few moments until she stretched up and whispered in his ear, "I don't know why you're doing all this for me, but...thank you."

"Yes, you do." He buried his face in her dark, tousled hair. Their deep kiss could have lasted for an eternity, but Sam forced himself to break away with a sigh of regret. "It's time. Wish me luck."

"I wish you weren't going."

"Lily..."

"I know. I know," she murmured. As he started toward the door, she stopped him. "Wait." She picked up a paper bag from the counter and thrust it into his hands. "I fixed you some lunch. You'll have a better chance to meet and feel out some of the key employees if you eat in the lunchroom with everybody else. They become more animated and informative over food."

"Thanks. Talk to you in a little while." Sam turned his briefcase so the lid acted as a shield when he opened it. He tucked the bag in the corner beside the gun. The last thing Lily needed was a pointed reminder of the way he had prepared himself against the potential of danger. He placed a chaste kiss on her forehead and headed out the door.

Lily watched Sam climb into Bean's low-slung sports car. The Porsche kicked up a cloud of dust, which obliterated its departure.

"Well, Mother. Did you get the boy off to school all right?" Bean stood in the doorway, running a hand through his disheveled white hair. Below his robe, he still wore last night's tights.

Lily suspected the robe's function wasn't propriety but to cover the rest of the costume he had evidently slept in. "Don't joke about it, Bean. This whole situation frightens me. What if he can't find the proof?"

Bean shrugged.

A voice came from the den. "Is he gone?"

Bean flushed and glanced at Lily before he answered. "Coast's clear."

Lily recognized the clank of coins which had been sewn to the hem of the gypsy outfit. Micki stepped into the kitchen, wearing a paler version of her perpetually brash expression. "Good morning," she offered, straightening the skirt of her wrinkled costume.

Bean shot Lily an embarrassed smile, then muttered something about a shower before he vanished, leaving the women alone.

Lily tried not to sound too presumptuous. "Good morning. You just missed your brother."

Micki's dress rattled as she dropped into a chair. "I know. I...I waited until he left. He doesn't appreciate a good hangover." She glared at Lily, drawing a deep breath before continuing. "I don't like what you've pulled Sam into."

Somewhere Lily found the strength to allow anger to fill the void fear had created within her. "I don't like the situation either, but it seems to be something neither of us can avoid."

Micki shook her head. "You don't understand. Sam's not ready to face that part of his life again." Tears formed in her eyes, and her face reddened to match her hair. "His world was shattered once. And he wouldn't let me help him pick up the pieces. He hid here with Bean rather than let me help."

Lily read the truth in Micki's bleary gaze. "You knew? You knew the whole time?"

Micki nodded. "Everything. I was devastated. Sam was hurting, but he didn't want me there. His own sister. Then I realized why." Her florid face softened. "I was the keeper of the flame. I remember the old Sam, the one who existed before his world caved in. I treat him no differently, make no allowances for what he's suffered. I yell at him, I bitch at him. I'm his link to his life before the incident. But now, you've come along..." Micki wiped her eyes on her sleeve, leaving a wet smudge on the material. "You've ruined everything."

"Me?"

Micki's posture stiffened. "Sam opened up to you, a virtual stranger. He's spilled out the most inti—" she stumbled over the word "—intimate details about a terrible period in his life. Details he hasn't even confided in me, yet."

"But Micki, you already know all about the problems he had."

Micki crossed her arms, more in a protective gesture than one of defiance. "But don't you see? Sam didn't tell me about it. Bean didn't tell me. I got it all from third parties. Even now, it would mean so much to me if Sam opened up and told me himself."

"Really, Micki..." Lily thought a judicious lie might be called for in this situation. "He hasn't told me too much."

"Yes, he has. And what he didn't mention, Bean probably did. Bean was there. *He* knows everything." Micki couldn't hide the venom in her words. "All the little triggers that cause a reaction in Sam. Like blood. Like a shattered window. You know, it used to be if Sam saw broken glass, he just stopped and stared at it. And sirens. He couldn't stand the sound of sirens." Micki's face hardened. "I wasn't supposed to notice his reactions. I was supposed to merely pretend I didn't understand." She turned toward the window, hiding her face from Lily.

"But Sam's overcome those things. He faced all of them to help me at the crash." Lily shivered at the memory. "The glass, the blood... the sirens."

"You're right." Resignation colored Micki's words. "He had to overcome them—without *my* help. During the past six years, he's lived in an emotionless, sterile environment with those damn computers where he didn't have to feel a thing. Desensitization, the doctors call it. But now everything's changed so fast, and I'm not sure Sam can take it." Micki pivoted and gave Lily a probing stare. "Exactly how much danger is Sam in?"

"I..." Lily's first instinct was to lie and reassure the woman there were no evils lurking in the halls of Bradley Pharm. Then her conscience took over. "I don't know. I wish I did."

"I was afraid you were going to say that." Micki's costume rattled as she snaked a hand into her skirt pocket. She held a key ring in her white-knuckled fist. "If anything happens, you'll call me? At work?"

Lily nodded.

The woman's face paled behind the smeared makeup. "If anything happens, I don't want to be on the outside looking in."

Lily reached over and gave Sam's sister a quick embrace. "I promise," she whispered. Micki scribbled a telephone number on a scrap of paper and shoved it into Lily's hand, then made a jangling retreat toward the door.

Lily tried to divert her thoughts by pushing herself into the automatic routine of fixing a cup of tea. But as the water heated, she stared out the window, trying to digest the curious exchange.

"Is she gone?" Bean rubbed a towel across the back of his neck as he entered the kitchen.

Lily poured the steaming water into a cup and took a tentative sip of her tea. "That seems to be the important question of the day. Yes, she's gone."

Bean stepped across the room. "I'm sorry if she unloaded on you. I tried to talk to her about it last night, but all we ended up doing was arguing over our drinks." He splayed a hand across his robed midsection. "I haven't tied one on in years! And to wake up in bed next to Micki..."

"Are the two of you—"

Bean interrupted her with a quick shake of his head. "No." His burst of nervous laughter faded away. "Not me and Micki."

A sudden flash of inspiration hit Lily. "How long have you had a crush on her?"

He winced. "Is it that obvious?"

Lily shrugged. "I know unrequited love when I see it."

He wandered to the counter and dropped to the stool Micki had vacated. "I fell in love with her when she was thirteen and I was eleven. But it was an unbridgeable gap in ages. And worse, I was her little brother's best friend." His expression grew more distant. "That's all I've ever been to her—Sam's buddy."

"But she and you . . . I mean, she came out of your room this morning."

He shrugged. "Absolutely nothing happened. Not one damn thing. I found her there last night, passed out across my bed. She knew right where to go. Good old Bean's room. Safe, reliable Bean." He released a sigh. "Bean, the eunuch."

Lily reached up and put a hand on his shoulder. "No. Bean, the trustworthy. Bean, the man who welcomes a complete stranger into his house. Micki came to you because she knew you wouldn't take advantage of her while she was vulnerable. She felt safe here, just like I do."

He wore a dreamy expression. "But I don't want her to think of me as safe. I don't want to be her best friend. I want to be her lover."

Lily wondered if he was aware he was verbalizing his thoughts. "You can be both friend and lover." For a brief moment, she flashed to her budding relationship with Sam. The forging of friendship with passion made their connection stronger, a bond with the potential to become permanent.

Bean gazed out the window at the fog-enshrouded city. When he pivoted back to face Lily, a faint grin replaced his woolgathering gaze. "We don't have time for this. We've got work to do today."

"What kind of work?"

"Anything we can find to keep ourselves busy. Neither of us needs to sit around and worry about what we can't change."

Lily nodded. "Agreed. It'll be hard not to worry, though."

He gave her a quick smile. "Listen, Lily. If anyone can get inside a stubborn computer and coax out some sort of incriminating evidence, it's Sam. He's got the touch. Simple as that. If the information is in there, he'll find it."

Lily rubbed her hands together, trying to warm them against a sudden chill. "It's not the machines that scare me. It's the humans."

Chapter Thirteen

The bright sunlight washed away Sam's more recent memories of Bradley Pharm. In the glare of day, the building appeared innocuous. He noticed the flag at half-mast. *For Lily...*

Parking in the lot nearest the main entrance, Sam paused for a last-minute check of his disguise. He damn near didn't recognize himself when he glanced into the rearview mirror. He made a quick mental reminder never to try to grow a real mustache. As he climbed out of the Porsche, another car pulled up next to him, and two women stepped out, already engaged in conversation.

"...one of the lucky ones because I found out before the fact."

The driver adjusted her scarf to ward off the sharp breeze. "I want to know why Mason didn't close down shop today."

"Because he's a cheap son of a bitch."

The other woman gave Sam a quick glance and signaled for her companion to lower her voice. "Sara, please!"

"Well, it's true. I can say it 'cause he's *my* second cousin, once removed. I think Mason rushed Lily's funeral just so he didn't have to give anybody the day off."

Sam reached the entrance ahead of the women but waited to hold the door open for them. "Ladies," he greeted them, adding a benign smile. He felt himself the subject of their curiosity. The taller of the two gave him an intense stare, which nearly melted his clothes. Suddenly, Sam understood the meaning of the phrase, "being undressed by someone's eyes."

Unfortunately, the woman at the reception desk, a matriarch before her time, didn't appear as receptive. "May I help you?"

"I hope you can. My name is Spencer Andrews. I'm looking for Mason Bradley."

Her voice dripped icicles. "Do you have an appointment?"

"Not really. When we spoke yesterday after the funeral, he didn't mention the necessity of an appointment." Sam leaned forward, and the woman matched his gesture. He spoke in a lower voice, trying to instill a sense of confidentiality. "Lily Bradley hired me Friday morning to be her assistant. Of course, this all occurred before her—her accident."

The icy facade broke, and a strong emotion flooded her face. "J-just a moment, please."

As Sam waited, he noticed the engraved nameplate sitting on her desk. Barbara Jean Bradley. He realized this was Lily's cousin, who'd been engaged to the late Lamarr Moody. Judging by her red-rimmed eyes, B. J. Bradley didn't look like she could handle any more bad news.

"Through the main room, second door on the left," she offered in a shaky voice.

Sam walked through the reception area and into the main office, gathering a substantial number of curious stares. Mason caught sight of Sam through the glass and greeted him at the office door.

"Mr. Andrews. You're prompt. That's always a good start for a new employee." Mason conducted him into the room, then closed the door, giving them the only measure of privacy possible with an office formed on three sides with glass. "Welcome to Bradley Pharm, Mr. Andrews. Please take a seat."

Sam shook the outstretched hand. "Thank you, sir." He sat down in the chair at the front of the desk.

"I didn't call the security company since you said you could gain entrance to the computer room...." Mason's voice trailed off, sounding dubious.

"I'm sure I can, Mr. Bradley. Depending on the sophistication of the equipment, it might take as much as an hour to break the code, but I'm certain I can get in."

"I hope so, Mr. Andrews. Your presence here hinges on finding verification of your employment in Lily's notes."

"Of course, sir."

Mason stood, then gestured at the door. Sam followed, noticing the group of women at the watercooler scatter as their boss approached. The man stopped at the nearest desk. "Marlena?"

The woman turned around to look at her boss. "Sir?"

"We'll be in the computer room if you need me."

She nodded. "Yes, sir."

"By the way, send Vance to Computer Ops when he decides to show up."

"Should my ears be burning along with my stomach?" Vance Bradley sauntered into the office, tossing his expensive briefcase in the general direction of a desk chair. "Sweetheart, find me something to extinguish this heartburn, okay?" He turned to face Sam. "Mornin', I'm Vance Bradley." The smile on Vance's face hardened a little when he looked above their handshake and into Sam's eyes. "Have we met before?"

"I don't believe so." *At least, we haven't been properly introduced. I'll wait until I can catch you in a dark corner.* Sam gave the man a bland smile. "I'm Spencer Andrews."

Mason crossed his arms and almost smiled. "Mr. Andrews will be heading up Computer Operations, starting today."

"My God, Mason." Vance clenched his hands into fists. "Lily's not even cold in her grave, and you've hired her replacement? I can't believe you!"

Sam watched Vance's reactions intently, surprised that the man's outrage appeared genuine.

Mason took a step closer to his partner. "Get control of yourself, Vance. I'm not that callous. Lily contacted Mr. Andrews last Friday before...before the accident and hired him as her assistant. It makes sense to retain him since she thought enough of his talent to hire him in the first place."

"You don't have to yell, Mason." Vance rubbed the heel of his hand against his stomach. "They can hear you all the way into the warehouse." He turned a sour face toward Sam. "I'm sorry, Mr. Andrews. I didn't mean to imply you weren't capable of handling the job. I just think it's a bit soon to haul in the temporary troops."

"Quite all right, Mr. Bradley."

Mason stepped between them, effectively cutting off any more conversation. "Please, there are too many Mr. Bradleys around here. We go by first names." Mason pivoted and glared at his cousin. "When Marlena returns with your hangover remedy, join me in my office."

Vance raised one hand in a careless salute. "Yes, *mon capitaine.*"

Mason ignored the comment and marched off toward the computer room with Sam following close behind. When they arrived, the man indicated the security keypad by the door frame. "If you are able to gain entrance easily, I may have to rethink our security system."

Sam opened his briefcase and removed a zippered tool kit. "I can make some recommendations if you feel you need them. But I think you'll find your existing system will keep out ninety-nine percent of the criminal element." Pulling out a screwdriver, he started on one of the four screws holding the metal frame in place. He turned back to Mason with a smile. "You might as well go for some coffee. This is going to take a while."

Mason nodded. "Just let me know as soon as you get the door open." He disappeared down the hall.

After dismantling the keypad, Sam allowed it to dangle by its collection of color-coded wires. Whenever anyone entered the hallway, he made sure he appeared deeply mired in either the circuitry or the schematic he'd spread out on the floor. Sam laughed to himself as one enterprising young man knelt down, consulted the schematic design, then shook his head in sympathy. "I don't envy you, mister. That's pretty complicated."

"You're right." Sam nodded, keeping a straight face. If he followed the old wiring scheme from his files, he'd be building a television cable converter, not recoding an alarm system. When Mason returned, Sam waited until the man was halfway down the hallway before punching in the security code.

"Got it, Mr. Bradley."

Mason nodded in encouragement as the door clicked and swung open. "Only fifteen minutes. I'm impressed. It makes me think our security precautions might not be as effective as we thought."

How true, Sam thought as he stepped back and permitted Mason to enter first.

The gray-haired man waved a hand in the direction of the banks of computers and sighed. "I can't pretend to instruct you about the computer operations. I know what comes out of this office, but I have no idea how Lily and her assistant generated the information. All I can do is turn you loose with her notes and your own abilities and sleuthing talents. Would you prefer to discuss salary right now?"

Sam shook his head. "Why don't I wade into the computer first and figure out how the system works? My level of involvement depends on the programming. It may be a matter of training someone how to input the data, allowing me to merely do periodic checks and updates to keep the system running."

"Good thinking. Anything else?"

"We'll see." Sam thumbed the master switch to turn on the system.

Mason paused by the door to examine the keypad and the locking mechanism. "I think I may call the security company and have them install a different type of cipher lock. Incidentally, I'll need the new code for this one."

Sam scrawled a series of random numbers on a piece of paper and handed it to the man. No one would get the real combination to the room until some answers were found.

"Thank you." The door closed behind Mason and locked automatically.

Now ... down to business.

LILY WAITED UNTIL ten o'clock to call Sam. She settled herself in Bean's leather chair and dialed the familiar number.

"Computer Ops, Spencer Andrews speaking."

"Sam?"

"That's one way of putting it. How you doing?"

"Well enough, considering I'm here and you're there. What's happening?"

"Mason turned me loose in the computer room. Vance is somewhere in the building, waiting for his hangover cure to kick in. I've been busy, checking the last eighteen months of narcotic records. The dollar amount is climbing exponentially. This may prove to be bigger than either of us imagined."

She found remnants of broken paper clips and began to reassemble them. "Has anyone mentioned who's going to replace me as the authorized DEA registrant?"

"No. Any suggestions?"

"Definitely Vance. He's an officer of the company so there shouldn't be any problem. Considering what he's done so far in the name of greed, he might believe it'll be a chance to control the entire narcotics operation."

"If he did become the registrant, he just might consider it a license to step up his operations."

"Anything to make this end quickly. Are you ready to download the files to me?" She heard a soft beep in the background.

"I'm ready."

Lily made one last check of the notebook computer. "Okay on this end."

"Here goes."

Fifteen minutes later, the end-of-file cursor flashed on the screen. Lily picked up the receiver. "Sam?"

"Got it?"

She swept the paper clips into the trash can. "Looks okay."

"Call me when you get through with that batch and I'll send you some more. Incidentally, have the pictures arrived yet?"

"No. Your friend called Bean a little while ago and said he was sending them by messenger later this afternoon. He said he's taking the extra time to make enhanced enlargements."

"Good. Call me as soon as you look at them. Even if you don't see anything suspicious."

"Okay. Sam, I…" She paused. "I don't want you to take any chances."

"No unnecessary ones, I promise. 'Bye."

Lily tightened her grasp on the phone. "Be careful." As the click ended their call, she added a silent *I love you*. The three words took her by surprise, but as soon as they crossed the barriers of her mind, they seemed natural, familiar. Honest.

Her fingers shook as she began to type commands into the computer. She couldn't help remembering the usual explanation for sudden shivers. *Someone is walking over your grave.*

AFTER THREE HOURS of scanning through data, Lily allowed Bean to bully her into a lunch break. When the phone rang, she nearly dropped her spoon into her soup. Bean answered the phone, then turned toward her. "It's Double-0 Seven."

She grabbed the receiver. "Sam, anything yet?"

"Not really. I haven't found any corruption in the programming. You?"

"Not a thing out of the ordinary. Did you have a chance to meet some of the players?"

"Yeah. Vance took me for a tour of the facility, and we became real chummy. Lunch with him was...interesting. Most of the ladies really seem to fall for his sleazy charm. He put his arm around every woman he introduced to me and called them sweetheart or honey."

The memory chilled her blood. "Half the time it's because he doesn't remember their names." In the distance, she heard a buzzer, belatedly realizing it originated from within the bar, not through the phone. Bean stood up and headed toward the service door. "Sam, someone's here. It might be the messenger with the photographs."

"I hope so."

When Bean returned to the kitchen, she could see the envelope in his hand. He quickly crossed the room and handed it to her. She balanced the phone between her shoulder and ear as she ripped open the paper flap. "I've g-got them." She hated how shaky she sounded.

"Just look at them one at a time, Lily, and tell me what you see."

"Okay." She took a deep breath and pulled out the first photograph. "The first one is a wide shot of the group at the cemetery. I don't see anyone or anything unusual. The next one...it's Mason talking to his wife. The third, I can see the man in the shadows of the tree but I can't make out his face. The next one...his back is turned to the camera, but I can see a piece of paper in his hand." When she saw the last picture, shock made her heart race and her throat close.

"Lily, what's wrong? Talk to me."

"Sam..."

"Tell me what you see, Lily."

"Oh, my God. It's him." Her hands began to tremble.

"Who, Lily? Who?"

Her mind screamed, but her voice came out in a whisper
"*Lamarr.*"

"Lamarr Moody? Your assistant?"

The room began to spin. "He's not dead, Sam. He's no
d-dead...."

"Who's he talking to in the picture?"

Lily fought to reclaim her composure, fumbling with the
phone.

"Lily? Describe exactly what you see."

She drew her strength from the concern in his voice. "I'm
sorry. This has ... caught me by surprise." She scanned the
photograph, trying to push back the sensations making her
stomach churn. "Okay. The person Lamarr is handing the
paper to—it's definitely a man's hand. And he's not wearing any rings."

"Right hand or left?"

"Left. No, right. Definitely the right. If we could only see
his face! I can't tell if it's Vance."

"But you're sure the other guy is Moody?"

"Very sure. What does this mean?"

"It proves you're not the first one to use an accident to
fake your own death. It also explains why the thefts didn'
stop when Lamarr supposedly died." Lily couldn't fathom
a response, and Sam continued in her silence. "Maybe La
marr wanted to give himself a chance to disappear before the
inventory check revealed the losses and the alarms went off
Could he have pulled off this entire scam by himself? With
out Vance's involvement?"

Lily tightened her grasp on the telephone receiver. "I
Vance isn't involved, then why did Lamarr risk being seer
at my funeral to pass a note to him? And what did the note
mean?"

An exasperated sigh echoed over the phone. "I wish
knew."

"Sam, I've got to go back through all that data again
I've been looking for amateur involvement, not corruptio
on the level of Lamarr's expertise."

"He was that good?"

"He was a hacker when he was fifteen."

"That doesn't mean anything."

"Sure it does. *You* never caught him." Lily regretted her biting words as soon as she spoke them. She drew a deep breath. "I'm sorry, Sam. I'm so frustrated just sitting here. I want all this to be over."

"I understand. You go over the data again and I'll do the same on this end. Maybe this time we'll find something."

"Okay." She paused for a moment. "Sam, stay in the computer room. I think you'll be safer in there."

"Don't worry about me. I'll be okay. I promise." A hint of strained laughter tinged his voice. "You just keep Bean in line. I'll call back later."

AN HOUR LATER, the phone rang in the computer room.

"Sam, I figured it out." Lily's voice was unnaturally high-pitched. "Lamarr's message, I mean. When I realized it came from him, I thought it might be related to computers. It's not run damn esta. It's Run D: Amnesia. The D hard disk drive contains the Schedule II inventory. Lamarr might have written an amnesia program that could either wipe out the entire memory or scramble it, removing enough key information so that we'd never get it straight. He was getting a message to Vance to tell him to run the amnesia program."

"That's got to be it. I'll search through the drive and find the program if it still exists. If it'd been my job, I would have embedded a command that would destroy the amnesia file as soon as it was completed."

"Lamarr was a great troubleshooter. It's entirely possible he wrote it to clean up after itself. Let me know when you find something."

"I will. Listen, do I inform Mason of a possible theft?"

She paused for a moment. "I don't know if there's anything he can do about it right now. My initial reaction is . . . no. Don't tell him yet."

"Okay."

In twenty minutes, Sam realized an amnesia program definitely had been run, making binary confetti out of the narcotic records. Luckily he discovered he'd created a protected backup file when he sent Lily a copy of the data by modem. Reconstructing the last three months of data, he compensated by using the protected data to replace the missing pieces of information from the main files.

He recognized a pattern that preceded the thefts. A large narcotic shipment would come in from the pharmaceutical manufacturers. A bogus order was inputted within a few days. The thefts didn't happen every week, but when the orders were "placed," they always occurred on Monday afternoons around two o'clock. The orders were filled by Tuesday morning and shipped out by that afternoon.

It wasn't hard to figure out the procedure. With Lamarr as an inside man, Vance would always know when the inventory levels were high enough so no one would notice an unexpected drop in stock. Since each order listed an identical terminal ID code, Sam realized the bogus orders were placed each time from the same terminal. But he couldn't find any listing of terminal codes or their locations in Lily's records or files. The amnesia program had conveniently wiped out that information.

Sam dialed Mason's extension and the phone rang several times before a female voice answered. "I'm sorry. Mason is away from his desk right now. Would you care to leave a message?"

"This is Andrews, in Computer Ops. I need to speak to him as soon as he comes back."

"Yes, sir, Mr. Andrews. One moment, please." The line was silent for a moment, then another voice spoke. "This is Mason's secretary, Marlena. I have some paperwork for you to complete. If you could come to my desk, it would make the entire process go a lot faster."

Sam glanced at the terminal where the pulsating cursor demanded his attention. "Well, I can give you ten minutes at the most. Be right there." Sam typed in an order which blanked out the monitor, hiding the numbers and figures describing the scope of the crime.

After too many minutes of paperwork, Sam excused himself, promising to return the next morning and complete the numerous forms. As he passed by the break room, Vance called out to him. "Hey, Spence. Come on and join us for a moment. You haven't met the data entry girls. Charlene, Melanie, Deanna and Janet. Girls, this is Spence."

Sam wondered if he could use the time to find out more about his adversary. He decided to join Vance and his bevy of beauties.

Vance propped his feet on the break-room table. "Tell us about yourself, Spence. Is there a little woman at home, cooking your supper?" The man laughed at his own joke and put a possessive arm around the nearest female.

"It's Spencer. And no, I'm not married."

Vance gave the women a big smile. "See, girls. Who says Bradley Pharm isn't responsive to your needs? You wanted some new blood and Cousin Mason provides. How's this for service?"

The women expressed various reactions to his comments, from laughter to embarrassment. "You see," explained a tall blonde, "Mason usually goes for the nerdy types when he hires. Of course Vance here doesn't mind that. He ends up with no competition." Her interested expression intensified, reminding Sam of a predator sizing up its next meal. "How in the world did Mason hook up with you?"

"Actually, Mason didn't hire me. I talked with Miss Bradley on Friday, and she hired me as her assistant." Sam watched Vance's smug satisfaction fade, and the women suddenly grow reticent. "Of course, when I read the paper Sunday and found out she'd been killed, I wasn't too sure I still had a position. When I called Mason and talked with him, he said to come on in today."

The women hurriedly made their excuses and filed out of the room. Vance stood to watch, evidently appreciating the angle of their exit but visibly upset at the abruptness of it. He released a long sigh. "You certainly know how to clear out a room, Andrews."

Sam shrugged. "They asked."

Vance shook his head and propped himself against the table, crossing his arms. "Allow me to explain the intricate politics of a family-run business. You have to remember we're not business partners because we chose each other. We've all been thrust into the business with other family members, whether we like them or not. Remember the old saying, 'You pick your friends, not your relatives?' It certainly applies in this case. Mason and I, we've never been what you might call buddies. I'm not too sure about the future of this company without Lily."

Sam saw his opening and went for it. "Tell me about her."

"Lily? Well, we always say, er, said, Lily was the oil that kept the machinery moving. She was bright, energetic. She had talent. You know what I mean?"

For a moment, Sam thought he read a flicker of pain on Vance's face. The man picked up a paper cup and began to tear it into pieces.

"She really took to the business, our Lily did. Even Mason finally admitted she'd probably learned more about the company in five years than he'd learned in twenty-five. She kept me from punching him out more than once and vice versa. Without her to run interference, Mason and I will be at each other's throats."

Vance stared at the pile of torn paper on the table, then found another cup, which he raised in mock salute. "Welcome to our happy little family, Spence," he said between the clenched teeth of his bitter smile. "You might think about coming to work armed for your own protection."

Sam thought about the revolver sitting in his briefcase. As his finger tightened around an imaginary trigger, he made no effort to disguise his sarcasm. "Thanks, I appreciate the update. I guess it's time to go back to work."

Vance glanced down at his expensive watch. "Naw. It's time for a drink."

Sam retreated to the computer room where he was surprised to see Mason standing beside the door.

"There you are. Barbara Jean left a message you needed me." Mason stepped aside, allowing Sam to input the entrance code. "What's up?"

Sam led the way into the room and sat in the desk chair. "I was wondering if you had a list of terminal codes."

The older man pulled up another chair and sat where he could see the monitor. "Terminal codes? What's that?"

Sam pointed to the pharmaceutical order on the screen, indicating the series of numbers at the bottom. "This is the pharmacy code that identifies which store this order came from." He pointed to a second series of numbers. "This series identifies the salesman."

"And you need a list of stores?"

"No, sir. A list of salesmen's terminal codes. The computer doesn't really identify individuals but the machines themselves."

Mason shook his head. "I had no idea." He pointed to the monitor. "You sure there isn't a list in the computer?"

"I'm afraid not. The system has a few glitches I can't go around."

The gray-haired man stiffened. "Glitches? Are you telling me there's something wrong with the computer system?"

Sam plastered on a quick smile, hoping he looked and sounded unconcerned. "It's just a few quirks Miss Bradley designed into the system. It's sort of a...programmer's signature. If you don't have the list, I can generate it some other way. I just thought I'd ask."

"Well..."

"Don't worry, sir. It'll sort itself out."

After Mason left the room, Sam dialed Lily.

"Are you any closer to an answer?" she asked quickly.

He could hear the anxiety in her voice. "Maybe. Do you know if you have a hard-copy list of terminal codes?"

"I don't think so. Did the amnesia program destroy that?"

"Yeah. I didn't send you those files so I can't reconstruct that part. But I was able to restore most of the narcotic data. Every bogus order originated from the same terminal and was always inputted on Mondays around two o'clock. I'd lay odds it's the same computer sitting on Vance's desk. I'll be able to physically check it out after everybody leaves."

"So once we establish opportunity, the next hurdle is motive?"

He allowed himself a small smile. *That's the spirit!* "Right. Can you think of any reason why Vance would need large amounts of money on a fairly regular basis?"

She hesitated for only a moment. "He's always had expensive tastes. Cars, women... What's the total so far?"

"The average retail cost for each theft was between two to three thousand dollars. Over a period of two years, it adds up to over a hundred thousand dollars."

"A hundred thousand..." Her voice trailed off.

"That's a lot of money to put into cars and women and—"

"Horses," she supplied in resignation. "He likes to play the ponies. But not to the tune of a hundred grand! I'm sure of that."

"Vance could be on drugs and stealing for his own use," Sam suggested. "Or using them to pay a debt to a bookie. No matter what, there's a lot of animosity between those two men."

"I bet he gave you the old song and dance about how you don't choose your relatives."

"You've heard it before?"

Lily sighed into the phone. "It's an ongoing theme with both of them. And I've always been caught in the middle."

"Well, I'm going to stay late tonight to finish this up. I need a chance to get into the empty office and run a code trace from Vance's terminal to the central processor." He paused. "You doing okay?"

"Of course." She sighed again. "Sam, I know I sound like a broken record, but please, be careful."

"I will. Promise."

As Sam hung up the phone, another call came in. "Computer Ops, Andrews," he answered.

"How is everything going, Mr. Andrews? Did you solve your problem with the terminal codes?" Mason sounded anxious.

"I thought I'd stay late and keep on working."

"If you feel the need . . ." Mason hesitated. "Most of the warehouse employees have already left, and the office staff will follow soon. The place will be completely empty in about a half hour. I'd stay, but I have an appointment I have to keep. If you have any questions, call me. Use my car phone." He recited a telephone number, which Sam scribbled on the nearest printout. "Good luck, Mr. Andrews."

I'm gonna need it.

Chapter Fourteen

The blade of the knife beat a steady rhythm as thin slices of lemon fanned across the wooden cutting board. Lily worked with a determined precision, hoping to keep her mind off Sam in the lion's den. She'd done what she could at her end and knew all she could do now was wait.

Bean had smiled when she offered her assistance at the bar. "Listen, I'd like the help, but I can't stay in the same room with you when you have a knife in your hand. Knives and vacant stares don't go together." He shuddered.

Left to herself in the kitchen, Lily glanced out the picture window, where late-afternoon clouds reduced the February sun to a feeble glow. In the valley below, tiny cars were caught in clogged queues on the freeways.

Are you down there, Sam?

She ached for reassurance. Not for her sake or safety, but for his. Lily reached into the mesh sack for another lemon and discovered the bag was empty.

"Bean! I finished the lemons. Bean?" she called toward the bar. She heard a thumping sound and knew Bean couldn't hear her over the competing noise. A small bowl of peaches sat on the counter, and she grabbed one as she headed out of the kitchen. She took a bite through the paper-thin fuzz, and juice dripped down her chin. "Bean, where in the world do you get such wonderful peaches in

February? Whenever I go to the store, they either look like shriveled Nerf balls or—'' Lily stopped.

A dark figure stood over Bean's inert body. The stocky man held up a short bat, as if Lily had interrupted him in midstroke. He turned a hideous face toward her, and she gasped before realizing he merely wore a grotesque Halloween mask.

When the intruder moved toward her, Bean suddenly sprang to life. He rolled over and wrapped his arms around the man's leg. ''Run, Lily!'' he yelled. Bean tried to pull the intruder off balance but the man kicked free.

Lily took advantage of the few precious seconds Bean gave her to shoot back to the kitchen and head for the parking lot. She sped through the room, dodging the counter and knocking over stools and crates in her wake. Stumbling off the concrete stoop, she saw a figure stepping out of an unfamiliar car in the lot.

Her momentary wish for a savior disintegrated when she realized the newcomer wore a mask, as well. *Two of them!*

Skirting the outside edge of the building, Lily headed for the dense stand of trees to her left. She darted between the trunks, slipping on the thick layer of pine straw and clutching at small, bare dogwood trees that dotted the sharp incline. Dead tendrils of kudzu clutched at her ankles, slowing her steps as she veered away from the building.

The terrain grew steeper, and vines gave way to rocks and bare patches of wet red clay. Lily lost much of her head start because of the slippery mud. She prayed her attackers would suffer the same setback.

Thorny bushes grew like monoliths on the mountainside, forcing her to navigate around their scratchy branches. Lily glanced behind her for a brief second, and felt the earth disappear beneath her feet. She sprawled to the ground.

Her lead pursuer covered the remaining distance between them and descended with force. ''Got her!''

Lily recognized the voice, only slightly muffled by the mask. The *late* Lamarr Moody. ''Get off me, Lamarr. And take off that stupid mask." Pine needles pricked her face as she struggled to escape his iron grip.

"L-Lily. I'm sorry."

"You're going to be sorrier if you don't let me up. My God, Lamarr! I trusted you. We were friends."

"Please..."

Another figure approached. Lamarr tightened his grasp and the blood began to rush through her ears.

"Hold her," the second man commanded in a gravelly voice.

She clawed at Lamarr, finding a foothold which helped her get leverage against him. But when a second set of hands joined Lamarr's, the opposition was overwhelming.

"I said hold her!" It was evident Lamarr's partner was trying to disguise his voice. The man placed a knee in her back, forcing her to remain facedown. A hand wound itself in her hair and jerked her head backward. Lily gave an involuntary gasp as a damp pad of cotton covered her mouth and nose. The sweet, cloying smell burned for only a moment. Just before she blacked out, her mind screamed a silent cry of anguish. *Sam! Help me....*

LAMARR PULLED OFF the annoying mask before he hoisted Lily's limp body over one shoulder. His partner negotiated a path with the fewest obstacles back to the parking lot, and during the brief trip to the summit, Lamarr's conscience surfaced.

Corrupting her inventory system had been a challenge. He had no trouble working out the details of the physical removal of the stuff. He'd been stealing all his life. It didn't hurt anyone; it was just a matter of diverting funds from the company to himself. But this?

He felt her arms dangle lifelessly against his back, and he involuntarily tightened his hold on her. Lily deserved more than this. She'd been his friend as well as his boss. They'd worked side by side. Had laughed together. Had even got drunk together once.

Lamarr carried her to the car, gesturing for his partner to open the back door. "Not there. In the trunk."

It violated Lamarr's sense of justice to do something so coldhearted to Lily, to treat her with such disdain. "Listen—"

"No, you listen!" Bradley ripped off his mask, fished in his pocket and pulled out a set of keys. "I don't have time for this. We agreed we had to do something about her. If you had found the files like I told you to, we wouldn't be in this situation."

Lamarr's stomach tightened as Bradley opened the trunk. "Put her in there." He laid her gently in the carpeted compartment, silently muttering his apologies. "Look in the glove box and get my extra tie," Bradley demanded.

After Lamarr returned, Bradley calmly forced the material between Lily's lips and knotted it behind her head. When Bradley allowed her head to hit the trunk floor, Lamarr flinched, his stomach turning in disgust. "Hey...don't be so rough." Lamarr stared at her pale features, feeling a tidal wave of remorse and sympathy. "You never said anything about involving Lily in anything like this."

"Shut up. It's part of the new plan." The man produced a length of rope which he looped around her wrists and tied tightly.

"Well, maybe I don't like the damn new plan." Lamarr stared at his partner, wondering what sort of man could treat his own relative with such detachment.

"Fine, Moody. Let's just give up now. Go to the police and tell them how you rigged the computer system so you could steal narcotics from the company. Tell them how you faked your own death by substituting your name on the flight manifest of the plane that crashed. Make sure you mention the half-million-dollar insurance settlement your sweet little fiancée is supposed to receive next month. Tell them about—"

"I see your point. But I don't understand why we have to drag Lily into this."

"She's a loose end." Bradley reached up and slammed down the lid of the trunk. "She knows too much, and what she doesn't know, she'll figure out. She and that damn detective of hers."

"What are you going to do about Markstrom?"

The man's face tightened. "He's too close to this whole thing for us to ignore him. I think I'll have to use Lily as a bargaining chip with him."

"All I know is no one could piece together anything from the narcotic data base. My program scrambled those records." He managed a proud smile. "Permanently."

"Don't be so damned cocksure, Moody. This guy used to head some sort of computer-fraud division in the police department, and he has quite a reputation. I won't chance it. We use Lily to take him out, then get rid of her."

"No. I won't do anything to hurt her." Lamarr knew his trump card would change his partner's mind. "And if you decide to set me up as a patsy, I'll drag you down with me. We never could've pulled this off without your involvement. You could have turned me in over a year ago when you tumbled to the scam." He paused for emphasis. "But you didn't." Lamarr smiled.

"That's the difference between you and me, Moody." Bradley reached into his jacket and pulled out a gun, leveling it at Lamarr. "You designed a unique option into the inventory programming, but you didn't have the guts to do anything but nickel-and-dime stuff. You should thank me...really thank me for letting you live a little of the good life."

Lamarr stared at the end of the barrel, mentally tracing a path between it and his chest. "What are you doing?" Vague plans of defense began to form in his mind, and he took a step to the side, but the gun tracked his movement.

His partner laughed. "Is this the part where you tell me I can't kill you? You idiot, don't you realize? You're already dead!"

"Now wait a second, Bradley...." Lamarr's voice rose as fear took over, blunting his control. His mouth dropped open, and he drew in his last breath. The echo of the explosion creased the heavy stillness like a clap of thunder. The sound reverberated in his ears, and he fell to his knees. As he watched his life ebbing away in bright red spurts, he heard the sound of an engine.

Lily...

SAM GLANCED AT HIS WATCH before he opened the computer-room door. Five-forty-five. The corridor was silent, robbed of the noisy bustle of the earlier part of the day. He let the door click shut behind him, then headed for the front of the building.

A single bank of fluorescent lights shone down the center of the open office area. Sam leaned over the railing that separated the receptionist from the rest of the office and studied the switchboard. No telephone traffic, a good indicator that no one was still hanging around after hours. He gazed out the office windows which overlooked the side parking lot. No cars, except for Bean's Porsche.

Sam turned his attention to Vance's desk. With a few keystrokes, the computer screen jumped to life. Sam typed in several commands that would send an interoffice memo to the computer room, a message containing Vance's terminal identification code. Sam knew a quick trip back to Lily's office would give him the final answer.

He entered the computer room and scanned the memo, running his fingers along the screen. *I got you, Van—*

The numbers were wrong.

Sam drummed his fingers along the side of the monitor. *What happened? Why doesn't this correspond?*

The simplicity of the answer astounded Sam. *Because it's not the right terminal.*

The orders weren't placed on Vance's computer. *Of course, that doesn't mean he didn't input the orders using someone else's terminal.*

Sam returned to the main office where he scanned the area, counting the dark silhouettes of desktop monitors. Twenty computers meant twenty electronic message-identification codes. Starting on the left side of the office, Sam worked clockwise, turning on each computer and sending a message to Vance's unit. Each computer identified itself with a sequence of numbers, but none of them matched the one from the bogus orders.

He dropped into Vance's chair and slammed his fist on the desk in frustration. "Come on, Markstrom, you know the answer is here...somewhere. What have I missed?" *What have I missed?*

He glanced through the darkened glass into Mason's office. *Everybody else has his own computer. Why not Mason?* Sam stepped into the office and reached for the light switch. An explosion of sound assaulted him.

Clangs, bongs, tinkling melodies, chimes. The clocks marked the hour with irritating, ear-shattering precision. Instinct pushed him into the shadows until he realized the source of the sudden interruption. *Damn clock collection...*

The sounds faded away. Sam rested against the desk, allowing himself a sigh of relief. He felt a smooth, cool surface beneath his palm. He glanced down and saw a monitor hidden beneath the glass-topped desk. The lap drawer extended to reveal the computer keyboard. When Sam flipped on the central power switch, the monitor flared to life. With only a few keystrokes, Sam sent a single-word message to the other computer via interoffice electronic mail: Mason.

When he read the string of familiar numbers on Vance's computer, a shiver raced up his spine. *Mason?*

It took a second or two before his thoughts coalesced. Sam recalled how he'd returned to the computer room and found Mason waiting patiently outside. Maybe Mason hadn't been so patient. But he didn't have the correct code for the door. *Maybe he didn't need one.*

Sam squeezed his eyes shut for a moment, hoping his gut instinct was wrong. He pushed back from the desk and stalked back to the computer room, cursing himself in advance with every step.

Habit, not necessity, had always made him type in the code to the cipher lock before reaching for the doorknob. He'd never tried simply opening the door without inputting the code. Sam took a deep breath. His hand closed around the knob. He pulled.

The door swung open.

Sam knew before he knelt down that he'd find tape covering the lock plate, preventing the bolt from being thrown. The oldest trick— Ripping off the tape, Sam wadded it into a ball and hurled it across the room.

Opportunity.

What about motive?

Vance was still the one with all the motives. Maybe Vance merely used Mason's computer. Maybe Mason had been simply protecting his company's interests by snooping in the computer room. Maybe...

Sam returned to the desk. If he could find out when the amnesia program was run, it would either help confirm or refute Mason's guilt. Sam hunched over the keyboard, alternately typing and scrutinizing the screen until he found the information he needed.

AMNESIA.EXE 01/12 18:46 02/22 12:40

The first and second sets of figures listed the program's creation date and time. The last two sets denoted the day and time the program was last run.

Today. At 12:40. The exact same time Vance was giving him the grand tour. *Damn you, Mason.*

Sam dialed the number for the bar and slammed down the phone when the sound of the unanswered rings burned into his brain. "Where in the hell are you, Bean?" he raged aloud. "And where is Li—" A fist of fear slammed into his heart. "Damn. What if Mason's found out she's alive?"

Impossible, he reminded himself. *He has no way of knowing she's alive, much less hiding at Bean's.* "But no one's answering the phone..."

His suspicion transformed into amorphous fears. Sam slapped the documentation into his briefcase and exited the computer room at a run. As he passed through the open office on the way to the front exit, he caught sight of a car pulling into the parking lot. When the car door opened, the interior lights illuminated Mason's harsh expression. Sam backed away from the door, hoping Mason hadn't seen him.

As long as Mason's here, Lily's safe with Bean. And if I can get back to her, I can make sure she stays safe. The last thing he wanted to do was confront Mason, much preferring to turn the information over to the police and let them handle it.

Sam retraced his steps to the computer room, then passed by the locked door, knowing it would be the first place Mason would look. The Porsche sat in the parking lot like a big red beacon, saying "He hasn't left yet!"

Pushing open the double warehouse doors, Sam slipped through the gap, closing it carefully. He grimaced as the cavernous room echoed his careful footsteps, making them resound threefold. He searched for a quick exit and he pulled at a door leading outside.

Locked.

He considered the loading dock but he gave it a pass. The man would be able to pinpoint Sam's location in seconds by tracing the racket from the metal overhead doors. He worked his way back to the shelves. Several fire exits perforated the two outside walls, but he knew each one was wired to an alarm system. He set down his briefcase, opened it, and pulled out a penlight. After a second thought, he removed his gun and slipped it into his waistband.

Examining the alarm contacts, Sam knew he could rig a bypass and get out without triggering the fire alarm, but it would take too long.

His muscles tensed when he heard a noise behind him. Sam retreated to a shadow along the wall moments before Mason opened the double doors and peered into the warehouse. Sam waited, holding his breath and praying the man didn't spot the briefcase in plain view on the workbench.

"Mr. Andrews, are you in here?"

Sam steeled himself to remain motionless despite the overwhelming urge to reach for his gun. Mason shrugged, pivoted and disappeared into the hallway. Arming himself, Sam slipped silently around the back of the shelf area and inched his way to the only exit. He peered through the small pane of glass to view the empty hallway.

Had Mason left?

Sam listened intently to the silence, straining to hear any telltale noises. Through the dock door, he heard a car start. He allowed himself to resume breathing. Five precautionary minutes later, Sam placed one sweating palm against the door and pushed it open. Silence greeted him. *He's gone.*

Sam crossed to the bench and retrieved his briefcase, returning the gun to its hiding place. He moved swiftly to the double doors, hoping to get out of the building as quickly as possible. He stepped into the hallway.

An arm closed around his neck.

With fears pushed back and replaced by survival skills, his body reacted with rusty instincts once honed by training but dulled by disuse. Unable to overcome the choke maneuver, he tried to ram the briefcase into the man's midsection, but his grip only tightened. Sam dropped the case and clawed at the hands slowly closing off his air. He dropped to his knees, hoping to pull his attacker off balance, but the man compensated, using the increased leverage to tighten his hold. A red cloud began to block Sam's vision as he felt the blood throb in his temples. A black cloud followed him to the floor.

SAM CAME TO AS THE LIGHTS of the warehouse were being extinguished by the closing vault door. He pushed himself slowly, painfully, to his feet, his pitch-black world spinning uncontrolled.

Reaching out, he discovered a metal wall. *The vault.* He groped for the light switch. Why hadn't he paid more attention when he was with Lily checking the narcotic inventory? Sam pushed at the foggy boundaries of his memory, trying to remember the layout of the safe. He inched along the wall until he found the switch plate.

Nothing happened when he pushed the toggle up. Even in the darkness, he could feel the room tilt on an odd axis, making him dizzy enough to sit until the gyrations stopped. "Damn!" His swollen throat issued no sound. As he held his head, waiting for the black void to stop swirling, he planned his next strategy, which included a thorough search of his prison. Starting at the door and working clockwise, he felt along, creating a mental map of the vault boundaries.

Maybe I can jump him when he opens the door. . . . If he opens the— Sam stumbled over something in the dark.

He froze when his fingers touched cool flesh. He recoiled, then pushed aside the boxes in his way, discovering a limp hand, bound to its partner by a rough cord. He hauled the body from the cramped space, wondering what unfortunate person had crossed Mason's path. An alarm started growing in the center of his body and spread outward when he noticed the familiar fragrance. He stretched a hand toward the person's face and traced the delicate features with the tips of his fingers.

Lily!

Chapter Fifteen

Rage exploded within him when he discovered the strip of cloth shoved in Lily's mouth. He cradled her head in his lap and tore at the knot. After untying it, he hurled the offending material into the darkness.

"Lily?" He tried to whisper, but his throbbing throat refused to comply. He raked trembling fingertips across her cheek, searching for signs of life. Her lips were cold and unresponsive against his.

Oh, God...I'm too late. Again. His tears became her blood. Sticking to his hands. Staining his soul. Memories began to merge, tangling together. He clutched Lily's limp body as he had held Walt's, knowing he had failed both of them.

I wanted to tell you...to say... Without a voice, he could only give the words sound in his imagination. He buried his face in her hair, discovering bits of pine straw and leaves matted in her curls. He gently shifted her so he could reach her bound wrists. Struggling with the ropes, he cursed Mason and his sadistic knots. *I'll kill the son of a bitch. I promise you, Lily, I'll—* Suddenly he felt her shift in his arms. A flare of hope burst into life within him. He placed two tense fingers alongside her neck and discovered the strong, steady pulse, which dissolved the worst of his anxiety.

Alive...

Lily jerked with a start, fighting against whatever forces held her in a half-conscious world. She muttered something and pushed his hand from her cheek. The darkness amplified every sound, including her sudden inhalation of breath.

And her scream.

Instinctively, he tightened his grip around her, deflecting the blows she tried to deliver. Her shriek of terror hurt more than her flailing fists. He wanted to yell her name, but he could barely croak. He chose the only way he could think of to silence her without letting go.

Lily fought him, sputtering indignantly and fighting to escape his kiss. Her thrashing subsided and she began to respond to the warmth of his lips. For one brief moment, they were transported beyond their dark prison, escaping on a promise of requited passion. When she finally pulled away, reality returned, along with his feelings of hopelessness and despair.

"Sam, where are we?" One cool hand remained, pressed softly against his cheek. He struggled to speak, but even a whisper was beyond his ability. "Sam? Answer me! What's wrong?" Fear and pain crept into her voice. "Why don't you answer me?"

Sam pulled her hand from his cheek and placed it gingerly against his neck where she would be able to feel the pulsating heat that radiated from his injuries.

"Are you trying to tell me you can't talk?"

Sam squeezed her hand, then shifted it to his cheek. He nodded yes.

Lily slid off his lap, and as they both stood, she clung to him, supporting and being supported. "Are we in the vault?"

He nodded again. *Yes. Lily, tell me you're all right. Tell me you can read my mind.*

"Vance put us in here, didn't he?" Her hand trembled against his cheek when he shook his head. "What do you mean? If it wasn't Vance, then who?"

His effort to answer her disintegrated into a painful fit of coughing that aggravated his throat as well as his protesting ribs.

"Don't try to talk. Just help me find the door. There's an inside release." They lurched forward. After a moment, he heard slow and hesitant musical tones from the combination keypad. The locking mechanism clicked silently beneath his palms and a slice of light grew around the opening vault door.

They crouched by the wall, listening to the uneasy silence that filled the warehouse. They'd escaped one prison to find themselves still locked within the chain-link fence surrounding the vault.

Lily clutched his arm, her gray eyes filled with confusion. "If it's not Vance, then who is it?" she repeated with increasing distress.

"Mason," he mouthed.

She stared at him in disbelief, then shook her head. "No. He couldn't..." She stared at Sam. "Mason? Why?"

Sam shrugged. *I don't know why.* They certainly didn't have time for a discussion of motives through charades. He mouthed the word "key," gesturing to the locked gate that imprisoned them.

She patted her pockets. "I don't have it. The spare is—" she grimaced "—in Mason's desk."

He was able to croak out a few words without triggering another coughing attack. "Up and over."

She grimaced at the chain-link fence, released a jittery sigh, then began the arduous process of climbing. Sam followed suit, cringing as the rattling of the fence echoed throughout the warehouse. If Mason was in the building, he'd certainly hear the noise. That realization made Sam propel himself over the top as quickly as possible.

"Hurry," he ordered in a raspy whisper, splitting his attention between Lily, stalled at the top of the fence, and the double doors leading to the offices.

"I'm trying," she replied, "but my sweater's caught."

"Get it loose!"

"I'm trying..." She clung to the chain link precariously with one hand, attempting to free the snagged fabric.

"Hurry!"

Protection. They needed protection. If only he could find—

My briefcase! He spotted his locked case, carelessly tossed on the conveyor.

"Lily, I'm coming up to—"

"Got it!" A moment later, she landed beside him.

He pushed her toward the fire exit. "Get out of here!" he rasped. Any alarms they set off now just might bring help. He headed toward the conveyor, hoping to retrieve his briefcase, not for its irrefutable proof, but for the gun locked inside.

"Sam, where are you—"

The crash of the double doors and Mason's shout interrupted Lily. Sam shoved her toward the first set of shelves, then dived behind the conveyer support seconds before Mason fired. Batting the briefcase down, Sam fumbled with the locks, praying he could arm himself before Mason reached him. The lid sprang open. Sam grabbed his gun and pivoted, bracing himself against the conveyor while he aimed.

Mason was gone.

The conveyor suddenly lurched to life, throwing Sam off balance. As he fell, the gun slipped out of his grasp. Mason charged toward him, wearing a malevolent smile.

"Sam, look out!" Lily's scream reverberated through the building.

Mason whirled around at the sound of Lily's voice and drew a bead on her position. With soundless rage, Sam leapt over the conveyor and dropped his adversary to the floor with a well-executed tackle. The force of the blow knocked the gun from Mason's hand, and the weapon disappeared underneath one of the shelf units.

Lily watched as Sam pulled Mason from the floor and landed a solid blow to her cousin's stomach. Mason doubled over but managed to knock Sam backward. He hit the conveyer support, and the air rushed from him with a sickening hiss.

She gasped involuntarily.

Mason moved toward Sam with both hands clenched together, and Lily screamed another warning. With her cousin's attention momentarily diverted, Sam rallied, getting in one solid blow before Mason reversed and backhanded him into the conveyor support.

Lily edged around the battlefield, wincing in sympathy when each blow landed, no matter the victim. Keeping an eye on the weapon, Lily crept alongside the conveyer belt, using it as a buffer between herself and the fight.

The gun rested beside one of the upright supports. The moment Sam drew Mason's attention, she made her move, sliding beneath the conveyer and heading for the weapon.

Her cousin moved faster than she expected, snagging her wrist as she lunged for the revolver. He wrenched it out of her hand and jerked her closer, tightening an arm around her waist.

"Let go of me, Mason." She struggled against the pressure pinning her arms down.

"No way, Lily. I've got too much at stake now. Hold it, Markstrom." Mason gestured with the barrel of the gun for Sam to move back. Then Lily felt a cold, lethal circle push against her temple.

Sam offered an empty-hand gesture and took a step backward. "Take it easy, Mason." Lily wondered how long his scratchy voice would hold out.

"Shut up!" Mason ordered. "I want those inventory files. They weren't in Lily's car after the wreck. Give them to me or she dies. Now!"

She caught her breath. Mason was asking for the impossible. Sam shook his head. "I don't have any files. I don't know what you're talking about."

"Don't stall. You were at the wreck. I know. I watched you mess around her car, then you disappeared. Give me the files." He punctuated the last word by jabbing the barrel of the gun into Lily's temple. He slipped his fingers from her waist to her throat.

Survival instincts made her grab his hand as it slowly tightened, cutting off her air. She watched Sam through a cloudy haze. Panic reflected plainly in his face. "For God's sake, Mason, let go of her!"

Her cousin's fingers cut into her neck like barbed wire, and any effort she made to talk became another desperate gasp for air. Black dots began to fill her vision, and she felt herself being lifted into the air.

"I said the files are in my briefcase!"

She could barely hear Sam's lie above the rushing of blood in her ears. Mason allowed her to fall to the warehouse floor. Her mind screamed *run,* but her oxygen-starved body couldn't comply.

"Get them." Her cousin's voice cut through the shadows like a steel blade. He reached down and pulled Lily to her feet, regaining his control over her with a white-knuckled grip on her arm.

Sam backed toward the conveyor where the briefcase rested. Screening his actions with the open lid, he shoved a handful of computer papers into a manila folder. When he spotted his tool kit, he formulated a hasty plan. *I hope this gives me enough time to get her away from him.*

He walked toward Lily and her captor with the files outstretched. "Here, take them. Just let Lily go."

"Don't come any closer," Mason warned. "Hand them to her." He wrenched her arm behind her and put the gun to the back of her head.

Lily's look of pain dug deep into Sam's conscience. They both knew the papers were fake, and they could guess what Mason's response would be when he realized he'd been tricked. Her eyes widened when she discovered the hilt of the screwdriver Sam had hidden within the folder. Silent communication passed between them.

Create a diversion and let me cover your escape. I won't leave you here with him.

Sam watched her hand shake as she clutched the files, blocking Mason's line of sight for a brief moment while she pushed the screwdriver up her sweater sleeve. "Here. You have the files. Now let us..."

A voice rang out from the loading dock. "I don't know what those papers are. All I know is—" Vance held up a folder "—these are the files from Lily's car."

Suddenly, light flooded the warehouse and revealed Vance standing beside a large electrical panel. He started to stalk toward the group, but froze in his tracks. His mouth dropped open and his face paled as if he'd seen a ghost. "Oh, God...Lily! You're alive! We... The wreck..." Unaware of the danger, he rushed toward them.

Mason made sure the gun was out of Vance's view as he prodded Lily viciously, whispering, "Not one word, either of you." Mason released her arm but made sure Sam saw the revolver pressed against her back.

"Am I glad to see you," Mason told Vance. "How did you know to come?"

Vance wore a smirk of triumph. "I knew I'd seen Andrews before. It hit me after I got home. He's the man I found going through Lily's stuff at the crash. Only his ID said Markstrom. Different name, fake mustache, but still the same guy."

"You couldn't have come at a better time. I just discovered this bastard trying to force Lily into opening the vault. Apparently he thought he could kidnap her and learn enough about the company from her to steal—"

Lily murmured a hasty prayer, slipped the screwdriver out of her sleeve and rammed it backward into Mason's stomach. She shouldered him away and fell toward Sam, who pushed her toward the shelves. He stumbled in his effort, but waved away Lily's help. "Get out of here!" he ordered between gritted teeth.

"Run, Vance!" she screamed over her shoulder, tugging at Sam's arm.

Confused and shocked, Vance turned to help Mason, who was doubled over in pain. At Mason's furious but wordless gesture, Vance picked up the gun he'd dropped. With little hesitation, he leveled it at Sam. "Hold it, Andrews... whatever your name is. Let go of her."

Sam froze, but Lily shifted so she blocked Vance from his intended target. "You don't understand, Vance. It's not Sam. It's Mason," she pleaded.

Vance shook his head, smiling sadly at her. "Lily, you're not making any sense. I was trying to catch up with you Friday night when I discovered your wreck and this guy prowling around it. So I slugged him, checked his ID, and took away the files he was trying to steal. The next day I couldn't find out any information about you at the hospital, so I drove to his house and tried to follow him, but he gave me the slip. Then he showed up this morning."

Vance glared at Sam. "The disguise may have fooled me but I still knew you were up to no good." Vance stepped closer to them, the gun clenched in his fist. "Move away from him, sweetheart. Mason and I will take care of him."

"You mean you didn't attack Sam and search his house?" Lily stared at Mason. "Then it had to be you."

Mason returned a cold, silent smile from behind Vance's back.

Lily stepped toward her nephew. "You've got it all wrong, Vance. Sam wasn't stealing the files. He witnessed my crash. Someone ran me off the road and shot at me. Those files you took prove Mason and Lamarr have been altering the narcotic inventory and stealing from the company."

The nose of the gun didn't dip as Vance motioned for her to move aside. "Lamarr is dead, Lily. Don't you remember? I know you loved him, but that doesn't change the fact that he's gone." His voice was soft and placating as if her denial of her assistant's death indicated her level of irrationality. "You'll have to accept his death, sweetheart, no matter how painful."

"Loved him?" she sputtered. "Why would you think that? I liked Lamarr until I found out he was an embezzler! He only pretended to die in order to cover his tracks. His and Mason's."

Mason stepped forward and held out his hand for the gun. "She's completely irrational, Vance. I suspect she's under this man's undue influence. Let me handle this." Vance relinquished the weapon, then suddenly found himself on the wrong end of the barrel. "Move over by them, Vance." Mason gestured with his other hand while he trained the gun on Sam. "Just stand there beside Lily."

Vance stared blankly at Mason. "Beside Lily? What's going on?"

Lily clenched her hands tightly into fists. "I told you, Vance. Mason and Lamarr have been embezzling from the company, and they've made it look as if you are the guilty party."

"Me?" Vance took a step toward his cousin. "How?"

"Shut up and turn around." Mason gestured with the barrel of the gun. "And put your hands on your head."

Lily continued her explanation, wondering how Mason would react to the bald truth. "The DEA narcotic inventory is due soon, Vance, and the discrepancies in the records would start a major investigation, which would end up implicating you. I found the evidence Mason planted to frame you."

Vance stared at their cousin. "She's starting to make some sense, Mason. I thought it was odd when you told me Lily had been upset over Lamarr's death...that she'd driven off the road deliberately. But she's alive. And what about Lamarr? Is he alive, as well?"

"No." Mason's voice boomed throughout the warehouse. "You were right the first time. Lamarr *is* dead. I didn't need him anymore."

Lily felt her throat close. If Mason had disposed of his partner after her capture, what chance did the three of them have now?

"Mason, we're family!" Vance lowered his hands and stepped toward his cousin. "I can't believe you'd risk everything in order to make a little extra cash." He advanced slowly, with his hands outstretched. "I know you, Mason. You're not a killer."

Mason blanched at the small insurrection. "Shut up, you idiot. You don't know a damn thing. A little cash? Try half a million dollars. And I deserved every penny of it. I gave up my life for this company. Sold my soul to the devil Bradley for a chance to be part of this business. And the son of a bitch left me nothing." He lifted a shaky hand and pointed at Vance.

"You're the reason I had to do it. You came into this company as the fair-haired child. No matter how asinine you acted or what stupid stunt you pulled, you always got away with murder with the old man." Sweat began to form on Mason's forehead. "I'll never know why Lawrence was so taken with a royal screwup like you. Then—" he pivoted to Lily, the gun trembling in his hand "—then, Miss Perfect comes into the picture, the new heir, leaving me with nothing. I work like a dog for twenty years, and what happens when the old buzzard kicks off? She inherits the stock majority."

He stopped talking to them and began to ramble aloud. Despite the insanity of his words, he kept a wary look in his eye. "He promised it to me. At Larry, Jr.'s funeral, he promised it all to me."

Vance held out his hands. "But, Mason, that was before Lily was born. He thought he'd never have another child. Jeez, she's his daughter! She deserves her share."

"She deserves it? No, I deserve it! I didn't kill Larry, Jr. just so she could walk away with everything! I worked the hardest. I deserved his trust and his loyalty and—"

Vance took a step forward, his face white. "You killed my father? The hunting accident . . ."

"Yes, I killed him. He was in my way, just like you are now." Mason's face twisted into a mockery of Vance's pain. "See? You're not the only one who can get away with murder around here."

Lily reached forward and grabbed Vance's coat, trying to pull him away from Mason. He shook off her grasp and took another step toward his cousin.

"It's such a sad story." Sweat began to pour down Mason's red face. "Vance and Lamarr conspired to steal narcotics from the company, but they had a falling-out. Poor Lamarr tried to fake his own death and cheat on his partner, but you know what? Vance wasn't quite as stupid as he seemed. He actually caught on to Lamarr's scam and killed him for real this time. Then . . ." Mason turned away from Vance and aimed the gun at Lily.

Sam stiffened and tried to shield her.

"Move back, Markstrom." His eyes lost their wild look. "Lily got in Vance's way. Both her and her investigator. So Vance eliminated both of them."

"No!" Vance lunged toward their cousin.

"Vance, don't!" Lily's words were drowned out by the sound of the gun. Vance was thrown backward by the impact of the bullet and didn't move after he hit the concrete floor. Mason seemed mesmerized by the bloody stain that grew across Vance's chest.

Sam pushed Lily aside and lunged for Mason. The men fought over the gun, hitting the heavy shelves with enough force to shift them a few inches. Boxes rained around them. Lily ducked, covering her head, then saw the butt of the second gun peeking out of the dusty darkness. She grabbed it and stood.

Mason and Sam were still tangled in a violent struggle. Sam knocked his opponent up against the conveyer, trying to force him to release the gun. Mason caught him in the stomach with a knee, and together they fell. When they hit the floor, the gun slipped from their combined grips.

Mason regained his footing first and scrambled toward the weapon, but Sam intervened. Lily drew a frantic breath when they pulled to their feet, and the gun disappeared between them. She raised her arms, prepared to fire a warning shot at the ceiling, when another explosion rocked the warehouse. She looked up slowly at the gun she held over her head, then realized she hadn't squeezed the trigger.

Mason bellowed with rage as he pushed Sam backward. Sam spun and fell to the concrete floor, facedown, and Mason used one cautious foot to nudge Sam's body.

Lily held her breath, waiting for Sam to leap up and resume the battle, but a bright, bloody stain decorated his white shirt. A tidal wave of emotions crashed over her, but the strongest of them—revenge—helped her aim the gun at her cousin.

Mason's sneer of satisfaction faded when he gazed at her, then the gun. She took aim at a large splotch of Sam's blood smeared across Mason's shirt. "You're a dead man, Mason." She used two thumbs to cock the weapon, and she prepared to fire.

His sudden, raucous laughter seared her ears. "You've got to be kidding. You can't pull that trigger. You don't have the guts to kill me in cold blood. No matter what I've done." He aimed his gun at her, then slowly pivoted until the barrel pointed to Sam. "You can't stop me. You're dead, remember? And I'll make doubly sure your expert joins you in the hereafter."

Lily pulled the trigger.

Her imagination provided the sound effects—a thunderous explosion to race from wall to wall with unending reverberations. But in reality, the only echo was of a harmless click.

Mason began to laugh. "You surprised me, Lily." The laughter died away. "But you'll never surprise me again."

Lily dropped the useless weapon and knelt by Sam. When she looked up, Mason had the barrel of the gun trained on her. A savage, evil grin split his face. He nudged Sam's inert body, then flipped him over with his foot.

Lily reacted. Simply out of anger, fear and a need for retribution before she died. She lunged for him, heedless of the gun, heedless of his threats. But before Lily could do any real damage to Mason, he batted her out of the way with a sweep of his arm.

She landed on the cold concrete floor in a heap.

When Mason pulled back his hand from his cheek, he exposed an ugly scratch, oozing blood. He stared at his reddened fingertips. "You bitch!"

"Good," she rasped, trying to catch her breath. "I bet you won't be able to come up with a good lie to explain that."

The jagged red gash that split his skin looked like a lightning bolt and matched his thunderous expression. He leveled the gun at her. "You'll never find out, Lily."

The air was filled with noise. She waited for an explosion of pain to rip through her.

But nothing happened.

Opening her eyes, she relaxed her tensed muscles, wondering if the process of dying had already started, preventing her from experiencing the sensations of pain.

She looked down at the front of her sweater. No blood.

She looked at Mason.

He dropped to one knee and began to laugh. It was a horrible, malevolent sound that continued in lingering echoes as he pitched forward, sprawling into the growing pool of his blood. The shreds of harsh laughter faded away and Mason remained motionless on the floor.

Lily suddenly remembered how to breathe. Apprehensively, she turned and stared at her fallen hero. She watched as Sam's fingers slowly uncurled and the gun dropped to the bloodied concrete. He drew a raspy breath, coughed, then grew eerily still.

The silence mocked her. Accused her. Blamed her.

"No!" She stumbled to him, falling roughly to her knees at his side. His lifeless expression frightened her.

"Sam...can you hear me?" she whispered. "It's over. You did it. We—we did it." She placed a cold, shivering hand on his cheek, mesmerized by the flicker of life she felt beneath her fingers. She pressed her ear to his chest to listen for his heartbeat.

I'm sorry...so sorry...so sorry....

Chapter Sixteen

Lily sat by his bed. The nightmares were coming more frequently now. The doctors had told her it was a side effect of the anesthesia, but she knew better. Bean had been the one to recognize the symptoms. After all, he'd been the one to see them the first time around. The tall man turned as white as his hair when Sam went through a particularly violent episode.

After it was over, Bean took refuge by the door. "I can't do this by myself again. I can't." His arms were folded tightly across his chest.

Lily gestured for him to lower his voice. "You don't have to, Bean. I'm a part of this now, but I'm not the only one who can help." She nodded toward the hallway. "It's time you talked to Micki. She knows everything."

Bean grabbed Lily by the shoulders. "You told her?"

"No. She's known all along. Talk to her, Bean. Don't keep her out of it this time. She loves him. Let her prove it."

"Micki knows...everything?" he repeated flatly. He sighed, reached for the doorknob and gave her a strained smile. "Wish me luck." His smile faded. "I'll need it."

After Bean left, Lily returned her attention to Sam, knowing she had to reach him...somehow. Dropping into the bedside chair, she waited for some sort of inspiration. How could she cut through the wall of guilt imprisoning him? The answer came after several furious minutes of thought.

With the truth.

She reached for his bruised hand, then took a deep breath. "Sam Markstrom? I know you can hear me." He didn't move.

"I'm alive because of you." No response.

"You saved my life, Sam." His fingers twitched in hers.

"You didn't save Walt because you couldn't." His grasp tightened perceptibly.

"But you did save me. And Vance." He shifted in the bed, responding either to her voice or to her words.

"Wake up, Sam. Come back to me, to us . . . now."

His eyes slowly fluttered.

She fought back the momentary thrill of success. She still had a more important task at hand. "Don't you dare feel sorry for yourself because you shot Mason. If you hadn't, I wouldn't be standing here, yelling at you."

His eyes opened.

"And don't try reliving the old days, reviving the old guilts. This time, it's totally different. You stopped Mason from hurting anybody else. From hurting me." Her emotions began to overcome her, and with them, her own sense of guilt. "I tried to do it myself. I tried to pull the trigger. I *did* pull the trigger but nothing happened. I tried to protect you—I really did, but I . . . I . . ."

Suddenly, she couldn't catch her breath. She grabbed the bed rail for support, barely aware of Sam's tight grip on her hand. Her world tilted for a moment as she realized what she was saying. Her conscience argued with itself.

You had to protect yourself.

I was willing to kill Mason.

You didn't shoot him.

I wanted to. I tried to.

She squinted with blurry eyes and watched her finger tighten on an imaginary trigger.

"L-Lily?"

She looked past her hand at Sam's expression of concern.

His voice was cracked and rusty. "Can't believe you . . . unless you believe yourself." His dark brows drew together as if he was either in deep thought or in great pain. He opened his eyes, catching her in an intense stare. "I'll for-forgive myself if you'll forgive yourself."

Tears trickled down her face.

He was right. She had fully intended to kill Mason. Point-blank. Without reservation. She was guilty of a double-edged crime: wanting to kill Mason and of failing to accomplish that very goal.

"L-Lily?"

"We did what we had to, didn't we?" she whispered.

He pulled her hand to his cracked lips for a kiss. "Yes."

His gesture gave her back some of her self-control. She wiped away her tears with her free hand and produced a quivery smile. "The doctors say you're going to be fine. The bullet hit your broken rib and exited without hitting anything else."

"What about Vance? Is he going to be all right, too?"

She nodded. "Thank heavens. But he's really upset. After all, Mason admitted to killing Larry, Jr. Neither of us ever . . ." The pain rose to choke her words.

Sam brushed away her tears. "Hurts, doesn't it?"

Lily gripped the bed rail. "Mason made us believe Vance was behind everything, and made Vance believe I was the criminal. We were nothing more than pawns in the hands of Mason, the master manipulator." A sudden wrench of pain twisted inside her. "I hate that bastard, that cheap, manipulative son of a—" She lost her fragile grasp of self-control. "How dare he? How dare he decide his financial needs were worth more than my life? How dare—" She broke into great, gulping sobs that racked her body.

Sam gently pulled her over until he had one arm around her shaking shoulders. His whispers of sympathy and support slowly cut through her anger and grief. After a while, she raised her head. Her mind flashed back to the terrifying events. All she could see was Mason's contorted face.

"You can't stop thinking about it, can you?" Sam asked in a low voice.

Emotion clogged her throat. "It's hard. I pulled the trigger. It was the gun's fault it didn't go off."

"We both have to remember to play the movie out to the end. We can't stop at the bad parts. If we do, we don't get to the part where the good guys win." His lips brushed temptingly near her ear and he spoke in a low, compelling rasp. "I want to get out of this place as quickly as possible. Together."

Together...

The noises in the hallway faded away as she became oblivious to everything but Sam. What she felt for him wasn't only a matter of letting ephemeral pleasures blot out fears. The passions they shared weren't merely temporary diversions to keep fear at bay. Her heart had demanded and continued to demand possession of him, just as her body did. She touched his face, running her forefinger over his lips.

He captured her hand and slowly kissed each sensitive tip. "I remember something you told me at the crash. Did you really mean it?"

"What?"

"You said 'Don't leave me.'"

"I meant it then. And I mean it now."

"Good." He tightened his fingers around hers. "Because I'm not going anywhere without you. Ever."

Valentine's Day was the best day of the year for
Dee's Candy and Gift Shop. Yet as the day drew closer,
Deanna Donovan became the target of
malicious, anonymous pranks.

A red heart was pinned to her front door with a dagger.

Dead roses adorned her car.

Soon, she was being stalked by her unseen admirer.

Suspicious of everyone, Deanna has nowhere to turn—and no
way to escape when she is kidnapped and held captive by her
Valentine lover....

#262

Cupid's Dagger

by *Leona Karr*
February 1994

You'll never again think of Valentine's Day without feeling a
thrill of delight...and a chill of dread!   CUPID

Take 4 bestselling love stories FREE

Plus get a FREE surprise gift!

My Valentine 1994

Celebrate the most romantic day of the year with
MY VALENTINE 1994
a collection of original stories, written by
four of Harlequin's most popular authors...

MARGOT DALTON
MURIEL JENSEN
MARISA CARROLL
KAREN YOUNG

*Available in February, wherever
Harlequin Books are sold.*

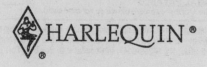

HARLEQUIN®

VAL94

HARLEQUIN®

Don't miss these Harlequin favorites by some of our most distinguished authors!
And now, you can receive a discount by ordering two or more titles!

HT#25409	THE NIGHT IN SHINING ARMOR by JoAnn Ross	$2.99	☐
HT#25471	LOVESTORM by JoAnn Ross	$2.99	☐
HP#11463	THE WEDDING by Emma Darcy	$2.89	☐
HP#11592	THE LAST GRAND PASSION by Emma Darcy	$2.99	☐
HR#03188	DOUBLY DELICIOUS by Emma Goldrick	$2.89	☐
HR#03248	SAFE IN MY HEART by Leigh Michaels	$2.89	☐
HS#70464	CHILDREN OF THE HEART by Sally Garrett	$3.25	☐
HS#70524	STRING OF MIRACLES by Sally Garrett	$3.39	☐
HS#70500	THE SILENCE OF MIDNIGHT by Karen Young	$3.39	☐
HI#22178	SCHOOL FOR SPIES by Vickie York	$2.79	☐
HI#22212	DANGEROUS VINTAGE by Laura Pender	$2.89	☐
HI#22219	TORCH JOB by Patricia Rosemoor	$2.89	☐
HAR#16459	MACKENZIE'S BABY by Anne McAllister	$3.39	☐
HAR#16466	A COWBOY FOR CHRISTMAS by Anne McAllister	$3.39	☐
HAR#16462	THE PIRATE AND HIS LADY by Margaret St. George	$3.39	☐
HAR#16477	THE LAST REAL MAN by Rebecca Flanders	$3.39	☐
HH#28704	A CORNER OF HEAVEN by Theresa Michaels	$3.99	☐
HH#28707	LIGHT ON THE MOUNTAIN by Maura Seger	$3.99	☐

Harlequin Promotional Titles

| #83247 | YESTERDAY COMES TOMORROW by Rebecca Flanders | $4.99 | ☐ |
| #83257 | MY VALENTINE 1993 | $4.99 | ☐ |

(short-story collection featuring Anne Stuart, Judith Arnold, Anne McAllister, Linda Randall Wisdom)
(limited quantities available on certain titles)

	AMOUNT	$
DEDUCT:	10% DISCOUNT FOR 2+ BOOKS	$
ADD:	POSTAGE & HANDLING	$
	($1.00 for one book, 50¢ for each additional)	
	APPLICABLE TAXES*	$
	TOTAL PAYABLE	$
	(check or money order—please do not send cash)	

To order, complete this form and send it, along with a check or money order for the total above, payable to Harlequin Books, to: **In the U.S.:** 3010 Walden Avenue, P.O. Box 9047, Buffalo, NY 14269-9047; **In Canada:** P.O. Box 613, Fort Erie, Ontario, L2A 5X3.

Name: _____

Address: _____ City: _____

State/Prov.: _____ Zip/Postal Code: _____

*New York residents remit applicable sales taxes.
Canadian residents remit applicable GST and provincial taxes.

HBACK-JM